The Message
... call me!

Mary Jane Forbes

Todd Book Publications

———

For those in the United States and
France who lived the event that
triggered the story…

…a bottle's journey through the waters
of the Atlantic Ocean containing a
message from the shores of a small
town in Massachusetts to the shores of
a beach south west of Paris, France.

———

The Cast

Newburyport, MA USA
Rawly Scott
Grammy Kathy
Meg Scott
Tyler Scott
The Beckers

Paris & Pornic, France
Leigh Dobrev
Eric Duris
Marie Binoche
Betsy Marceau
Gerry & Shelby Depardieu

The Message

... call me!

Prologue

December 28, 1999

THREE DAYS TO NEW YEAR'S EVE!

Such a fuss.

Personally, I like to put a bag of popcorn in the microwave, open a mini-bottle of bubbly, settle in front of the television in my flannel jammies, and watch the fireworks cascading over Boston, New York City, and Washington DC.

I'll be sixty three!

It's a wonderful date to be born. The whole world celebrates. This year is especially great. My sister Miriam and her husband Dick flew in from Seattle to celebrate with me—on the couch watching TV, popcorn and bubbly—the works.

But today, three days before the world's big event, my son Michael is bringing my two grandsons, Rawly and Tyler, nine and eleven, to visit us. Peeking out the window this morning, I had hoped to see a foot of snow—none had fallen this winter and none fell last night.

Chuckling, I set the coffee pot to perking. When you have houseguests, as well as young grandsons, visiting, you have to be ready.

And, I was ready.

The setting for our activity was perfect.

You see, I live in a red-brick townhouse, built in 1850, in the little city of Newburyport, Massachusetts. The town is nestled along the Merrimack River which flows into the Atlantic Ocean four miles due east of my home.

Over the months leading up to my birthday I had saved several wine bottles—empty after drinking my obligatory glass, or two, each evening. Scrubbing the bottles clean, I stored them in a big wicker laundry basket along with the other paraphernalia required for the day's project.

While we adults were enjoying cranberry muffins with our morning coffee, there was a knock on the door immediately followed by a blast of winter air—Rawly and Tyler scrambling in with their father.

After hugs for everyone, we settled at my big round kitchen table.

Tyler was the first to spot the laundry basket in front of the kitchen's open fireplace. At eleven, he noticed everything. Rawly, nine, looked the other way—if it didn't fly like one of his model rockets, or roll like a ball, he wasn't interested.

"What are we going to do with those bottles, Grammy Kathy?" Tyler asked grinning at me.

Everyone turned in my direction, eyes wide, questioning. What did the matriarch have up her sleeve today?

"Tyler, hand out the bottles," I said smiling back at him. "There's one for each of us. And, Rawly, please bring the rest of the items in the basket to the table."

"Okay. But what are we going to do with all this stuff?" Rawly asked transferring a box of rice, a bag of corks, and an envelope stuffed with pieces of paper on the table.

"Give me that package of wax, Tyler," I said.

Taking the package labeled paraffin from his hand, I walked over to the stove, put the wax in a small pan, and turned the burner on low. "We're going to put messages in these bottles, seal the corks with melted wax, and toss them into the ocean tomorrow morning at high tide. Michael, it's your job to check exactly when that occurs."

Rawly, now perched on one of the ice cream chairs ringing the table, swinging his legs, looked at me. "Grammy Kathy, what's the rice for?"

"I know, I know," Tyler said waving his hand. "It's for ballast."

"What's ballast?" Rawly asked.

Tyler rolled his eyes.

"Gives it stability—steady as she goes in the water," Uncle Dick, an ex-Navy man, said with authority.

"Rawly, please hand out the pieces of paper in that envelope. I typed the messages for us but, as you can see, I left space at the bottom if you want to add some words of your own, and your telephone number. If someone finds your bottle, you want them to have a way to get in touch with you. Right, Rawly?"

The kitchen was quiet as everyone read the message I had typed.

> *To whoever finds my bottle, I wish you happiness, health, safety and prosperity. I launched this bottle on December 29, 1999, with the outgoing tide of the Atlantic Ocean from the mouth of the Merrimack River in Newburyport, Massachusetts, USA. Please call me with your whereabouts so I know how far my message traveled. Hope to hear from you, somewhere out there.*

"Grammy Kathy, we should put a dollar in the bottle for the phone call," Tyler said matter-of-factly as he signed his name and wrote his telephone number.

"I'll get my purse," Miriam said. "I know I have some dollar bills." She went upstairs, returned with her purse, and laid several dollars bills on the table.

"How about a penny for good luck? I think that would be nice, don't you, Grammy Kathy," Rawly said holding the pen with his fist, lips pulled tight in concentration as he printed his name.

Tyler watched him. "Why did you print Rawleigh? Why not Rawly?" Tyler jerked the pen from his brother's hand.

"Gimme that back. I'm not finished," Rawly said, pulling a tough face.

Tyler raised his brows, touched the pen to his cheek then laid it in front of his dad.

"Come on, Ty. Give the pen back to your brother," Michael said frowning.

Tyler again raised his brows, picked up the pen with two fingers and laid it down on Rawly's note. Legs swinging under his chair,

Rawly picked up the pen and added two words after Rawleigh Scott: *"Call me."*

"Sis, do you have some pennies in that purse?" I asked stirring the paraffin.

"Sure do," she said dumping several shiny copper pennies onto the blue-and-white-check tablecloth.

Michael had set up his laptop and was accessing the internet to determine the best time tomorrow morning to head to the beach based on the tide table. "Looks like, if we leave the house at nine-thirty, we should hit it about right—as the tide turns, begins to go out."

"Here's your bottle, Dad," Rawly said.

"I'll just help you guys," Michael said smiling at his youngest son. "Why didn't you sign with your nickname—Rawly?"

"I don't know. Rawleigh looked more important," he said looking up at his dad.

"I know what you mean," Uncle Dick said. "I signed ours Miriam and Richard, not Dick. We're launching one bottle from the two of us." He smiled knowingly at Rawly.

Rawly grinned at his Uncle as we began the serious business of preparing the bottles.

We added the rice using a funnel, dropped a penny in each, popped in our rolled up messages with a dollar bill inside, and then shoved the corks in the top. Michael checked all the bottles giving each cork an extra nudge. The paraffin had melted and one-by-one I poured the hot wax around each cork to make them very watertight. Michael turned the bottle over the pie plate I had placed on the counter to catch any wax drippings. After each bottle was sealed, Rawly and Tyler took turns setting the bottles on the kitchen table.

Finally, four bottles stood ready to be launched on their journey.

———

Dawn, December twenty-ninth, ushered in more frigid air but no snow.

After breakfast we headed for the beach dressed for the cold in our jeans and heavy winter jackets. The boys pulled on their gloves, and with green pompoms swinging from the top of their red stocking caps, they trotted to the car.

It was a beautiful, sunshiny winter morning but very cold. Michael drove to the beach, parked his van at the top of the hill bordering the sand. We were the only car. We were the only ones on the beach. Laughing, we piled out into the fresh salty air and began trudging across the packed sand, to the waves rolling along the shore.

The first action on the list, Rawly wanted to shoot off his latest model rocket. It was a perfect launch, rising, rising, rising into the blue sky. At the apex of its flight, a small parachute popped open allowing the little rocket a smooth descent to the beach. Tyler ran with Rawly to retrieve the rocket, then ran back to their dad, Rawly with a big grin on his face.

Then it was time for the big event.

Rawly and Tyler, and my sis and I clutched our bottles chattering, pointing to the best spot, most strategic to toss our bottles into the rolling waves.

Miriam and I asked Michael to start the action by throwing our bottles so the boys could see how much strength it took to send them far enough out to catch a wave.

With a pretty good heave, Michael tossed my bottle into a wave as it pulled back over the sand, and then tossed his Aunt Miriam's. The waves were noisy splashing on the beach, but they were far from the monster waves the Atlantic is known for in this area. Nonetheless the first two bottles were caught by the receding tide, dipping under then resurfacing as the waves rolled in and out.

Tyler was next. He gripped the neck of his bottle, drew back and threw it. He didn't have a clean release. The bottle barely floated a few feet, but the next wave coaxed it away from the shoreline.

It was now Rawly's turn.

We watched as he stepped up to the plate, pitching his bottle into the surf only to see it wash back. But each subsequent wave slowly worked his bottle down the beach until it finally drifted out to sea.

Lost in thought, the waves lapping at our feet, we stood in a line watching in silence, straining to see our bottles bobbing on a wave, vanishing, bobbing up again, until finally all of our bottles had disappeared, leaving only the surf ebbing and flowing, sparkling in the sunlight.

Shivering, I wrapped my coat tight against the frigid air wondering where the currents would take the bottles, wondering where or if they would come ashore—maybe north thirty or so miles to the beaches of Portsmouth, New Hampshire. Or, somehow drawn south eighty or so miles to Provincetown, Massachusetts, or maybe they would wash ashore a few yards down the beach on the next incoming tide to be found by a jogger or a dog walker.

Oh, I had a plan alright, and my family joined in the fun, performing magnificently.

I just didn't realize that executing my plan on this day would change our lives, setting them on a different course ... especially for one of us.

Part One

Chapter 1

———

April 2001

Pornic, France

SPRING WAS IN THE AIR.

A lovely Sunday afternoon for a picnic on the beach, The Atlantic Ocean twinkled in the bright sun lapping the shores of Pornic, a fishing village on the coast of France. Leigh, a young French girl, ten, and her school chum Eric, eleven, raced down the steep rocky-path ahead of Madame Dobrev, laughing as they ran to see who touched the water first.

Leigh's paternal grandmother, Madame Claude Dobrev, smiled at the children as she carefully picked her way down the path in her sneakers, trying to avoid a stumble on a loose rock here and there.

Winning the race, Leigh tapped the surf with the toe of her sneaker then ran back up the path to where she set the wicker picnic basket. Grasping the basket's handle, she threaded her other hand through her grandmother's arm. Glancing down at the beach, she smiled as Eric took off his sneakers and splashed into the cold water.

"Oh, Grandmama, it's such a beautiful day," Leigh said, her smoky-blue eyes twinkling up at the silver-haired woman.

Leigh, orphaned at the age of six, her parents dying in a horrible car crash, had no family except her grandmother and grandfather in Nantes—forty miles east of her school in Pornic. She was growing up under the custody of her teacher, Marie Binoche, who had eagerly stepped forward to raise the girl, her favorite student since enrolling in the school. Grandfather Dobrev was not a well man which prohibited him and his wife from taking care of the child when her parents died.

Madame Marie Binoche, divorced with two grown sons, delighted in having the precocious little girl in her life. Leigh was imaginative and friendly, but reserved after the death of her parents. Due to the distance between home and school, Leigh had already been in the habit of spending two to three nights a week under the teacher's care so she eased into the broadened adjustment quickly.

On the other hand, Eric was boisterous, looked for trouble and usually found it, except when it came to Leigh. The boy saw himself as her protector but Madame Binoche felt anxious when the two played together. He was growing into an angry young man, blaming the military and the French Government, anyone in authority for his parent's untimely death. His family had rendezvoused at the army base near Paris and was traveling by train back to Pornic for his father's two week's leave. The train, traveling at too high a speed, derailed rounding a sharp curve. Eric's right hand was severed at the wrist trying to save his parents. As a result of their deaths, Eric became a ward in a foster home. His new guardians had their hands full with the rebellious boy.

Grandmother Dobrev stepped onto the sandy beach holding a red-plaid blanket under her arm. "Eric, come here, s'il vous plaît. Help me spread out this blanket so we can sit and enjoy our picnic. Then we'll take a short walk," she said breathing in the cool salty air.

"Okay, Madame." Taking a corner of the blanket from the woman's out-stretched hand and giving Leigh a hip bump, he helped the woman shake it out letting the cover flutter down over the sand.

"Stop that, Eric. You want me to drop this basket?" Leigh snapped.

"Oh, tsk tsk. Here, let me help."

"No, thank you," Leigh said dropping to her knees on the soft fabric. She gave Madame Dobrev a hand as she settled on a corner smoothing out her tan slacks and sweater. Eric in a pair of cut-off jeans squatted beside Leigh.

"There's a ham and cheese sandwich for each of us, a bottle of water, and an apple. *And* a treat—fudge that Leigh whipped up early this morning," Madame said handing out the bottles of water as

Leigh placed a sandwich and an apple in front of them on a paper plate. The fudge was on a china plate covered with plastic wrap.

They were the only people on the beach—Madame Dobrev relishing the solitude. No one to bother them as they sat eating their lunch ... gazing at the sparkling water, the waves softly lapping the sandy shore. Eric, finishing first, jumped to his feet, ran into the surf tossing his apple core out in the water, his red hair glistening in the sun's rays.

"Eric, why did you do that?" Madame admonished. "What if it drifts ashore? Garbage for someone to see."

Eric ran up to Leigh, grabbed her half eaten apple, scampered back to the water, raised his arm to toss the apple as Leigh ran up grabbing his hand. "Come on, Eric. Don't be a tease."

He turned, looked at Leigh with a devilish grin. Laughing they ran back to Madame as she uncovered the fudge. Leigh was known for her fudge so there was no clowning around when her candy was offered, usually of the chocolate variety. The creamy candy melted in their mouths like butter. Madame closed her eyes savoring her piece of fudge as did Eric.

"Umm, Leigh, this is the best batch ever," Eric said.

"You always say that, but thanks anyway," Leigh said, her eyes crinkling at the corners.

"All right, let's pack up the wrappings so they don't fly around, and then we can take a walk," Madame said opening the lid of the basket.

"Can we leave the basket under those bushes, Grandmama? No one's here," Leigh said glancing around at the empty beach.

"Certainly, we won't be going far," her grandmother replied.

"I'll take it for you, Madame," Eric said, graciously picking up the basket.

Leigh smiled at her grandmother, their eyes locking. Maybe there was hope for him.

As Eric set the basket on the sand under the bushes, Leigh started to run. "Beat you to that boulder," she yelled taking off down the beach to a large outcropping of rock some thirty yards ahead.

"Oh yah," Eric yelled. But there was no catching her, her inky black hair waving in the wind as she streaked down the beach, sand flying off her feet as she ran.

Just before she reached the rock she suddenly stopped, fell to her knees, her hands scooping away the sand from something embedded in front of her, sand piling onto her jeans, onto her white turtleneck shirt. Eric caught up to her, sat on his haunches, watching her work at freeing the object in the sand. Madame Dobrev, breathing hard from running, feared Leigh had hurt herself.

"Oh my, you gave me a fright. What's that you're digging out?" Madame asked slumping to the sand to watch with Eric as Leigh pulled a pale-green wine bottle from her excavation.

"Eric, look, there's something inside. Wait, let me rinse off the sand." Leigh pulled off her sneakers, ran into the surf, dunked the bottle several times, and returned, sliding to a stop where the bottle had been lodged.

"Grandmama, there's a coin inside, and it looks like there's a piece of paper. I bet it's a note. Eric, I found a note, a message. Look at all this wax," she said her finger tracing over the lumpy wax sealing the bottle.

"Let me see it, chèrie." Her grandmother carefully lifted the bottle from Leigh's fingers. "It certainly could be a note. But it's sealed tight. We'll have to break the bottle if we want to see what's inside. Come on, let's go back to the basket for one of those plastic bags. Eric, you find a rock so Leigh can break the bottle."

"Why Leigh? I want to break the bottle."

"No, Eric. I found the bottle ... I break it," Leigh said glaring at him.

Opening the basket, taking the big plastic bag that had held the three sandwiches, she put the bottle inside the bag, then wrapped it in a towel in case a shard of glass pierced the bag.

Placing the covered bottle on a flat surface of one of the boulders, Leigh took the rock Eric handed to her. Smiling up at her grandmother who nodded to her to go ahead, Leigh giggled then raised her hand in the air and swiftly brought it down with a smashing blow. She felt the glass give way and quickly discarded the towel around her hand. Carefully unfolding the other towel around the plastic bag she revealed the broken bottle inside.

The bottom and neck of the bottle were still intact but the rest of the glass was a mound of sharp splinters where the belly of the bottle gave way. Leigh carefully reached into the bag and picked up a dollar bill, gave it a little shake over the bottle's carcass and handed it to her grandmother. She inserted her hand once again into the bag and slowly lifted the piece of paper, opening each fold with a gentle shake to free any glass that might have punctured the paper, a small piece of glass falling onto the mound of glass in the bag.

Sitting on the sand, Leigh glanced at her grandmother, then Eric, and then read the note written in English out loud to her audience.

> *To whoever finds my bottle, I wish you happiness, health, safety and prosperity. I launched this bottle on December 29, 1999, with the outgoing tide of the Atlantic Ocean from the mouth of the Merrimack River in Newburyport, Massachusetts, USA. Please call me with your whereabouts so I know how far my message has traveled. Hope to hear from you somewhere out there.*
> *Rawleigh Scott*
> *Call me!*

Leigh gasped along with her grandmother. "Grandmother Claude, we have the same name," she whispered.

"Rawleigh is hardly Leigh," Eric snapped.

"Leigh is my nickname, silly."

"Oh, Leigh, it's like a sign from heaven … that this bottle should travel so far … to your hands … traveling more than a year."

"Oh, I know," Leigh said clapping her hands. "Do you think I should call?"

"But of course, you will call, ma chèrie."

Chapter 2

Nashua, New Hampshire

THE RING OF THE telephone cut through the silence in the modest condo. Tyler Scott, marking his progress in his math study guide, reached for the phone hanging on the kitchen wall thinking it was his mother calling to say she would be home soon with Rawly after his baseball practice.

"Hello." Tyler looked at the clock. 4:28 p.m.

"Bonjour. I'm calling for Monsieur Rawleigh Scott? Are you Monsieur Scott," a woman asked, a lilt to her voice, rising slightly on the last word of each phrase.

"What? I don't understand," Tyler said straining to decipher the heavy French accent.

"Mademoiselle Dobrev is calling from Pornic, France, for Monsieur Rawleigh Scott. I am Madame Marie Binoche, her Professeur. Mademoiselle Dobrev found Monsieur Scott's bottle."

"Oh, my God. She … the Mademoiselle … ah … ah found the bottle? I'm Tyler, Rawly's brother. He and my mom are at baseball practice. Ah … can you call back? Wait. Wait. What's your name and where do you live?" Tyler asked fumbling with his pen as he tore a sheet of paper from his notebook.

"My name is Professeur Marie Binoche. I'm Rawleigh Dobrev's English teacher. She asked me to place the call. We are in Pornic, France."

"France? Oh, my God, Can you spell that? The city?" Tyler asked holding the phone to his ear with his shoulder.

"P.O.R.N.I.C."

"Please spell Rawly Dube … her name?" Tyler's brows scrunched in concentration.

"First name is R.A.W.L.E.I.G.H. Last name is D.O.B.R.E.V.

"Thank you," Tyler said looking at the letters he wrote. "This is very strange."

"What is strange, Monsieur?"

"Rawly's name, my brother, his first name is Rawleigh ... the spelling you gave me."

"Yes, I agree, Monsieur. It is quite a coincidence."

"Can you give me your phone number? I know my mom will ask."

Madame Binoche gave Tyler a string of numbers, explaining that the first two were the country code for France.

"Can you call back in an hour? Please. An hour?" Tyler asked his fingers twisting the curly telephone cord, rocking in his sneakers toe to heel to toe.

"Of course, Monsieur. But it will be after midnight here in France. We'll call back tomorrow morning at 7:30. It will be 1:30 in the afternoon in France. Is that all right?"

"Yes. Yes. 7:30 ... in the morning."

"Au revoir, Tyler Scott."

Tyler, his heart beating faster than he ever thought it could, punched in the numbers for his mother's cell phone.

"Mom, Mom, you aren't going to believe what just happened. France called."

"Frances who?"

"No, no, a call from France. Someone found Rawly's bottle on the beach and she's calling back at 7:30 tomorrow morning," he shouted twisting the phone cord again. Rocking again.

"Oh, my God. Call Grammy Kathy ... and call your dad. We'll be home in an hour."

————

The headmaster of the Pornic grade school, hearing of Leigh Dobrev's discovery, immediately granted Professeur Binoche's request to use his office phone to place the call to the United States, and also suggested she bring her entire English class of sixteen students to the office with her.

Entering the Headmaster's office, the students huddled around his desk the model of decorum—no sharp elbows into a classmate's ribs. Leigh, holding the receiver tight to her ear, watched her teacher dial the phone.

"Hello," Rawly said smiling at his mom and brother.

"Hello. My name is Rawleigh Dobrev and I'm ten years old. People call me Leigh."

"Hello, Leigh. I'm Rawly Scott and I'm ten years old, too. I like your accent."

Leigh giggled. "I like your accent, too."

"Hello, hello, Rawleigh Scott?'

"Yes, who's this?"

"Professeur Binoche. I'm Leigh's teacher."

"Here's my mom ... Mrs. Megyn Scott." Rawly shoved the phone to his mother's ear. "Here, Mom, you talk. I don't know what to say. She said they call her Leigh."

"Hello. I'm Meg Scott, Rawly's mother."

"Madame Scott, so nice to speak with you. I'm Leigh's English teacher, Professeur Marie Binoche, but please call me Marie."

"We were so excited to receive your telephone call last night, Marie, and please call me Meg. Where did Leigh find the bottle?"

"She was with her grandmother on the Saint Jean de Monts Beach, about an hour's drive south of Pornic where Leigh goes to school," Marie explained.

"Oh, my, Marie ... so many coincidences. Same first name, same age, and both were with their grandmothers. This is an expensive call. Can you give us an address so we can exchange letters?" Meg asked snapping her fingers at Rawly for a piece of paper and something to write with.

"Can you repeat that, Marie?" Meg listened intently as Marie repeated her address and then asked Meg to do the same. Rawly and Tyler on either side of their mother, leaned against her, watching as she checked the address.

"I think we have it, Marie. We'll send a letter shortly. Bye."

"Au revoir, Meg Scott."

Hanging up the phone, Meg smiled down at her two boys. "Well, how about that—"

Interrupted by the ring of the phone, she picked up the receiver but before saying a word Grammy Kathy blurted out, "Did she call ... the teacher. Did she call?"

"Yes, and you aren't going to believe what she told us," Meg said, her free arm around Rawly's neck as he grinned up at his mother, his big dark-brown eyes shining.

Chapter 3

——

BY MID-MAY, two communications—a letter received and an email sent—seemed innocent enough at the time. But, in fact both pushed forward the story of the bottle's journey to the opposite side of the ocean.

The letter arrived with a photo of Leigh Dobrev. Her smoky-blue eyes and pretty pink lips smiled out at Rawly. Rawly, almost eleven years old, took her picture to school. His classmates, especially the boys, marveled at his pretty French pen pal. Some teased him, saying Leigh was his girlfriend. He didn't care because he thought she was beautiful.

In her letter, Leigh explained she lived with her teacher, Professeur Binoche as her parents died in an automobile accident. She liked to make chocolate candy, and studied a lot, paying more attention in her English class now that she had a friend to write to. It was a short letter but she did ask him to send her a picture.

Rawly shared the letter with Grammy Kathy, who had a thought that the local media might be interested in the connection with a young girl in France because of the bottle—a nice human-interest tale. And, the story might grab the attention of others in her little town of Newburyport. After all it was there that the story began. And, maybe people in Nashua, New Hampshire, where Rawly lived, would like to read about his adventure. She sent an email to WBZ, a Boston television and radio station. They did not respond.

The Nashua Telegraph, a local newspaper, got wind of the story from a student at Rawly's school. A reporter called Mrs. Megyn Scott to schedule an interview with Rawly and Tyler at their home.

Mayhem was about to erupt at the Scott's Nashua condo.

On June third, a Sunday, the Nashua Telegraph article appeared as the lead headline on the front page of Section B. Rawly was set to go to a friend's birthday party but during the morning the telephone began ringing—ringing off the hook.

The media had engaged.

This was a happy story, no gloom and doom, a reprieve from blood and death.

The Associated Press picked up the story from the Nashua Telegraph and immediately put it out on the wire. CBS news, ABC's Good Morning America, and NBC's Today show were three of the callers that morning. ABC and NBC asked if they could schedule an interview in New York City with the boy whose bottle was found on the coast of France.

The phone continued to ring. WMUR News out of Manchester, New Hampshire, requested an interview that afternoon.

Meg called Grammy Kathy telling her about the phone calls, pleading for her to make the hour's drive to Nashua as soon as possible. Meg needed support.

Kathy said she would leave immediately.

Meg took Rawly to the birthday party, dropped off the present and promptly left with a piece of birthday cake wrapped on a Lion King paper plate. They had forty-five minutes to drive home before the WMUR interview.

———

Grammy Kathy turned right at the top of the steep hill leading down through the row of condos on either side of the street. She immediately saw the television news van at the bottom of the hill. The news crew had set up a staging area: white umbrellas to control the lighting, cameras, and cables strung from the van to the middle of the Scott's driveway. The filming of the interview was underway with Rawly and Tyler perched under the umbrellas on high stools, scrubbed and dressed in matching red and green-striped long-sleeved polo shirts over tan cargo pants. Their sneakers rested on a rung, sometimes swinging to the side unable to hold still. The reporter held out a microphone to the boys as they related the day the bottle was launched.

Smiling, excitement flowing through her body, Grammy Kathy parked her car at the same time Rawly pointed at her. "That's Grammy Kathy. Just ask her what we did."

Grammy Kathy's black slacks fluttered in a breeze, her white turtleneck shirt guarding against a chill as the reporter whisked her under the white umbrellas, peppering her and the boys with more questions.

Meg opened the front door, telephone to her ear, the curly telephone cord stretching from inside the house, waving frantically at Kathy who was now having a casual conversation with the reporter.

Kathy broke away, feeling a few drops of rain as the news crew began packing up their equipment. Stepping inside, Meg, covering the mouthpiece of the receiver with her hand, spoke very fast in a hushed voice explaining that Good Morning America had first wanted the family to come to a studio in Manchester, New Hampshire, but the home of the show was in New York City and they didn't want an offsite interview and were now asking the Scotts to come to New York in the morning … and that Good Morning America was prepared to send a limo tomorrow afternoon to take them to Boston's Logan Airport to fly down to New York City. The limo driver would have the tickets and an itinerary.

Meg, her hand over the mouthpiece, stopped talking, looking with raised brows at Kathy—Good Morning America, or The Today show?

Whispering back and forth, Kathy thought Michael should be included in the trip as he was with the boys when the bottle was launched, and then with a nod, a return nod from Meg, Meg removed her hand and accepted the invitation from the Good Morning America reporter saying the Scotts would be a party of five—Grandmother Scott, Meg and Michael Scott, Rawly and Tyler Scott.

Meg hung up the phone, her hand clinging to the receiver in the wall cradle, nodded to Kathy, both women bug-eyed. They were going to New York City tomorrow.

WMUR's interview was aired that night on the eleven o'clock local news. NECN (New England Cable News), and WNDS out of Concord, New Hampshire, left messages the next day requesting an interview with Rawly and Tyler Scott, and to please call back with the best day and time.

The whirlwind continued.

Chapter 4

New York City

IT WAS A PERFECT day to fly—nothing but blue sky.

The black stretch limo, gleaming in the sunlight, rolled passed the tan wood-sided building, turned around, and then pulled up and parked in front of the driveway at the end of the condo-lined street.

Rawly and Tyler peeking out of the living room window announced the arrival of the limo shouting to the three adults in the room—their mom and dad and Grammy Kathy. Meg hustled to the window and looked out over Rawly's head.

The driver stepped out of the limo wearing a big smile, donned her black cap on top of her auburn hair, squaring it with a tug on the bill. Her black jacket and trousers were sharp against a white shirt, sturdy black shoes grounding her. Kathy Scott mirrored the driver's outfit—black slacks, and white blouse. Kathy and Michael had left their rolling carry-on cases on the doorstep beside Meg's large suitcase packed with extra clothes for the boys. Rawly and Tyler had crammed sweaters and games into their green backpacks.

The limo driver, Monica, loaded the suitcases in the trunk with Michael's help, then opened the limo's doors and with a chuckle invited the Scott family to climb aboard for the first leg of their adventure—Boston's Logan Airport to catch a flight to New York's LaGuardia Airport.

Rawly and Tyler were wound up and immediately began exploring all the compartments in the room-size limo. Tyler discovered a well-stocked bar with glasses of all shapes and sizes. The boys slid along the black-leather seats, from one side to the other. Michael finally laid down the law ordering the boys to sit still. For a while, the boys stretched out on either side of the limo. But then it was Michael's turn to fiddle with the gadgets in the vehicle. Kathy rolled her eyes. Her son was a typical engineer.

The limo arrived at the airport's departure area. Monica unloaded the luggage, wished the Scott's a good trip, waving goodbye as she drove off. Time swept by and the party of five soon found themselves seated aboard the plane. This was the maiden flight for Rawly and Tyler, both aware that their mother was a nervous flyer. Tyler spotted the barf bag in the seat pocket, waved at his mom, and told Rawly to be ready to grab his if he thought he was going to vomit. Fortunately, Rawly did not follow through with the power of suggestion, but held the bag next to his chest just in case. His face turned a little green as the plane gathered speed for takeoff, but he managed to keep his nerves and stomach under control.

Landing in New York City, a cab whisked them over the Queensboro Bridge into Manhattan, and to a hotel across the street from the ABC studios. A packet of instructions had been left at the hotel's reservation desk confirming that an ABC guide would pick them up in the lobby at 8:00 a.m. escorting the Scotts across the street to the interview with Charlie Gibson, the host of Good Morning America.

———

The next morning, as scheduled, the guide, an intern for the network, greeted the family, chatted with the boys and dropped everyone off at the first stop: Makeup. The boys' hair was spiffed up and faces powdered. Kathy purred under a full makeup treatment— foundation, blush, eyes lined and shadowed.

Next stop: The Green Room. The room the Scotts were to wait to be taken to the studio. The boys rushed up to the tables set against windows overlooking Times Square. The tables were laden with doughnuts, croissants, bowls of fresh fruit, sodas, and coffee— treats for everyone, especially two energetic, always hungry, growing boys.

Their guide stepped into the green room to escort the Scotts to the interview. Along their walk they were given a souvenir of their visit—Good Morning America coffee mugs.

It was time to tell their story.

Meg and Michael Scott stood off in the wings, as Rawly, Tyler and Grammy Kathy were led to a couch centered in a brightly lit, living-room-style television set. Charlie Gibson sat in a chair facing the trio over a coffee table as microphones were tucked in place on his guests. Gibson asked a few questions to put them at ease and then it was show time. The boys warmed up quickly telling their incredible story of the bottle. A few times Gibson addressed Grammy Kathy but for the most part it was the boys who related the story. Addressing Rawly, Gibson asked with a chuckle, if he planned to learn French.

"Bonjour, Monsieur Gibson," Rawly said grinning, leaning forward then back, shaking his leg. "I just learned those words. Mom signed me up to take French in the fall."

Then, as quickly as the interview started, it was over.

Kathy sighed in relief as the microphones were removed. Meg and Michael rushed on to the set hugging their two boys. The guide signaled the Scotts to follow her back to the hotel. On the way she told them that the show was supposed to air live but had been bumped for a breaking news story. The bottle segment had been taped and would be slotted sometime in the next seven days.

ABC's Good Morning America had managed to grab the story before other media outlets, but the urgency to get the story on the air had evaporated.

The Scotts quickly found themselves standing alone in the hotel lobby with their luggage. Exhausted from the whirlwind of activity since the story broke, the Scotts piled into the limo that pulled up to the curb to take them to the airport for the first leg of their trip home. In Boston, another black stretch limo drove the family back to the quiet, condo-lined street in Nashua, New Hampshire.

———

Chapter 5

France – November 2003
Two and a half years later

THE MORNING SUN filtered through the trees outside the window of Marie's cottage as she padded to the kitchen. The sweet scent of chocolate had roused her out of bed. Her young friend under her guardianship was melting chocolate again.

Leigh glanced up from stirring the creamy chocolate in the double-boiler over the stove's gas flame. She smiled in greeting. "Bonjour, Marie. Your coffee is ready as you like it. Shall I pour for you?"

"No, I'll fix my cup," Marie said observing the assortment of candy-making tools and ingredients spread out on the old pine kitchen table. Adding a shot of cream from the carton in the refrigerator, she sauntered to the far side of the table stopping on the way to give Leigh's shoulder a squeeze.

"Do you have enough room?" Leigh asked. "I can move the molds to the counter."

"I'm fine, ma chèrie. I see you unpacked the box your grandmother gave you."

"Oh, Marie, so many treasures. Grandma Claude told me several times that my Great Grandmother Dobrev was known for her chocolates. When she and Great Grandfather helped with the French Resistance word spread about her—a bright spot in their struggle. Grandma Claude says I take after her. Hearing the stories of her chocolate candy makes me want to be just like her."

"Follow in your Great Grandmother's footsteps?"

"Oui. Working with her tools, especially in your little kitchen, I feel she's instructing me. Look at these molds—starfish, little bars, little animals like this bear. They're very old."

"Has Claude told you stories about what her mother and father did in the resistance?"

"Oui. They were members of a small cell, mostly farmers. They published an underground newspaper with information about the allied soldiers as they progressed through France after the invasion of Normandy."

"It must have been very dangerous," Marie said gazing around the kitchen. "Allied soldiers who had been trapped during the occupation hid in this house."

"This stove ... someone fixed meals. If only it could talk. Grandmama said her father worked with some of the men in the resistance sabotaging the electrical and transportation facilities." Leigh paused, running her fingers over the starfish mold. "It's really a miracle that her tools survived. But she kept making chocolates. She said there were several times, fearing they would be shot, she bribed some enemy soldiers to let them live."

Leigh dipped the edge of the spoon into the creamy chocolate ganache—a mixture of chocolate, butter, and cream—touched a spot to her tongue and, satisfied it was a perfect consistency, poured it into a bowl. Covering the bowl she put it in the refrigerator where it would stay for the next three hours to chill until firm.

"What will you do with the ganache?" Marie asked.

"Today, I'm creating one-inch round balls, nice bite-size truffles. We can take them to church with us tomorrow. Parishioners will have a chocolate with their tea and coffee after the service."

"They'll love the treat," Marie said. "How many of your Great Grandmother's chocolate recipes survived?"

"Quite a few. Grandma Claude thinks there are a few additional boxes in the attic. Maybe I'll find more recipes and molds. She's going to bring them to me on her next visit."

"That's nice, chérie," Marie said softly, her lips spreading into a grin.

Leigh looked up hearing a lilt in Marie's voice. "What? I know that look."

"I have a secret. A secret surprise."

"What? Tell me. Even your eyes are grinning at me."

"An email came to me yesterday. From Kathy Scott."

"Rawly's Grandmother?"

"The very one. You must promise if I tell you what she said that you will keep it a secret. Can you do that? Not your classmates. Not Rawly. No one."

"What about Eric?"

"Especially not Eric. He's ornery enough to try to spoil the surprise."

Leigh pushed the sack of sugar and tub of butter to the side. Pulled a chair up close to the table, leaned forward hands folded in front of her resting on the table. "Okay, I'm ready. Tell me, Marie," she said giggling. "It must be a big secret … you're being so coy."

"Madame Scott wants to give a very special Christmas present to Rawly, Tyler, and their mother."

"What does that have to do with you?"

"Remember, chérie, a secret," Marie said raising her brows.

"Oui. Go on."

"She asked if she could bring the boys and their mother to France—Paris and Pornic, to meet you during the boys' spring school break in April."

"Oh, Marie," Leigh gasped. Jumping up, she twirled around the kitchen then flung her arms around Marie's shoulders from behind her chair. Quickly resuming her seat, Leigh looked intently into Marie's eyes. "You said, yes?"

"I said, yes, and invited them to stay with us … here … in this house."

Leigh again popped up, squealing as she twirled around the kitchen, the ties from her white apron flipping with each whirl, then scooted back to her chair. "Tell me everything she said."

Marie laughed. "You have more chocolate on that apron than you poured into the bowl. I'm going to find you a black one, or brown if they have it. Then you can wear it for more than one day."

Sipping her coffee, Marie gazed out the window. "Well, none of them have been out of the States ... have to get passports, tickets, plus the hotel in Paris. Kathy wants to spend two days in Paris, and a day and night here in Pornic. Considering the limited time for such a trip, she wants them to see as much as they can. Anyway, she said she was asking me first before saying anything to Meg and the boys. If I said it was okay, which I did, she plans on asking Meg if she thinks it's doable, and then divulge the whole trip as a gift to the boys on Christmas day."

"Less than two months to Christmas," Leigh said clapping her hands. "Too bad they weren't here two months ago for my birthday. Rawly must be thirteen, too ... err, maybe not ... I have to find out when he was born."

"Not now, chérie. Remember," Marie twisted her fingers over her lips.

Leigh giggled and locked her lips with her fingers mimicking Marie.

"She wants to meet your grandparents. You can call them today if you like. Kathy wondered if they should drive to Pornic from Paris but I said better to take the train—much faster given their short trip. You and I can meet the train, drive to Pornic, take them back to Nantes the next day to see your grandparents. After that we'll drive them to the train for their return to Paris." Marie finished her coffee, putting the empty cup in the sink. "We have time to work out the details. The main thing, Leigh, you are going to meet Rawly."

With a happy heart, Leigh set about cleaning up the kitchen— the bowls, scrapers, measuring spoons and cups—from mixing the chocolate truffles. She couldn't stop smiling and every so often Marie heard her clapping her hands, or saw her twirling, or skipping as she dried the dishes, putting them back in the cupboards.

I'm going to see Rawly, Leigh thought. He's so cute, at least in his picture. Oh ... maybe he's a brat. She frowned for a second, followed by a big grin. No ... not the boy in the picture. We'll walk down the hill to the beach ... it looks just like the beach where I found the bottle. I'll take the soccer ball ... with Tyler and Eric we can kick it around.

Frowning again, Leigh flopped on the chair as Marie came into the kitchen juggling a handful of her student's test papers she was grading.

"Chérie, why the frown?" Marie asked measuring the grounds in the basket for another pot of coffee.

Leigh stared down at the table, her pink lips in a pout. "Six months to April is forever away."

Chapter 6

———

April 2004
Six months later

THE BULLET TRAIN SPED through the countryside from Paris to Nantes. Kathy and Meg gazed out the window transfixed as little villages appeared, disappearing seconds later under a sun-filled April sky with only a few cloud skiffs darting about. Farm buildings and yellow fields of rapeseed better known as canola, dominated the landscape. Field after field of the bright, brassy-yellow flowers would be harvested for their oilseed pods sometime in July or August.

Rawly and Tyler sat unaware of the majesty of vibrant colors and villages outside the train's windows, their ears plugged into an electronic game device, their fingers magically moving figures around the tiny screen. The newest game technology was in their hands, yet outside were centuries old buildings.

The two hour trip on the TGV Eurostar, a sleek, silver bullet high-speed train, streaked south from Paris.

Slowly rounding a bend, the train entered the Nantes station, jerked and hissed to a stop. Rawly and Tyler pulled on their green backpacks. Meg adjusted their straps, and they lined up behind the other passengers exiting the car.

Leigh saw Rawly first, waved as she dropped her grandmother's hand and ran up to the Scotts just as Meg stepped off the train. Leigh stopped abruptly a few feet from the smiling foursome with a sudden case of shyness.

"Rawly?" she asked looking at him.

Rawly grinned. "Yup. Leigh?"

"Oui."

"What?"

"Yes," she giggled. "I'm Leigh."

He giggled too. "I like your silver chain," he said another grin filling his face.

Leigh smiled, "Merci, it was my mothers. I always wear it."

Marie and Leigh's Grandmother Claude rushed up hugging Kathy and Meg and Tyler and then the two thirteen-year-olds who couldn't stop giggling.

The connection was made, all because of a wine bottle, that battled who knew what, brought them together.

Kathy put her hand through Claude's arm, handing off her rolling suitcase to Tyler. Rawly and Tyler trudged along, weighted down with their backpacks and rolling suitcases, following Leigh up the length of the platform, into the terminal, and out into the parking lot. Marie immediately became translator-in-chief with Leigh a close second. Having grown up with her English teacher definitely had its advantages.

The two grandmothers, Claude and Kathy, smiled a lot—the language barrier was evident. Meg stayed close to Marie as did Leigh, Rawly and Tyler. Leigh slid into English punctuated with French and giggles. Kathy had not expected to meet Claude until the next day and was thrilled to walk along beside her if only to smile.

They piled into two cars—Claude driving Rawly with Leigh translating in one car, and Marie, Meg, Kathy and Tyler in the other for the forty-five-minute drive to Pornic.

After stashing the luggage in Marie's charming French cottage, Leigh grabbed the soccer ball and started running, yelling for Rawly and Tyler to follow her. In a line they all streamed down the steep hill lined with dense spring foliage to a path that opened at the bottom onto the beach and the sparkling water of the Atlantic Ocean.

Kathy noticed a boy with red hair, a head taller than the others, had joined Leigh and quickly all the young people were running around the small beach bordered on both sides by a high outcropping of rock fringed at the top with lush bushes and trees.

Kathy, Meg and Marie tossed their shoes under a bench and strolled with Claude to the edge of the water. Meg and Marie chatted quietly while Claude and Kathy, arm in arm, smiled and gazed out at the water. Kathy was sure they were thinking the same thing: *How did this happen?*

Kathy looked at Claude out of the corner of her eye as Claude, grounded in sturdy black shoes, stood stoically looking out at the sea, strands of her silver hair moving slightly in the soft breeze. Kathy could only wonder what was going through the woman's mind. What had she seen, witnessed, during the horrors of a world war.

Tired of kicking the ball, the three boys and Leigh sat on the sand cross legged—talking punctuated with occasional laughter. Leigh said something to Rawly and they both dashed to the wet sand where the tide had receded, both picking up something, exchanging whatever they had picked up and raced back to Tyler and Eric, the redhead.

With the sun slipping below the horizon the group made their way back up the path, up the hill to Marie's gate, and up another path to her house. Marie suggested Kathy and Meg take a few minutes for themselves as she showed them the bedrooms and bathroom all with fresh linens and towels. With the excitement of being in Pornic, Kathy and Meg quickly joined the others in the living room.

The party had grown to eleven.

Sensing the language barrier was causing a strain on her guests, Marie had enlisted the help of a friend and her husband. With their translation assistance the party turned lively with chatter. Kathy and Claude now being able to converse through Marie's recruits.

Marie set the stage for the evening. The sun long gone, the room was cozy in the flickering light of candles—candles grouped on the long table laden with numerous varieties of cheeses, pates, bite-size rounds of bread and crackers. Candles enhanced the rich colors of various wines—red, white, and a sweet dessert decanter on another table. Goblets twinkled in the flicker of more candles as well as sodas and sparkling water.

Throaty French ballads by European songstresses such as Marlene Dietrich floated quietly over the gathering.

With several explanations, giggles and laughter, gifts were exchanged.

The Scotts presented to Claude and Leigh a ship in a bottle handcrafted by a ship-model artisan in Newburyport. There were numerous scented Yankee candles for Marie. The Dobrev's set a large box on Meg's lap which held a clock fashioned as a ship's wheel. Leigh then gave all the Scott's her chocolate truffles in white boxes, tied with silver ribbon, each containing eight pieces in silver paper cups.

Everyone chuckled as Leigh unrolled a Red Sox poster of Nomar Garciaparra, Rawly's favorite baseball player. "Merci, Monsieur Rawly. I will tack this to my bedroom wall. The player … he … he looks just like you. I have a gift for you, Rawly, but you must wait until tomorrow." Grinning at each other, both slid their hands into their jean's pocket fingering the small polished stones they had exchanged earlier on the beach.

The mood to her liking, frenetic conversations and translations slowing between new friends, guests mellow with freshened goblets of wine, Marie asked everyone to take a seat. She said it was time the two grandmothers told the story of the bottle.

A hush fell, candles flickering in the shadow-filled room, children sitting on pillows leaning back on the couches where the adults had snuggled to hear their story.

Grammy Kathy began telling of the day they prepared the bottles, then tossing them into the ocean off the shores of Newburyport. In French, Grandma Claude picked up the story relating the exciting day she and her granddaughter found the bottle in the sand of Saint Jean de Monts Beach, and having to break the bottle to retrieve the message inside.

At each phrase, Marie translated speaking in a soft voice.

A magical night.

———

The next morning, the three women enjoyed a second cup of coffee at the kitchen table chatting about the séance-like gathering the night before. The youngsters took advantage of the quiet time and ran down to the beach.

All too soon, it was time to leave.

Claude had driven back to Nantes the night before accompanied by the couple who had joined the party as translators. She had to rise early with her husband Narcisse to prepare supper for Marie and the Scotts.

Marie, Leigh and the Scotts arrived at the Dobrev family home to the delicious aromas of a six-course supper, glasses aligned at the adult settings ready for special wines to be poured in a fresh goblet with each course. Marie took a bite now and then between translations, oohs and aahs requiring no translation. Dessert was served on china platters set in the center of the table presenting Leigh's chocolate truffles nestled among various French pastries.

Leigh excused herself, quietly leaving the table while the sweet delicacies were passed around. She returned holding what looked like a jewelry box tied with a gold bow. "This is for you, Rawly. Don't you dare forget me."

Rawly took the gift from her hand, carefully untied the bow, and lifted the lid. Inside was a man's sterling-silver chain necklace. He smiled at Leigh fingering her silver chain, his big dark eyes crinkling in the corners. "Merci," he said in a perfect French accent. "Merci, Mademoiselle." Suddenly shy, he handed the chain to his mother who fastened it around his neck.

Silence fell over the room.

The last drops of wine were sipped.

The visit had come to an end and it was time to leave for the train station.

Claude drove Leigh and Rawly in her car followed by Marie with the rest of the Scotts.

A pall had fallen over everyone. Was this the end of the magic, the bottle's magnetic field bringing them together?

Rawly was the last to mount the steps onto the train. He turned to Leigh. "I'm coming back after college—will you be here?" He called from the top step.

"Probably, but I dream of being a chocolatier in Paris," she replied smiling.

"I'll find you," Rawly said, then turned down the aisle to his mom.

On the train, sitting on long bench-like seats facing each other, Rawly looked out one window, Tyler the other. Outside on the platform, Claude, Marie, and Leigh were lined up staring back at them. The train hissed, jerked, then slowly began to move. Rawly put the palm of his hand on the window. Leigh raised her palm as if to touch his.

Kathy and Meg locked eyes.

Were these thirteen-year-olds ever going see each other again?

Part Two
Chapter 7

Pornic, France
High School Graduation – May 2008

THE LACE CURTAIN fluttered in the morning breeze. Leigh rolled to her side clutching the down-filled pillow to her chest. Sunbeams danced across the floor, specs of light and shadow slipping through the lace in the open window.

It was May and she was graduating from high school today. For the first time since she was a little girl she would be in charge of her life, her destiny. She smiled hearing the songs of the birds heralding her new day.

A wonderful new day.

Her passage from a school girl to a young woman, a young woman filled with dreams of building a business plying tourists with her chocolates.

The aroma of brewing coffee floated under the door, Marie's start of the day. Padding barefoot over the centuries old chestnut floorboards, Leigh entered the kitchen. Marie turned and embraced the young woman. Leigh hugged her back, kissed her cheek, and picked up the coffee Marie had poured for her—coffee in a special china cup and saucer for a special day.

"I'm sorry your Grandma Dobrev won't be able to join us for your graduation ceremony," Marie said setting a plate of whole-wheat toast on the table.

Leigh slathered the toast with soft creamy butter and raspberry jam. "I know she wanted to come," Leigh said. "But all the walking, the push of people ... it would have been too much for her."

"I hear there are several parties," Marie said, adding a splash of thick cream to her coffee. "Are you going?"

"Eric is taking me to dinner … at the hotel, mind you. A celebration he said."

Marie frowned. "He's trouble that one. I hoped you would accept one of the party invitations," Marie said, absently stirring the cream into her coffee.

"We might go to one after dinner. Don't worry, Marie. Eric's always considered himself my protector … and … don't wait up for me."

They grinned at each other. It was such a simple phrase, *don't wait up*, but the words carried a new meaning today. Leigh would turn eighteen in September. Already of drinking age in France, and now graduating from high school, her life was changing.

Even though the day flew by, Leigh tried to enjoy every moment, wanting to feel the transition of school girl to young woman. The graduation ceremony was memorable only in that she was one of the graduates. Marie gave her a nosegay of violets, a quick kiss, a hug, and wished her a nice evening. Leigh thanked her, threw her another kiss out of the window of Eric's relic of a car as he pulled away from the gaggle of graduates, their families, and friends.

Leaning back in the seat of his car she sniffed the lovely scent of the violets, smoothed the creamy-white chiffon skirt of her halter dress, her lips curving up.

"I hope that smile is for me," Eric said navigating the windy, narrow roads to the hotel.

"Today, Eric, I smile at everyone and everything, and that includes you, my friend." She was pleased that he wore a pair of long tan trousers instead of his usual cutoff jeans, even though he continued to wear his sneakers.

Eric pulled around to the back of the hotel, the employees' entrance to the kitchen. The sun was low in the sky casting long shadows over the pavement as they strolled to the open door. The kitchen staff were racing around as chefs shouted instructions, often cussing out a sous-chef for a prep error. Now two hours into the dinner service the kitchen was running full tilt.

The beat of the music, drums, symbols, guitars, an electronic keyboard, penetrated the walls into the kitchen from one of three small bands scheduled to entertain the diners throughout the evening. Eric's small group was to perform later—their set scheduled to last about an hour, give or take, the length of time depending on the reaction of the diners and the dining-room manager.

Eric grasped Leigh's hand. The couple continued through the kitchen, into the dining room, and to a small table to the side of the waiter's double swinging doors—through one side carrying trays laden with plates of food prepared to order for the guests, and waiters rushing back through the other side of the swinging doors with empty trays.

"I hope you don't mind the table," Eric said indicating Leigh should sit in the chair opposite him. "I've already ordered for us. Dinner is part of my tip for playing tonight."

Leigh was disappointed but tamped down her feeling of not being able to sit among the candlelit tables with small vases of flowers. At least the table had a white cloth, well, only a couple of spots. "Excuse me a minute," Eric smiled. "I'll go get us a glass of wine. After all, this is a celebration, a special day for you."

Leigh glanced around the tables out in front facing a small stage where a young male singer was belting out a lively pop song to the beat of the band.

Eric returned with a bottle of red wine and two goblets. The wine had been opened and Eric poured two glasses toasting her with a nod as he took a sip. "Are you ready to eat? You must be famished?" he asked reaching across the table for her hand.

"Yes, I am hungry. Whenever you're ready," she said taking another sip of wine and then another. This was not how she envisioned the evening, but she was determined to make the best of it.

Eric left the table returning with two dinner plates—rounds of pork tenderloin, golden roasted potatoes, and green beans. Eric poured another round of wine and smiled warmly as Leigh tried the pork.

She had to admit it was delicious and she was famished.

"Our group is scheduled to play next but you can sit right here … enjoy the music. I'll bring you a dessert and some more wine. The group following us asked to play early so I should be finished in less than an hour. Okay?"

What was she supposed to say—*no, I want to leave?*

When Eric's little band began their set, couples rose to the slower music and began to dance. Leigh had heard Eric play before but not with a group. She marveled at how well he handled the guitar—picking the strings, playing the cords with his left hand, the instrument tucked under is right arm hitting the guitar with his stump. She was amazed at the soft sound he produced and seconds later, hitting the body of the instrument harder, producing a loud swell.

Leigh recognized a family, one of her classmates with her parents. She was dancing with a boy from their class. Leigh pushed her chair back, shrinking into the shadows, watching. At the end of the number Leigh rose, filled her wine glass, and retreated into the shadows.

Time passed.

Eric returned to her as the next collection of musicians began playing. He pulled her to her feet and into his arms, swaying with the music. It was nice. At last she was dancing, being held, this was much better. The music continued. Eric drew her closer. She felt wonderful, her body melting against his. He kissed her cheek as they swayed.

"Leigh, let's leave, go someplace where I can hold you. My place," he whispered.

"Umm."

Eric, his arm around her, guided her to his car and drove down the road bordering the harbor where small sailboats and private fishing boats were docked. He pulled in back of a two-story building, parked, and helped her up the stairs to a hallway. The second floor, over several shops below, consisted of small rooms rented to service staff in the town.

Leigh stepped through the door into a room brightly lit with a bare bulb hanging down in the center. A futon couch was against one wall, a kitchen sink, a hot plate and a small refrigerator sat on a counter in the corner. An open door revealed a small bathroom to the left. The room was clean except for an ashtray filled with cigarette butts. Eric lit a few candles, turned off the ceiling light.

Leigh set her purse on a small table by the door as Eric retrieved a bottle of champagne from the refrigerator.

"I bought this today for us. I hoped you would come here with me," he said. Holding the bottle tight under his right arm, he managed with the strong fingers of his left hand to uncork the champagne. He poured the golden liquid into two plastic footed tumblers, the bubbles twinkling in the candlelight.

Leigh sipped the champagne, the bubbles tickling her tongue. She wrinkled her nose as Eric, fumbling a bit, lifted the glass from her hand setting both of their glasses on the little table.

Leigh hadn't spoken since they left the hotel. Dancing with him, the wine, the champagne, she wanted him to kiss her. She wanted to lie down, feel him holding her. He reached around, his shaky fingers fumbling, unsnapping the halter at the nape of her neck, her dress dropping to her waist revealing her breasts, the breasts of a woman.

"Leigh, you're beautiful. I've wanted you for so long … but I wanted … waited for today. You are a woman. School is behind you. Now, we can have a life together."

He pulled her to him, nuzzled her neck, reached around pulling the zipper of her dress down allowing the creamy chiffon to puddle on the floor.

She gazed at him, her eyes glassy, arms hanging to her side as he removed her panties. Holding her, guiding her with only a slight stumble to the futon, lowered her to the bed. Excusing himself, she heard him in the bathroom, opening and shutting a cabinet, tearing a wrapper, then he returned.

Her eyes closed.

She felt nothing.

———

A dull ache consumed her head. The room was dark. A street lamp filtered through the window with a soft light. Eric was lying beside her, a soft snore emanating from his throat with each rhythmic breath he took.

Was this love? Was this what she had read about in the novels on Marie's bookshelf?

She knew, her groin sore, she was no longer a virgin. This was no storybook romance. Eric, two years her senior, was a friend. Nothing more. Never anything more. Definitely not a lover.

Inching away from the man lying next to her, she left the bed. Her clothes lay on the floor where she had left them, creamy-white in the soft light from the street. She quickly dressed, grabbed her purse off the little table, picked up her shoes and tiptoed out the door closing it softly behind her. She ran down the steps, out of the building, then to the street that bordered the dock, the harbor. She ran to the split in the street, veering to the right and up the hill.

"No, that was not love, you stupid girl," she muttered.

The wind suddenly whirled around her body. A light rain began to fall. The waves in her long black hair fell in wet shanks down her back. Tears streamed down her cheeks, creamy-white chiffon whipping her legs as she ran to Marie's gate, up the path to her sanctuary. She tiptoed inside, silently closing the door behind her, her breath coming in gulps. Her bare feet tender, scraped from the rough street pavement, she climbed the stairs of the familiar soft wood of the old chestnut boards, into the room she had occupied for thirteen years. She slipped into bed burrowing under the covers, sobbing into the down pillow.

———

Marie heard Leigh quietly climb the stairs, heard the creak of her bed.

"Thank God, you're home," she whispered as she turned her head to the clock.

Three a.m.

She rose and shut her window against the advancing storm off the Atlantic, a pelting rain washing away the dust and grime of the night.

Chapter 8

―――

A SUNNY SUMMER DAY.

The beginning of July.

Marie stirred a shot of cream into her thick coffee, took a sip peering over the rim of her cup at Leigh. Something was wrong. She had noticed a change following her graduation from high school, but whenever she asked, Leigh brushed her off.

Maybe it was the sudden let down with the end of high school. This summer was different than the previous summers. It marked the beginning of the next phase of a young person's life.

"What are you going to do today, chérie? A skirt and blouse ... you must have plans." Marie asked, her voice cheerful, trying to coax a positive response out of the pathetic looking girl sitting across from her.

"Monsieur Linden, the manager at the souvenir shop, asked me to stop in. He said something about needing more help," Leigh replied. "And, Eric has been asking me to have coffee with him ... again. I keep turning him down. But he's very persistent, so I told him I would meet him at the café by the dock. Outside."

"Sounds like a busy morning. By the way, I have a favor to ask. I've accepted an invitation from a friend in Paris. I'll be gone for about five days. Will you be okay watching the house for me? I could ask—"

"Marie, you know I'll be glad to take care of things. Don't ask anybody to stop by ... an intruder."

"Our neighbor is not exactly an intruder." Exasperation was creeping into Marie's voice.

"I'm sorry. I didn't mean the way it sounded. I'd better get going. See you later." Leigh took her cup to the sink, gave Marie's shoulder a pat, and was out the door.

Walking down the hill to the harbor and the souvenir shop, she chastised herself for her behavior. "Marie's only trying to help," she mumbled. "I wish I wasn't seeing Eric today, but we keep bumping into each other. I need to clear the air."

Monsieur Linden was harried trying to take care of a group of tourists. When another couple strolled in, looked around, interrupting the first group with questions, he tried unsuccessfully to remain cool. It was at this moment that Leigh walked in. Linden rolled his eyes at her, and then turned back to the group of four leaving the couple with an unanswered question.

Leigh immediately saw his dilemma and stepped in to answer the woman's question. Satisfied, the woman sidled up to the counter chattering to her companion that she had found the perfect gift for her niece. Linden excused himself from the group, collected the money from the woman, put the gift in a plastic bag imprinted with the shop's name, thanked her and invited her to come back anytime. Meanwhile the other tourists left the shop empty handed.

Linden sighed, looked at Leigh with a kindly expression, hope in his eyes, and asked if she could start tomorrow. He needed help. Leigh returned the kindly look and accepted his job offer. Tomorrow was just fine.

Stepping out into the sunshine, the little harbor bustling with activity, Leigh saw Eric on the other side of the parked cars. He was sitting on the cement wall with iron knobs for boats to tie up, and ladders over the side used to climb onto or out of a boat. Seeing her, he stood holding up a large foam cup of coffee.

She walked up to him, took the coffee he extended to her and sat on the wall looking down at the ripples of water splashing against the stones. Removing the lid, taking a sip, she looked at him. "Thanks."

"Leigh, about that night ... I'm sorry. I thought—"

"Eric, I want to be friends. Just friends. I had too much to drink. It was my fault ... you misunderstood ... I shouldn't have ... I would like to forget that night ever happened. Can we do that? Can we be friends?"

"Uh, sure, but, Leigh, I want to be more than friends. I—"

"Eric, if you can't accept me as a friend, then I don't ever want to see—"

"Okay, okay. I get it." Scowling, he looked at a fishing boat pulling out of the harbor. "I'm not good enough for you. Is that it?"

"Don't be silly."

"I wish I was more like you. You have dreams. I drift from one day to the next."

"What are you doing this summer?" Leigh asked.

"The Le Varech bar hired me to play on the weekends, outside on the patio. I have a regular gig at the hotel lounge during the week. I hate it when the French soldiers come to the hotel on leave. They're boisterous ... think they're so smart. I hate them."

"Come on, Eric. Stop blaming the army for your father's death. It was an accident."

"Well ... both my father and mother were killed ... if he wasn't in the army ... given a leave, we wouldn't have been on that train. They wouldn't have died. And, I wouldn't have lost my hand. But it doesn't matter anymore. I have friends."

"I haven't seen any soldiers in town, at least not in uniform, and what new friends are you talking about?"

"Guys. Just guys getting together, spending time before they go to Paris. They have a leader they want me to meet. They like that I can speak French ... theirs isn't so good."

"So, they aren't French? What are they?"

"It doesn't matter what they are, or where they're from. They're my friends. We stick together."

"Well, if you like them, then I'm happy for you. Thanks again for the coffee. Friends?" Leigh stuck out her hand.

Eric took her hand, gave it a pump. "Friends," he said trying to smile.

I hope he means it. We've been part of each other's lives for such a long time.

Leaving Eric, Leigh decided to take the path down to the beach before going home. The air was warm and a melancholy feeling swept over her.

I wonder what Rawly is doing today? I bet he has a summer job. I should send him an email ... it's been a long time since I've heard from him. Maybe he's forgotten about me? He planned to go to college. And, what am I doing? A job in a souvenir shop. What about your big dream of becoming a chocolatier, Leigh Dobrev? Yes? What about it? I wish my mother were alive. Dad. Did I call him dad or daddy? Stop it! Marie is more than a mother to me. She's a friend. I know she's worried about me.

What's the matter with me? You're pitiful, Rawleigh Dobrev. Pitiful! Are you just going to let your life drift by like Eric? You always had dreams. Eric even said so. What happened? So you made a mistake that night. Get over it. Don't you dare disappoint Marie … or yourself.

"Oh, my God," she whispered. "What if Marie feels she's done with me. Wants to be done with me, but doesn't know how to tell me. I finished school. Time to move out?"

Leigh brushed the sand off her knees, stared momentarily at the waves lapping the shore, turned and ran up the path. Bursting into the kitchen where Marie was peeling potatoes for dinner, Leigh took the half-peeled potato from her hand putting it in the bowl of cold water, the peeler to the side. "Marie, I have something very important to ask you," she said pulling her to the kitchen table, to a chair. Leigh pulled another chair grasping both of Marie's hands.

"Chérie, what's the matter?" Marie asked, her brows drawing together, questioning.

"I've been very selfish. I assumed I could continue to live here … with you. I never asked you if I could, if it was okay with you. I know my grandparents send money to you every month, provided by my mom and dad's estate. But … now … will that continue? Maybe there are other things you want to do. You're going to see friends in Paris. Were you trying to tell me something?"

"Ma chérie, you silly girl. This is your home … always will be."

Leigh threw her arms around Marie, hugging her tight.

"Now," Marie said stroking Leigh's silky hair away from her eyes, "tell me what this is all about? Did you get the job?"

"Yes. But, more than that … I've been thinking." Leigh jumped up, walked to the sink and back. Sat again. "I'm going to go on the computer and look up schools in Paris that offer classes for a chocolatier. I've been acting foolishly, selfishly. Will you forgive me, ma mere?"

"Oh, ma chérie, of course I forgive you. I love you," Marie said wiping a tear from her eye. Leigh had never called her mother before.

"That's good, because I plan on making candy to sell. Besides the job at the souvenir shop, I'm going to have to save lots of money if I plan to go to school. Do you mind if I turn your kitchen into a mini chocolate factory?"

Marie laughed laying her hand over her heart, thanking God for returning Leigh's spirit. "A little chocolate factory? Sounds like fun."

Leigh kissed both of Marie's cheeks, then began opening cupboards pulling out measuring cups, mixing bowls and Great Grandmother Dobrev's candy molds and recipe cards.

Chapter 9

Boston, Massachusetts

SEPTEMBER—SUMMER HEAT had waned and the crisp air of fall seeped throughout New England. Mother Nature began tinting the countryside with gold, red, and bronze.

Rawly embraced the change. Excitement coursed through his veins. He had been accepted into the Air Force ROTC program at Massachusetts Institute of Technology—a full scholarship with a four-year commitment after graduation to serve his country.

With a major in Electrical Engineering, and a schedule of ROTC classes consisting of one hour of classroom work and one to two hours of leadership training each week, he knew he was in for a tough time. But his tuition would be paid in full, not like most of his classmates who would face an education bill of more than sixty-thousand dollars.

Tyler urged his brother to minor in Computer Science. Rawly listened, but also squeezed in a political science class. He wasn't certain as yet which career path he wanted to pursue once his active-duty ROTC commitment was fulfilled. He might even decide to stay in the Air Force.

With his freshman year of college now underway, Rawly vigorously threw himself into his studies. Tyler was a Junior at Babson and Rawly was matriculating only a few miles down the road at MIT.

A group of Rawly's classmates in his Poly Sci class urged him to run for Freshman Class President promising to help with his campaign. Their professor sweetened the pot by challenging them: if they took the opportunity to work on the campaign they would earn extra class credit almost assuring them an A grade. Rawly and his classmates accepted the professor's challenge.

The experience whetted Rawly's appetite for politics. The experience made him think about why he sought the office of class president, made him hone a campaign message. He had to articulate succinctly what he and the other class officers might do, what the whole class would do that could make a difference, leaving behind a legacy.

The U.S. 2008 presidential campaigns were discussing how to make the environment and the world a better place, homeland security, immigration, the economy and taxes made up the candidate's talking points. Rawly wondered where energy fit into the debate. The economy was in free fall so that was certainly a hot topic, and he could foresee that the senior class was going to have a hard time finding jobs. He decided to use that issue as the main plank of his platform: run a job fair for seniors.

Rawly won the election—President of the Freshman Class!

This is easy, he thought.

True to the promise his campaign made, he and his classmates ran a job fair for the seniors. It proved to be a big success. Dozens of companies in the area, around the state, and neighboring states participated.

The following fall he ran for Sophomore Class President.

He lost!

Maybe running for office wasn't so easy after all.

But something bigger than school politics stirred inside him, something bigger than the fun of running for a class office, or the thrill of winning. He saw that by working with others through the planning and execution of the job fair, that he could make a difference. Maybe he could make a difference for his country.

Calendar pages flipped month-to-month, year-to-year. Tyler graduated setting a high bar for his brother when he accepted a job in a small database company on the twenty-third floor of the John Hancock Building. The building was known for its glass facade providing a view of Boston's business district with the backdrop of the Atlantic Ocean to the east. The rapidly-growing company was happy with their new hire, and Tyler zealously dug into his job of mining data for statistical trends leading to targeted marketing programs for the company's expanding client base.

Rawly's junior year began with a full schedule.

He added another Poly Sci course to his already heavy load of electrical engineering and computer science classes.

A few of his fellow ROTC cadets didn't like the drills, the marching, but Rawly enjoyed the physical workouts. Both his mom and dad had remarked more than once that his physical appearance was rapidly changing—the skinny boy, now six-foot-one, had broader shoulders, muscular arms and legs. The girls noticed too. They were attracted to the good-looking guy with the easy smile.

He was restless, had been since starting college even though he was active in study groups and managed to take part in the campus social scene, on a limited scale. He didn't think he was any different than his classmates, but gradually he could see they were calmer in adapting to the routine of classes, summer work, more classes and the hours of study each class required if he was going to attain his goal of straight A's. His junior year would end with a four-week ROTC summer camp, a mandatory program for all individuals qualified to pursue an Air Force commission through AFROTC .

Rawly enjoyed the parties and the girls, especially the girls, but rarely dated the same girl more than twice. Christmas holidays were around the corner and one of the girls he asked to a dance invited him to her house for dinner before the event. She lived nearby—her parents were traveling so they would have the house to themselves. Rawly eagerly accepted her invitation. They never arrived at the dance, and Rawly learned that sex, while pleasant enough, only added to his restlessness.

The handsome, smart, going-places Rawly Scott had no trouble finding women. He could have what he wanted, with whomever he wanted. However, if he thought his ease with girls would calm his restlessness, it did not. He continued to fidget, jumping at the completion of one project into the frenetic activity of the next assignment.

———

It was Saturday and Boston's Quincy Market was buzzing. The first week of April and residents, visitors, and students, especially the students, wanted out of confinement and into the balmy spring air.

Rawly saw his brother waiting for him at the outdoor café, kicking back, enjoying his Saturday morning coffee in the sunshine.

"Hi, Bro, trying for a suntan?" Rawly asked, slumping into the chair beside Tyler.

"Very funny. You're late," Tyler said taking a sip of his coffee.

"How soon you forget those early Saturday morning sessions with a study group. Mine was longer than usual today. Must be nice to be out working instead of studying for the next exam," Rawly said leaning his head back for a warm beam of sunshine.

"Spring break starts next week?" Tyler asked.

Rawly snapped straight in the wrought-iron chair, cradling his foam coffee cup in his hands. "I've been thinking."

"Uh oh. Who is it this time?"

"Seriously thinking."

"Uh huh."

"I've decided to go for my Masters in Engineering, Electrical Engineering."

"What? How can you do that? I thought you had to start serving your four years with the Air Force after graduation and your commissioning."

"Dad thought it was a good idea. He did it. He was commissioned as a Second Lieutenant and then studied for his masters. That's what I'm going to do. I asked for a one-year deferment."

"One year? Rawly, a master's takes two years. Sometimes more."

"Not if I cram. I talked to my professor. He said I can do it." Rawly sat back. Sat forward. Walked to the railing around the café's patio.

Tyler watched him, shaking his head in disbelief.

Rawly turned back, a grin on his face as he rejoined Tyler. "I'm going to do it, Bro. The ROTC Captain already checked, put in the request, and they gave me the one-year deferment. This summer I go to Texas for twenty-eight days—the ROTC summer camp. Then back for my Senior year.

"If you're still alive. Geez, Rawly, there's more to life than school."

"Exactly. Last night my two roommates and I were chatting about our senior year. It was exciting, but then we started talking about graduation, and one thing led to another."

"It is what it is, Bro—excitement and responsibility. Believe me, I know what you're talking about. As they say, been there done that, still doing that and will be for several years to come."

"That's just it, Ty—responsibility, no time to kick up our heels. We started throwing around ideas. Why not travel through Europe during our spring break … before graduation? By planning now we think we can take some early finals."

Rawly stood, raked his fingers through thick, dark-brown hair. Pacing again to the edge of the café, looking out at the eager shoppers, he strolled back to Tyler. Sat down.

"By formalizing our plans now we can save up for a week's excursion, maybe ten days, two weeks, I don't know. I've certainly earned a little fun … don't you think?"

"Geez, Rawly, you really think you can afford it?"

"We'd stay at youth hostels, eat two meals a day. A beer for dinner." Rawly chuckled. "We put together an itinerary. Here, take a look." Rawly jammed his fist into his pants pocket, pulled out a wrinkled piece of paper, smoothing it out in front of Tyler. The paper was a printout of a map of Europe. Two countries were circled in red.

"See, begin in France then across to England," Rawly said pointing excitedly to France.

"Wish I could go with you," Tyler said. "Which is exactly why you're doing it—go before you can't go because of your military commitment … wherever that takes you."

"I knew you'd understand, Ty. During the night I had another thought."

"Really?"

"Maybe my buddies should fly to London I'll meet them there after a quick stop in France."

Tyler smiled, closed his eyes, fingers to his forehead. "Let me see. I think I see something. Yes, yes, a girl. A scrawny girl with buck teeth. She's thirteen. Ah, yes, it's clear. Her name is Rawleigh Dobrev."

"She's not thirteen now, gypsy fortune teller. She's twenty … same as me. I could retrace the trip we made seven years ago. I told her I'd be back."

"Not keeping a promise, especially to a buck-toothed girl with your name, would doom you to purgatory forever." Tyler smiled at Rawly. "As you said, you deserve a little fun."

That night Rawly wrote Leigh a letter, dropping it in the mailbox on his way to class the next morning.

Chapter 10

———

Pornic, France
April 2011

CANDY MOLDS, MIXING BOWLS, spatulas and a sundry of other candy-make tools covered every flat surface of Marie's kitchen and dining room. A selection of classical piano music—Chopin, Beethoven, Rachmaninoff—was playing softly from the computer sitting on the counter next to the breadbox.

Marie leaned against the door jamb to the kitchen sipping her morning coffee, watching Leigh engrossed in painting a mold. She had turned Marie's kitchen and dining area into a veritable candy factory in order to maintain a stock of chocolates in the two shops by the harbor. Well, one souvenir shop and the Le Varech pub.

This morning she was performing a new technique she had read about—painting leaves inside two metal molds of her great grandmother's. The molds had twelve small leaf cavities, each with intricate details—grooves showing the veins of the leaves. A plate with ten hollows, similar to a deviled egg serving dish, sat on a heating pad to maintain the paint at the proper temperature so it wouldn't harden. Three of the hollows contained a thin melted-paint mixture of white chocolate, a few drops of vegetable oil, and powdered food coloring—apple green, cherry red, and lemon yellow.

Bending over the mold, Leigh picked up a brush and tapped a small red dot from the red mixture onto the bottom of each leaf, repeating the process with the yellow. Using the green mixture, she stroked color into the grooves, veins, of the leaves. With the yellow, she brushed a petal on each side of the red dot covering the green vein, repeating the technique with the red paint on either side of the yellow dot.

Standing straight, rubbing her back, she glanced up at Marie. "This painting stuff is tedious. There's another method where I can drop a color into each cavity, smooth it around for a very thin veneer effect, or there are transfer patterns—each little pattern goes in the bottom, then the chocolate fills the cavity. After the completed mold cools in the refrigerator for thirty minutes, I turn it upside down, tap it, and voila, the chocolates fall out showing the pretty decoration—paint, veneer, or transfer pattern. I think I'll do the veneer method for the next couple of batches or I'll never be able to deliver them today. What do you think, Madame Binoche?" Leigh chuckled.

"Sweet little Monet masterpieces, ma chérie. I can see why you painted the green veins first … working in reverse so you see the detail when you pop the candy from the mold. Coffee?" Marie asked.

"Oui, s'il vous plaît. Now, I temper the chocolate, spoon it over my paint, scrape off any excess so the bottom of each piece is perfect, and pop the mold into the refrigerator." Leigh was talking more to herself than Marie as she sipped her coffee, engrossed in the art project.

"Tempering chocolate for a solid, molded piece of candy … tricky?" Marie asked.

"It's all in the heating and cooling. Mainly, melt the chocolate to about 110 degrees, cool to about 85 by constantly agitating it with a spatula so the temperature is even throughout the mixture, and then pour it over the paint in each little hollow. The tempering step is critical for a solid piece of chocolate. The candy should snap when you bite it. I'm also adding a little cherry flavoring."

———

The April air turned chilly. Leigh bundled up in jeans topped with a smoky-blue turtleneck sweater matching her eyes, and a jacket zipped to the top. She quickly dropped off a box of chocolates at her first stop, and then drove to the Souvenir Shop where she worked. She admired an addition to the window display—a wide-brimmed yellow straw hat just like one she had dreamed of her mother wearing.

Leigh mentioned the hat to Monsieur Linden as he paid her for last week's chocolate sales. He suggested she try it on and if she liked it she could have it—a bonus for her hard work. It was perfect and she strutted out of the shop feeling like she had drifted out of a lovely dream.

Her lips curved into a smile as she carried her basket of chocolates into the Pornic hospital, a brilliant white, austere building with a red-tiled roof rising at a sharp angle on one side.

"Bonjour, Mademoiselle. Pretty hat." The information desk attendant scurried around the counter. She knew what the basket held and was pleased to receive the delicacies.

"Bonjour, Pati. Candy for your patients … fresh this morning." Leigh set the basket on the floor transferring two large rectangular white boxes to the counter. Inside, each piece was nestled in a little white paper cup.

"Merci, Mademoiselle Dobrev. And I have your empty boxes from last week in case you wish to fill them again," Pati said with a wink. She fully anticipated that Leigh would return with more of her chocolates. The delivery had become a weekly habit.

The hospital's administrator had quickly agreed to Leigh's offer of complimentary boxes of chocolates if in return the nurses would give the patient her business card along with the candy. The two establishments in Pornic where her candy could be purchased were printed on the back of each card.

The marketing plan was working.

Leigh strolled out of the hospital to her used Smart car parked in the lot. Another one of her marketing schemes—buying the little car through a Pornic dealer from the Smartville manufacturing facility in Hamburg, France, and painting the white exterior with *Dobrev Chocolates* in the center of a cluster of chocolate truffles.

Stashing her basket, now filled with empty white candy boxes gathered from her three stops, on the front seat of the car, she drove back to the main street and up the narrow hill to Marie's cottage.

Entering the house, she hooked her hat on the corner of a chair and headed for the kitchen following the aroma of fresh coffee.

Setting the basket on the floor next to the back door, she pulled her wallet out of her shoulder bag and stuffed several bills into a big pink piggy bank that had been her mothers. Running her fingers over the pig she sighed—it wasn't much but each bill represented a step closer to her goal of going to Paris.

"You have a letter, chèrie. You'll never guess who it's from so I'll tell you ... Monsieur Rawly Scott," Marie said handing her a mug of coffee.

Leigh's brows shot up over a broad toothy grin. She turned, spotting the white envelope propped up against a stubby red candle in the center of the kitchen table. The two women had made it a habit of eating dinner in the kitchen and always by candlelight. The two swapped stories about the day's events over a glass of wine. Receiving a correspondence from Rawly was definitely an event.

"Marie, I don't believe it." Leigh laughed picking up the envelope, her finger tracing her name and his return address. "How long ... seven years?" She carefully pried open the flap, withdrawing a card. "Look, a cute airplane in the sky ... across the miles," she giggled. "There's a letter inside."

> *Hi, Leigh,*
> *I told you I'd be back some day. Long time no see.*
> *I'm graduating from college next year and two of my buddies and I are planning a last-hoorah trip before we receive our diplomas in July.*
> *Our hooray's destination of choice is Europe: France, England, maybe Germany if our money and time allows.*
> *Even though it's almost a year away, next April, will you be in Pornic or at least somewhere in France? If that bottle of mine could land on a beach near you it's the least I can do to try to find you again.*
> *Please send me an email sometime—snail mail is too slow.*
> *Can I put your name on my itinerary?*
> *Your American friend,*
> *Rawly Scott*

Chapter 11

———

LEIGH STARED AT THE LETTER. *Rawly … graduating from college. What have I done? Nothing. Making candy. Giving most of it away.* Her eyes tortured, she faced Marie.

"Did Rawly's letter bring bad news?" Marie asked reaching out, covering Leigh's fingers holding his letter.

"No. Not bad news. He's graduating from college next year. He may come to see us."

"But that's wonderful. Why the long face?" Marie smiled, a bright smile matching her yellow shirt, so pretty against her dark cap of hair curling forward over her ears.

"Graduating from college. He's making something of himself. I've done nothing. I'm the same little girl I was when we met years ago."

"Oh, chèrie, not so. You graduated from high school. You're building a business … selling your chocolates."

"I'm kidding myself, Marie." Leigh looked around the kitchen, through the archway to the long dining room table covered with oil cloth to protect the antique patina from spills, from a hot pan placed too quickly before it had time to cool, a pot of creamy yellow butter melting the cloth but not marring the wood underneath.

"Look what I've done to your home … made a mess of it … clutter. Nothing but clutter. Marie, I'm sorry. You never complained but I should have seen I was taking advantage of your kindness."

"Nonsense. Now you listen to me Rawleigh Dobrev. You are my joy. I love you like my own daughter. You turn those pretty pink lips up into a smile. If you aspire to move your passion forward, the passion to take the little cacao bean and transform it into something delicious, to cause a person to put your chocolate on their tongue closing their eyes as it melts against their palette, then you must take steps to do something about it. And, not just tiny steps. Think big. I mean think really BIG."

"But what, Marie? I'm saving to go to Paris, to go to school, to be a true chocolatier, but the savings I'm putting aside from my candy sales are mere pennies. I need more, much more." Leigh's shoulders slumped as she gently pushed Rawly's letter back into the envelope.

Marie bustled to the coffee maker starting a fresh brew. "I've been researching an idea and I think it's time I tell you what I've found and what I'm prepared to do ... providing you're up to the challenge."

"What idea? We tell each other everything ... well, almost everything. You've never mentioned anything to me about an idea."

Marie's fingers tapped nervously on the counter as she gazed out the window at the late afternoon shadows. *Time to test the ambition of the girl. Does she have what it takes?* "An online course to establish your credentials as a chocolatier. You can keep working. This will give you the flexibility to schedule your studies around your work routine. The school is well known in the States, France, other countries. The online chocolatier curriculum is available twenty-four hours a day, seven days a week, no specific time do you have to sit in front of your computer.

"A one or two-hour session is perfect to learn and retain the material and techniques. I'm a teacher you know," Marie said whirling around to face her former student. "Understand that if you enroll you have to spend the time, be committed to this chocolate-making program to succeed. Leigh, it's a way to bring your dreams to reality."

"What's the name of school?" Leigh asked, skepticism written across her face.

"Academy of Chocolate Arts. Wait, let me get the folder. It's in my desk ... I sent for information but I didn't want to tell you until I checked it out ... that the course would give you what I think you need."

Marie trotted off to her office as Leigh paced to the kitchen window framed with a lace curtain held to one side with a floppy green satin ribbon. Her heart hitched up a beat with optimism but her head spun with doubts. *Online classes might not be as expensive as actually attending a school in Paris. No room and board. But online? How do you melt chocolate online? Ask the teachers if the consistency is too thick or too thin?*

Marie returned pulling papers from a manila folder. "Here, take a look." She laid out several sheets along with brochures picturing various types of chocolate candy—a treat for the eye. "Regarding the curriculum, this brochure states that the program contains over a hundred learning activities to make sure you develop the expertise you need."

Marie looked over her glasses to see if there was a display of interest from Leigh. There seemed to be. She wasn't staring out the window, had come to the table, picked up a brochure with a beautiful picture of chocolate truffles on the front—the solid chocolate candy coated with coconut, slivered almonds, or powdered chocolate.

Scanning the course description, Leigh's fingers traced down each line, then back to the top. "The chocolatier program is only three months long. It can't possibly give me all the training I need to become a professional—design candies for a shop, or start a real business." Leigh set the brochure aside, shuffled through the other papers Marie laid on the table.

"Their chocolatier program is only a foundation—a start," Marie said. She wasn't giving up. "Somewhere I saw where you don't need special skills or qualifications to take the course. The instructor begins with the basics and builds to more advanced work. All at your own pace but you have to finish in the timeframe they set for the class. Also, because you're working in my kitchen you can repeat the lessons over and over until you master the technique. You certainly are not, I repeat, chérie, you are not a beginner, but you are self taught. While the basic skills may include techniques you already know, there will be others you don't know. And completing the course will give you credentials to show to potential employers, or ..." Marie smiled, her eyes sparkling, "or a banker to loan you money for your own shop."

"I don't see anything on what techniques will be taught?" Leigh tried to tamp down the adrenalin slowly inching up through her body. *Could this really be a way to become a professional candy maker? A chocolatier?*

"Ma chérie," Marie pulled another brochure from the bottom of the papers, pushed her glasses up on her nose, and began to read out loud in her teaching voice. "This course includes the consistent production of fine chocolate bonbons, confections and bars beginning with an in-depth understanding of chocolate, then moves from that foundation into professional production skills, modern decoration techniques, equipment and supply sourcing, and production and marketing issues involved in opening a chocolate business." Marie looked up, smiling. "Sounds pretty comprehensive to me. How about you?"

"Sounds very different than online courses I've heard about where you start anytime. This school's online courses are offered on specific dates, kind of like a real school. When does the Chocolatier Program start?"

Picking up another brochure, Marie opened it to the information she wanted. "August. It's followed with a course on the cacao bean, and a quality control program, and, you'll like this, a program for starting a business, pulling together a business plan ..."

"Sounds expensive. More coffee?"

"Don't change the subject, Leigh. Oui, a little more coffee, s'il vous plaît, and hand me the cream pitcher ... here this sheet gives the tuition for each program. The first one, the Chocolatier, is $685 plus equipment and ingredients." Marie looked around at all the bowls, mixers, molds, pans, and baking sheets. "I think you have the equipment covered, so then it's just the ingredients. And, with the new techniques you can push a new line of holiday chocolates for your current clients. You'll make a killing, you clever girl."

Leigh chuckled, "Really, Marie, that's a stretch even for you. But it doesn't matter. I may have eighty-five dollars but not six hundred."

"Oh, I'm sorry. Silly me," Marie said feigning surprise, her hand on her chest. "I forgot to mention that the initial tuition is on me, and if you pull an *A,* as you did in school, then maybe there will be more. There's time to save for follow-on courses. Now get busy and fill out these forms. By the time that Monsieur Rawly arrives you will have finished at least three programs." Marie took a sip of coffee as a smug look crossed her face.

"And, I also forgot to show you, if you finish successfully … and you will …" Marie sorted through the papers and brochures, finding what she was looking for, pushed it in front of Leigh, then leaned back. Bringing the coffee cup to her lips, she finished her sentence, with a glint in her eyes. "You will be eligible for an internship. The school will sponsor you. But I can't think about that because that would mean you'd probably move to Paris."

Paris! Adrenalin shot through Leigh like a bolt of lightning. *Paris!*

Lighting the dinner candle with the scent of cinnamon, Marie added, "When you write to Rawly, tell him I won't hear of his staying in a hotel. He'll bunk right here with us as he did when he was thirteen."

Leigh, unable to sit another minute, jumped up, ran around the table dropping to her knees beside Marie wrapping her arms around her waist. "Merci, merci, merci. I love you. I promise I'll work hard."

Marie patted Leigh's shoulder, kissed her silky head. "I know you will, chérie."

Leigh stood, kissed Marie on both cheeks, then clapping her hands twirled like a little girl around the kitchen, stopping abruptly at the counter. She lovingly caressed her great grandmother's leaf mold she had painted and filled with chocolate that morning. A feeling of warmth flooded her body—a connection to a woman she had never known.

———

To: RawlyScott@yahoo.com
Date: April 15, 2011
Time: 9 p.m.
From: LeighDobrev@gmail.com
Subject: Your letter
Monsieur Rawleigh, hi back at you.

I eagerly read your letter—long time no see is an understatement. A trip to France—I wonder if we'll recognize each other?

As of now I will be in Pornic and Marie asked me to tell you that you are welcome to bunk with us if you will be staying overnight. Her exact words.

Marie has been making plans for me behind my back— several online courses to become a professional chocolatier. Not sure how that will work in actually learning new techniques but I'm going to give it a try. You can taste my new chocolate truffles but only if you promise to rave over them.

I look forward to hearing the details when your plans crystallize—dates and stuff. You now have my email address. :)

Your friend,
Leigh

Chapter 12

—

To: LeighDobrev@gmail.com
Date: October 5, 2011
Time: 10 p.m.
From: RawlyScott@yahoo.com
Subject: April Trip
Hi again.
Can't believe it's October, October of my SENIOR year no less.

First, and most important, how does the first week in April look? My buddies and I are planning on taking our second semester finals as early as possible which will give us ten days to cruise Paris and London. If the date works for you, then I plan on making Pornic my first stop ... well, after I land in Paris. Ha-ha. My buddies will fly straight to London and I'll catch up with them a couple of days later.

Please thank Marie for her offer of a bunk. Ha-ha again. I'm thinking of arriving as early as possible, as fast as the train will roll from Paris to Nantes. Should I rent a car? Will stay with you and Marie that night and leave late the next day.

Yup, my senior year. However, it won't end school for me. I'm going for my masters in electrical engineering—another year, but I'll be a commissioned officer, Second Lieutenant in the Air Force. The AFROTC offered me a full scholarship—started my freshman year. So, I guess we never stop learning. Tyler says I should get a life which is why I'm coming to see you.

I ran for senior class president and won! I kind of like this politic stuff but will give you more of my thoughts when I see you.

One more thing on the political subject. I began working as a volunteer for a candidate from Massachusetts. He's a businessman running for the U.S. Senate in next year's election.

How about you? Did you take the chocolatier course? I bet you could have been the teacher. I seem to recall you said something about chocolate truffles waiting for me.

Glad we're using email. Don't forget to let me know about the date.

Rawly

———

To: RawlyScott@yahoo.com
Date: October 6, 2011
Time: 8 a.m.
From: LeighDobrev@gmail.com
Subject: Re: April Trip
PEN me in on your itinerary, Monsieur.

Anytime the first week of April works for me and for Marie. Forget about renting a car. Marie and I will meet your train in Nantes no matter the date or the time with a little white box of my chocolates. And with a sad face we will return you to the station the next day.

Rawly, the first chocolatier course was incredible. I had my doubts, you know the online method. But it worked. There was an online chat room setup with the instructor. I learned so much. I hope you don't get sick of chocolate because as April draws closer, I'm saving samples of my class work for your critique.

Senior class president. Very impressive. Does that mean I have to address you as Monsieur President? Sounds to me like you have the political bug big time. It wouldn't surprise me if one day I can say I knew you when. Wow! Not only class president but a lieutenant in the U.S. Air Force. Wait till I tell Grandma Dobrev that tidbit of news. Your email *contained so much information!! Air force, electrical engineering, masters, politics—whew. No wonder you're ready for a holiday. I'm anxious to hear how you intend to fit all these pieces together.*

Yes, I'll still be in Pornic in April, but, and this is a big BUT, as you start your masters program I'll be going to Paris for an internship. At least that's the plan. I get goose bumps thinking that Paris may actually be in my future. We'll both be in a big city!

That's it for now. No, wait. One more thing. I'm starting another course: Specialty Candy, Creating Holiday Magic. Marie is urging me to offer a new line of chocolates to my customers for Christmas.

Have a nice day, Monsieur President.

Leigh :)

Part Three
Chapter 13

——

France – April 2012

THE EUROSTAR HIGH-SPEED train streaked south from Paris. Gazing out of the window at the countryside, Rawly smiled warmly at the rolling fields of yellow oilseed rape. As a boy of thirteen, he and his brother had been too busy with their GameBoys to notice the passing landscape, but he remembered Grammy Kathy remarking about the vibrant yellow fields. He began feeling anxious about seeing Leigh, wondering why he had altered his trip, why he was spending a day with Leigh when his buddies were on their way to London. Well, no matter, one night in Pornic and then he'd be back on the train to catch up with his friends.

He felt the train reducing speed as it rounded the bend and then jerked and hissed to a stop in the modern train station of Nantes. Rawly glanced out the window as he pulled his bag from the steel rack above his seat, swinging it over his shoulder.

People stood on the platform waiting to meet friends, family, business associates. Most were smiling, some holding babies in their arms, or a child's hand. It suddenly occurred to him he had no idea what Leigh looked like other than black hair. She stood a head taller than he eight years ago. She told him in her last email she would be holding a white box of chocolates—a way to recognize her.

The porter swung the steps down in place from the body of the train to the cement platform. Passengers began shuffling ahead of him to the exit. It was his turn. Gingerly stepping off the train Rawly immediately spotted Leigh two cars back—a beautiful woman, not a girl, holding a little white box. With a broad smile, he strolled in her direction.

THE MESSAGE | 65

Leigh caught sight of the handsome man coming her way. Stunned, her eyebrows hitched up, and with a musical laugh she quickly closed the distance to him. He dropped his bag on the cement, hugged her, held her away, his head shaking back and forth. They were a matched pair—both in dark-blue jeans topped with white turtlenecks. The only difference, his shirt stretched over broad shoulders and hers followed womanly curves. His black leather sport shoes anchored him firmly to the ground, but her black heels accentuated the beautiful body they held.

Laughing, they sputtered at the same time, "You've changed."

Still laughing, she extended her gift.

He lifted the box from her hand, his eyes remaining riveted to hers. She pointed to the box which was now open. Chuckling, he saw four chocolate truffles with an *R* painted in a ribbon of gold. Holding a hand up to stop any further conversation, Rawly picked up one of the candies, put it in his mouth and immediately closed his eyes as the chocolate melted on his tongue. Savoring the sweetness he picked up a second chocolate, nodded for her to open her mouth and placed the truffle on her tongue.

His lips drawn to a smile, he gave her a peck on the cheek, and closed the box. "That's all you get of my candy, young lady. No more sharing." Unzipping a side pocket of his backpack, he stashed the little box and closed the zipper.

Out of the terminal, Leigh's truffle-decorated Smart car sped down the road away from Nantes to Pornic. Playing tour guide, she pointed out a few places of interest but mostly they talked about where his buddies were, that they had agreed to meet in London, and that he looked forward to seeing the sights of Paris after they left Great Britain.

"If it's okay with you, we'll go to Marie's first. She can't wait to see you. I thought she might come with me to meet your train, but she said she'd wait."

"Sounds good. Mom, Tyler, and Grammy Kathy—"

Leigh laughed, "Grammy?"

"Hey, you're never too old … well, maybe. Tyler and I call her GK … Grammy just slipped out. But *my family* told me to give Marie a hug for them. Not one hug, mind you, but one from each."

Leigh couldn't help stealing glances at the grown man with a deep voice, muscles, and warm brown eyes sitting next to her. Each time she glanced at him, he was smiling at her not at the point of interest they were passing. She was his point of interest.

———

Retrieving his bag from the car Rawly stood on the street in front of Marie's gate, his eyes following the path on the other side up to the French cottage. "This I remember," he said with a melancholy sigh. He looked at Leigh standing next to him, her scent fresh, sweet, with a hint of jasmine, teased him.

They stood in the street. Held in a trance—dazed. No longer children, they marveled at the transformation that had taken place—boy to man, girl to woman. Years had unfolded, but here they stood as if it was yesterday ... back at this gate ... once again standing beside each other feeling the incredible magnetism they had the first time when she found the bottle he had thrown into the ocean, guided by currents—his hand to her hand.

Rawly felt his heart seize, then relax. Leigh had blossomed into a beautiful woman. She had curves, lovely contours, and her beautiful face, her silky black hair in soft long waves falling around her shoulders one strand flicking up in a curl from a puff of wind, her long eyelashes fringing big smoky-blue eyes. But it was her mouth. Oh, those soft pink full lips. He wanted to run his thumb slowly over those lips yet he held back, hesitated. Who was this beautiful person? He'd never hesitated before. Why now? He'd never really looked at a woman's lips before. Kissed them quick, sometimes hard in lust. But a man could lose himself here.

Leigh pulled her eyes away, opened the gate nodding for him to follow. He let her lead the way, swinging the ornate iron gate shut with the toe of his shoe.

"Bonjour, Rawly Scott," Marie called out waiting on her porch for him in her jeans under a flowered apron, her arms open wide. "This can't be the thirteen-year-old Rawly Scott, surely not," she said her brown eyes crinkling in the corners as he dropped his bag and enfolded her in a bear hug. Another squeeze. Another squeeze. "And here's one more hug from Grammy Kathy."

"Oh, how wonderful," she said gazing up into his handsome face. "So tall. Come, come, inside. I'll show you your room so you can freshen up if you like. Leigh, I put the kettle on. I'm going to hold you two for a cup of tea before you run off and start swapping stories of the years since you were here last. I know you want to head down to the beach, even though it's chilly. Nice sun, but the breeze off the ocean ..."

No further than the living room, the three chattered rapidly—a mixture of French and English. Rawly asked Marie to repeat what she said a few times, her accent masking the words as he tried to follow what she was saying. "You've been studying French, young man," Marie said unable to resist hugging him. "With a slight American accent," she laughed scooting him up the stairs to the bedroom. "Second door on the right."

Leaving him to freshen up, Marie joined Leigh in the kitchen.

"Chèrie, oh, my. Rawly, he is so handsome, yes?"

Leigh turned away from the stove, stepped close to Marie, and whispered. "Marie, I don't know what's the matter with me. I can't take my eyes off him. He keeps looking at me, I mean into my eyes, like ... like he wants to kiss me but can't move." She thought about the stray lock of dark brown hair falling down on his forehead, his dark brown eyes. He was now way taller than her five-foot-three.

"I can see he is attracted, and you, too?"

"But, Marie, I've never felt like this. I don't care about boys ... men ...never ... but ...

"Okay, I'm ready for that tea—followed the trail of orange down the stairs. Then I'll be ready for that walk to the beach." Joining the women, Rawly lifted the kettle from the stove, strolled to the pine table, smiling.

Leigh and Marie, rooted to the floor, watched the man.

Chapter 14

———

A SWISH OF CHILLY AIR entered the cottage with the laughter of reunited friends enjoying a private joke. Marie was setting three places for dinner when Rawly swooped in, picking her up, swinging her around.

"Oh, no, Madame Binoche. No slaving over the stove tonight. I'm taking you and the mademoiselle to dinner."

"But, I already—"

"The Scott clan would skin me alive, if I didn't take you to dinner," Rawly said setting Marie back on her feet. "They all chipped in specifically stating that the money was to treat you two, and I was not, I repeat, I was not to blow it on some girl I met on my travels."

"I suggested Le Bistronomi'k," Leigh said with raised brows over a wide smile.

"Oh, my, well, give me a few minutes to spruce up," Marie chuckled. "Help yourself to tea while I change."

"Hold on, I'm changing, too." Leigh said both women chuckling as they dashed out of the kitchen. "Teabags are above the stove, Rawly," Marie called over her shoulder.

The evening air was brisk, the sky clear, as Leigh parked Marie's car across from the harbor. Tables with sets of turquoise chairs dotted the outside patio, but with the cool air patrons had opted to dine inside.

The trio was greeted by a friendly hostess who showed them to a table next to a wall washed with soft light, a small votive flickering in the center of the white tablecloth. Rawly took in the attractive decor punctuated with an imaginative use of wood tones. The food was being prepared by the chefs in an open kitchen at the rear.

"The owner and her staff speak fluent English so don't hesitate to ask about any of the dishes that catch your eye," Marie said opening her menu.

Marie ordered a cod andouille entrée, Leigh stuffed clams and shrimp brochette marinated in lime, and Rawly a beef brochette. Deferring to the ladies fish, he asked for a carafe of white wine, and a glass of robust merlot.

The goblets of wine twinkling in the soft light, Rawly raised his glass. "Here's to Leigh's chocolates. I hope there will be more because I polished off the box."

Over dinner Rawly related how much he had enjoyed seeing the antique houses, stone walls, and yellow fields as the train whizzed through village after village. This led to a discussion of his growing interest in history. "Marie, tell me about the French Resistance … stories of their escapades in Pornic?"

"Well, now, as a teacher, I've heard stories. For instance, I've heard it said, that Saint Nazaire, a port on the mouth of the river Loire, and the area including Pornic, were liberated by the Allies very late in the war. Oh, and in Pornic, August of 1944, Germans came looking for a man they considered a spy. Because they couldn't get him, they asked all Pornic residents to gather at the harbor. It's said they took sixteen hostages. Eventually the hostages were freed. There was also an exchange of prisoners, which was rare during this war. Sixty-four Germans were exchanged for thirty-two French plus thirty-two Americans. What happened has not really been written officially but the information comes from several different sources."

Rawly topped off their wine glasses and signaled the waitress for another glass of the Merlot. "What about your parents, Marie?"

"My mother, who used to live in Vendome near the Loire Valley, helped save American pilots. And the way it happened and the consequences have had a big influence on our family."

"Sounds as if we must go out to dinner again." Rawly smiled but noticed Marie's eyes were tearing so he quickly changed the subject to a jovial discussion of his successful class president campaigns, and the not so successful campaign, since he began matriculating at MIT. And, he regaled Marie with tales of his professors. He held back talking about the Air Force and his future commitments.

———

Dinner was lively, except for Marie's stories of the Resistance fighters. After a delicious grilled pineapple dessert and a cup of espresso, they left the restaurant, Rawly sauntering between Marie and Leigh, his arm relaxed over their shoulders. Holding the car door open for Marie, Rawly asked if the little bar she had taken his family to so many years ago was still open.

"Oui, but I have to teach tomorrow, so drop me off at the house. You two can go back to the harbor and visit Frédéric," Marie said resting her head back on the seat. "Rawly, be sure to thank your family for our dinner, especially that cute little brother of yours."

Rawly squeezed into the back seat and shut the door, hugging his knees.

"Tyler's not so little anymore, Marie." Leaning forward Rawly laid a hand on each of their shoulders. Marie patted his hand, a warm companionable gesture.

Turning up the hill Leigh stopped in front of Marie's gate. Rawly jumped out of the car, took Marie's arm, and walked her up to the front door.

"Did you say you were leaving tomorrow?" Marie asked turning the knob on the door.

"Well, yes, but I may change my plans. I'll call my friends on my cell in the morning … see where they are."

"You're welcome to stay here as long as you want," Marie said stepping into the house.

———

The Le Varech bar was quiet. Only one couple sat in the corner, holding hands across the table, whispering to each other. Rawly glanced at the pair as he guided Leigh to a little round table-for-two next to the bar.

Frédéric's face lit up as they entered. "Well now, Mademoiselle Dobrev, who is this stranger?" Frédéric asked, his blue eyes twinkling over rosy apple cheeks.

"You met him eight years ago, Frédéric—the bottle—"

"Came back did you, Monsieur? Nice to see you. Are you the one who threw the bottle in the Atlantic?"

"That would be me," Rawly replied shaking Frédéric's outstretched hand.

"Well, your drinks are on the house. What would you like?"

"Leigh?" Rawly asked laying his hand on hers.

"A coffee with Baileys would be wonderful. A bit chilly tonight," Leigh said.

"Bailey's Irish Crème with a little shaved chocolate on top?"

"Oui, s'il vous plait."

"Two, s'il vous plait," Rawly grinned. "*Please* is one of my French words."

Frédéric returned with two footed glasses of coffee, each topped with frothy cream and chocolate shavings.

"Merci, Frédéric," Rawly said raising his glass to Leigh's and sampling a sip.

"Still pursuing the training to be a professional chocolatier?"

She reminded him of Marie's gift, and, yes, she had started the online course. "It's so exciting, Rawly." He felt the adrenalin race from her arm to his. Pulling away, looking at him with bright eyes, and then leaning close again.

"I'm learning so many techniques. Did you notice the new equipment and tools on Marie's dining room table?"

"I did ... a chocolate candy-maker's toy box."

Finishing their drink, and saying goodbye to Frédéric, Rawly tucked Leigh's arm through his. "Up for a walk?"

Nodding, yes, they strolled down the narrow street which led to the lampposts along the harbor their lights twinkling on the rippling water.

Feeling Leigh shiver, he removed his jacket wrapping it around her shoulders, his arm holding the jacket in place to keep her warm, while he continued peppering her with questions. He had called his friends from the men's room in the bar. They had a few more days before visiting Paris and the flight back to Boston.

Returning to the house Rawly paused at the iron gate, turning Leigh toward him. He felt a wash of warmth envelop him. What's happening to me? I've never stood still looking into a girl's eyes, wanting an evening to never end. No, I always looked for a graceful escape. But not now. Not tonight.

He wanted to learn more about this beautiful girl standing in front of him. He believed she was feeling something too. Looking into his eyes, her eyes were warm, her lips so close he could feel her breath, breath accelerating.

"Leigh, would you mind if I stayed a few days?"

"Of course, I wouldn't mind ... but I thought you said you were meeting your friends?"

"I called them from the bar. I said that, if you didn't mind my staying, I would meet them in Paris."

Leigh closed her eyes and in that moment Rawly bent his head and softly touched his lips to hers. Opening her eyes, her lips bowing slightly in the moonlight, Rawly pushed open the door. They stepped inside, said goodnight, parting to their separate bedrooms.

Chapter 15

OVER THE NEXT FOUR and half days Leigh introduced Rawly to her world. After Marie went off to teach her classes, and after a strong cup of coffee and biscuits slathered with butter and jam, Leigh donned a plain black bib apron handing another to Rawly to pull over his head tying both in the back. He wanted to help with the day's chocolates for the hospital and her customer's orders.

Clumsy at first Leigh started him slowly, gently stirring the chocolate—tempering, melting the chocolate, then agitating the thick mixture with a whisk so the temperature remained consistent throughout. Rawly transferred the pot to a heating pad still stirring as Leigh worked with the fruit. This morning her plan was to coat the fruit, dipping strawberries and maraschino cherries into the melted chocolate.

With the chocolate at the perfect temperature, Leigh held the cherries and strawberries by the stem dipping them one-by-one while Rawly continued to agitate the mixture. Wiping the bottom of the fruit against the rim of the pot, she set each piece on wax paper holding the stem upright for a couple of seconds to make sure that the cherry or strawberry stood straight. After letting the dipped fruit set for ten minutes at room temperature, she transferred the coated fruit to white paper cups lining the white boxes—this time only one layer because of the stems.

Leigh finally sat down rubbing the small of her back waiting for the coffee to perk. They had laughed a little but mostly Rawly was intent on what she showed him, the techniques, explaining what she learned from her online class. He smiled at the streak of chocolate on her cheek which he gently removed with his thumb and then kissed the spot.

After coffee, they discarded the aprons and set out to deliver the fruit-dipped candy.

———

Leigh chose a different restaurant on the waterfront for dinner. Being a fishing community they both ordered delicate fish entrees with a carafe of Chardonnay, and shared a decadent chocolate fudge cake with whipped cream and chocolate sauce drizzled in ribbons around the small white plate.

Walking along the dock for the second night Rawly talked about his family. His mom, who Leigh had met when they were kids, and his dad were divorced but seemed to get along. He lived with his mom but saw his dad often. Growing up he had been into model rockets and there wasn't a sport he didn't excel at. Everyone close to him was surprised when he suddenly became disenchanted with sports, but kept on building rockets filling the bookcase in his bedroom, the ceiling holding a mass of rockets ready to rain down.

Like Leigh the evening before, Rawly spoke in excited tones of his course in political science and how he was now helping a state-senate candidate's campaign. Holding her hand, he punctuated his thoughts—swinging their arms, small fist pumps.

Once again before stepping into the house they said goodnight, Rawly gently putting his hands on either side of her cheeks, thanking her for a wonderful day, his lips brushing hers.

———

The next two days flew by. Leigh showed him around her hometown of Pornic explaining the city was known in ancient times as a pirate haunt before welcoming British, Dutch and Scandinavian merchant ships. It had since become an ideal site for regattas, bright sails dotting the little harbor as they filled with a breeze pushing the vessels out to sea.

From the top of the cliffs rising from the ocean's pounding waves, they gazed over the red and blue rooftops—terracotta and slate. They could see several beaches and orange-tinted sandy creeks. They strolled around the old town with all its medieval charms as well as visiting a few fishing boats that had remained in the port. More than once, he swung her into his arms, laughing, enjoying her excitement for her town, kissing her sweet lips, or cheek, then strolling on.

Stopping at a café for a cappuccino, they bumped into Eric. Leigh gave him a hug and asked him to say hello to Rawly, who stood to shake his hand. Eric said hello but kept his hand stuffed in his pocket. Rawly was surprised at the grown-up Eric—still red hair but now sporting a brush of a beard across his chin. No handshake, he sat back down watching the two exchange words in animated French.

Rawly had diligently studied the language in high school but couldn't decipher the words if spoken rapidly. Eric's body language told Rawly that the redhead had feelings for Leigh as he touched her arm. She didn't move forward or away from him. Eric kept chattering as she looked at him with steely eyes. He gave her a perfunctory peck on the cheek. She drew back. He said goodbye. Eric sauntered out of the café without a backward glance at Rawly.

"Sorry, Rawly. Eric forgets his manners."

"What was that all about? I only caught one word—guitar."

"He reminded me he was playing at a cafe down the street next week."

"How does he manage with one hand?"

"He's very gifted, also very moody, angry at times."

"He likes you, Leigh. I could see it in his eyes, the way he looked at you."

"Not really," Leigh said looking down into her coffee cup.

"My guess is it's more than friendship on his side. It's none of my business but do you see him? Outside of occasionally bumping into him?"

"Never!" she said emphatically, took a sip of coffee, looked out the café window, then turned back to Rawly "We're just friends. We talk over coffee, which is why he was probably here. He's never been mean to me, quite the opposite, but the way he talks scares me sometimes. Scares me for what he might do, for what he talks about, seems capable of doing."

"Doesn't sound good. Like what?"

"I don't know. I can't really explain it. He's two years older than me. Maybe he talks the way he does wanting to get even, revenge because of the way his parents died. He's an orphan. Was brought up by quite nice foster parents but they were very strict. He moved out of their home before finishing high school. He receives some kind of a stipend from the government which is why I don't understand his hatred, especially toward the military. I don't dare mention anything about the army. He holds them responsible for his parents' death. Horrible train crash on their way home from his father's army base. That's how he lost his hand. He tried to save them."

"Hey, enough of Eric. No more bad thoughts." Rawly wasn't sure what was behind Eric's words, but Leigh's eyes had narrowed while they were talking. It was time to lighten the air.

The next day they drove to Nantes to visit Leigh's grandparents. Marie played chauffeur—a basket of side dishes on the front seat to add to Claude's lunch of roasted lamb. Over dessert and into the late afternoon Claude and Narcisse relived their parents' days and their own as children in answer to Rawly's questions about the history of the French Resistance fighters and the Allies marching north from Normandy.

Marie's eyes darted from one to another translating their conversation—questions and answers rapidly spilling from one subject to another, many times circling back to where they began. Leigh spoke up with an occasional question of her own. It was the first time she had heard many of the stories.

It was a nostalgic goodbye, Claude and Narcisse hugging Rawly in a warm embrace as if he were their own grandson, a delightful grandson who showed an interest in them, their lives. Rawly returned the embrace wondering if he would see them again. He ambled to the car following Marie and Leigh. Before climbing into the back seat with Leigh, he turned, waved to the silver-haired couple nearing their nineties, his arm around his wife, still protecting her, still in love with her.

Marie waved goodbye as she pulled out of the driveway under the light of a full moon as it rose joining the stars in the black velvet sky.

Chapter 16

———

RAWLY TOPPED OFF Leigh's second mug of morning coffee as Marie bustled into the kitchen. "Can't believe I overslept. But, it's for the best—no long goodbye." Setting her briefcase on the kitchen table, Marie stepped into Rawly's open arms, hugging her to him. Stepping back, smoothing her hair, she said. "So … you're leaving us this afternoon. It's been wonderful having you here again. But don't you dare wait another eight years before coming back. You hear?"

"Yes, I hear, and thanks for everything, Marie."

Her eyes glistening, Marie picked up her briefcase and, with one last look at the pair, hustled out of the house.

Rawly sighed, drinking the last of his coffee. "I think you mentioned something about driving down to the beach, Saint Jean de Monts Beach, where you found my bottle," Rawly said.

"That's right, Monsieur. Get your things because we'll not have time to pick them up later."

This time Rawly drove Leigh's little car, joking he felt like he was driving a go-cart. Leigh giggled seeing his hair graze the ceiling of the car. He had managed to make her laugh again. He loved her laugh. Light, musical, bubbling up from inside. Her eyes danced, and when he took her hand he noticed her cheeks turned warm, a delightful peach matching her silk blouse and slacks.

At the beach, breathing in the fresh salty sea air, they kicked off their shoes, spread out a blanket on the sand, and sat watching the ebb and flow of the tide as they broke chunks of bread from a loaf Marie had set aside for their lunch. She also cut a brick of cheese into small slabs, put a small bottle of red wine beside the picnic basket ready for them whenever and wherever the whim took the couple.

"Rawly, you haven't told me about the Air Force, the ROTC— when did you sign up and why?"

Not an unexpected question, but one Rawly had been wrestling with since the first day of his visit, since he had laid eyes on Leigh standing on the train platform holding the little white box of chocolates. His future had seemed certain, the path he had chosen exciting, but it was a path for one. He never saw anyone else in the picture, no one standing beside him, like Claude and Narcisse standing together ... their love still strong. Suddenly, he wanted that kind of love.

Turning, he laid on his elbow facing Leigh, to answer her question. "Well, some of it was money. A college education is very expensive. But I've been interested in flying, space, since I was a kid launching rockets on the beach every chance I got. Even the day I sent that wine bottle on its way to you."

Rawly stood, walked toward the water, picked up a stone slinging it with a baseball player's right arm over the incoming waves. He ambled back to Leigh, his eyes seeking hers, sat Indian style on the blanket searching her face.

Leigh said nothing. Looked back into his eyes. Waited.

"I kept thinking about what I wanted to do with my life—I couldn't figure it out. Then ideas started to click, things I liked to do began to fit together. The Air Force ROTC was a way to train for something important—maybe fly, maybe space exploration, and a way to serve my country. The ideas really began to gel once I started at MIT. Electrical engineering gave me a good grounding for the advanced equipment, newest technologies, evolving technologies used in aircraft, spacecraft. Sophisticated equipment I would be working with once I was commissioned."

He took a sip of wine, looked out at the waves. "Then along came the political stuff and I saw the two coming together—exploration and serving my country ... understanding the first to better serve the second. Of course there was the military component, the weapons training on the firing range and making sure when you're armed that the weapon is ready to fire with pinpoint accuracy."

"What happens when you're commissioned?"

"Nothing at first. I'll be a second lieutenant but I have a one-year deferment to work for my master's in electrical engineering. Then there's a four-year commitment, eight if I go to flight school, in return for the education I received. Deployments last about three years at each base, deployment where I'm needed. Dad stayed state-side, Mom, too. They met in the ROTC."

"I didn't know that. Your mom was an officer?"

"Yup. With all that's going on in the world, I may deploy overseas somewhere."

Unable to sit still, his breathing rapid, Rawly sprang to his feet, dashed to the water, hesitated a second then stripped to his briefs running into the surf, swimming away from shore.

Leigh watched him, wondering if he was fighting some kind of demon. One minute he was talking with great passion about his future, the next his face seemed full of doubt as he searched her face for …for what? Leigh could see he was excited about his future and understood his excitement. But she didn't know how or if there would be room for anything else, or anyone else in his life. He seemed to have it all mapped out.

Rawly swam back to shore, picked up his clothes and trotted to the car. Toweling off, he dressed, and returned pouring the remainder of the wine into their glasses.

The waves lapped the shore as they watched a couple of seagulls riding the wind. He had been talking non-stop and now they were silent—his words remaining, loud and clear. Rawly leaned forward picking up two small stones, polished, washed smooth. He gave one to her. "Remember today … with me," he said smiling. "Add it to the one I gave you eight years ago."

Rawly now appeared relaxed, breathing normal as he tilted her chin up looking into her smoky-blue eyes, kissed her, their kiss becoming warmer than the brushing of lips before.

Her pulse hitched up as he slowly drew back, his hand sweeping her hair gently from her eyes.

"Leigh … if I gave you a ticket as a Christmas present, would you fly to Boston for the holidays? Stay with Grammy Kathy, in Newburyport? I know she'd be thrilled to have you."

"Any candy shops in Newburyport?" she asked grinning.

"I can think of one that would rival Paris. These few days with you—Marie, your town, your delightful candy making, and your grandparents—I can't leave without knowing if ... no, not if, when I'm going to see you again. When I get on that train I have to know I'll see you soon, not another eight years."

"I admit I wondered if there was someone special back home. You never said and I was afraid to ask." Leigh watched a wave roll in, held her breath. *Was there a sweetheart he hadn't told her about?*

"No. There's no one. Think about it. Christmas is a magical time in New England. I'll have almost two weeks off from school. Tell me now that you'll think about it."

"I don't have to think about it. Yes, Rawly. The answer is, yes. And now, Monsieur, we have a little more than an hour's drive so we'd better get going or you'll miss that train of yours."

Chapter 17

———

THE SUPER-TRAIN picked up speed heading north to Paris. The silver cars were taking Rawly away from her but not for long. She knew in her heart that they had experienced something magical, but neither had said the word love.

Leigh wrapped her arms around her body as if holding him. Yet, her eyes sparkled, breathing even. Her posture was straight, head held high, a slight smile etched onto her lips. Her hand plunged into her pocket, fingers searching for the stone. *There it is ... smooth, warm.* Images coursed through her mind—the beach, the man. She vividly saw every feature of his face: square jaw, unruly shock of dark brown hair falling forward on his forehead, his eyes riveted on her, and his smile. A kind smile ... strong, confident.

She watched the train disappear around the bend, then turned and strode away from the empty tracks. Her stride lengthened as she marched through the terminal to her little car. Pulling out of the parking lot she headed west to the seacoast mentally compiling a list of tasks. Christmas was a little over eight months away and there was much to be done.

Bursting into the kitchen, she gave Marie a fierce hug, twirled around the kitchen lovingly touching every piece of her candy-making equipment, running her fingers over her great grandmother's molds, the whisk that Rawly had held in his hand.

Marie poured tea from the steeping pot into two china cups and saucers then sat at the table and waited, watched as slowly the girl's energy waned and she sat opposite her.

"Rawly asked me to spend the Christmas holidays with him in Massachusetts," she said her face glowing at the thought.

"And you said?" Marie asked seeing the answer in Leigh's beaming face. The child had grown into a woman, and the woman was tasting love.

"Yes! Marie, I said, yes." Leigh reached across the table, grasped the hand held open to her. "I have so much to do ... finish the chocolatier program, go to Paris for internship interviews. Then there's the Chocolatier Business Plan program ... and other courses. What do you think, Marie? Am I doing the right thing?"

Before Marie could answer Leigh shot up from her chair, placed her hands on her hips as she slowly walked to the stove, turned, faced the only mother she had ever known, tears gushing from her eyes. "How can I leave you," she whispered, the words strangling in her throat.

Pulling a hanky from her apron, Marie quickly went to the young lady, mopping the tears as she had so many times when she was hurt, crying. This was a different kind of pain ... for both of them. The excitement of going forth into the next phase of her life, leaving the little girl behind to take on new responsibilities, joys, and the pains of adulthood.

"Oh, chèrie, I'll always be here. I'm so proud of you, your imagination, the way you turn melted chocolate into pleasure for the soul. You are going to do great things, I know it."

"And Rawly?"

"Through the will of the heavens above, I believe with all my heart that God had a hand in guiding that bottle of his to the beach that day ... to you. Rawly has grown into a fine young man. I feel you are destined to be together."

———

Chapter 18

To: LeighDobrev@ gmail.com
Date: April 8, 2012
Time: 11:30 p.m.
From: RawlyScott@yahoo.com
Subject: Miss you

Hi, made it to the airport without a hitch. My buddies had already checked in but I told them I had to send a couple of emails and am now down at an internet kiosk.

Just to let you know it took all my will power not to pull the cord to stop the train. I didn't want to leave. I'm not sure the train had a rip cord, but I wanted to get off. Hope you made it safely back to Pornic.

Christmas seems like a long time away.

Rawly

———

To: RawlyScott@yahoo.com
Date: April 9, 2012
Time: 8 a.m.
From: LeighDobrev@gmail.com
Subject: Re: Miss you

... miss you too.

Drive home was quick.

Rawly, the thought of Christmas in New England is thrilling. We both have so much happening over the next few months that I'm hoping the time will speed by.

I told Marie of our plans. She was excited for us. I had a moment of sadness—thinking of going to Paris for my internship, and then to see you, I felt I was leaving her forever. She said that was silly, but our lives are changing—

yours and mine. All for the good, I think, but change also holds the bitter with the sweet.

Please, please let me know as soon as you can that your plane made it across that huge body of water—I guess if a bottle can make it your plane can. I'm a little nervous about flying.

Leigh :) :)

———

To: LeighDobrev@gmail.com
Date: April 9, 2012
Time: 12:10 p.m.
From: RawlyScott@yahoo.com
Subject: Re: Re: Miss you

... back in my dorm, safe and sound. Flight was smooth and uneventful. Tried to sleep. Leigh I kept seeing your beautiful face and I swear I felt our kiss.

I'm diving into my studies and upcoming finals ... maybe that will help make the time buzz by. BUT there's summer in between. Can't think about that now.

Rawly

———

To: RawlyScott@yahoo.com
Date: April 9, 2012
Time: 2:05 p.m.
From: LeighDobrev@gmail.com
Subject: Re: Re: Re: Miss you

... same here ... diving into my studies. I hope to finish the first chocolatier program before the end of June which means I'll be contacting the school on what I have to do to begin the internship. I presume I will have to interview first.

Good luck with your finals.

Kisses,

Leigh :) :)

Chapter 19

DONNING JEANS UNDER a white T-shirt ready to begin the day, Leigh picked up the printouts of the next project—how to create soft centers with different flavoring oils: orange, cherry as well as caramel—soft centers encased in syrup and then wrapped in milk chocolate with a slight swirl on top. The directions instructed her to wear special white cotton gloves to keep fingerprints and smudge marks from the beautifully finished chocolates as she placed the delicacies in individual cups so they didn't stick to each other. Then the man, woman, or child, picking up the finished candy will savor the taste and texture of the chocolate delighting in the surprise of the soft-center flavor.

Leigh checked the ingredients making a list of what she was missing before darting out the door. At the grocery store, she checked the packages, never buying the cheapest but sometimes passing up the most expensive if the package the next price down held the same ingredient or mixture.

"Leigh, bonjour." Eric sidled up to her, spreading his feet as he rocked back and forth, arms folded across his chest. "Finally, alone. Did the American leave town?"

"Oui, a couple of days ago. How are you?"

"Okay. Time for coffee?"

"A quick cup. Let me settle up with the cashier. I'll meet you at the café next door."

Eric smiled and strode out the door. Leigh watched him as he left. He seemed to be in good spirits. His red hair was secured neatly in a short ponytail, his shirt cuffed at the end of his stump.

Catching up with him a few minutes later, setting her bundles beside the chair, she took a sip of the coffee he'd given her, vapors of steam escaping from the edges of whipped cream.

"You look happy," Eric said, raising his cup of black syrupy liquid to his lips. "What brings that skip to your step? Seeing me?"

"I am happy to see you, Eric, but I'm also excited about a new candy project. That's why I was in the store. Needed some special flavorings. But, I'll let you in on my plans. I'll be going to Paris soon, on an internship."

Eric's brows drew together, his head tilted to the side, eyes questioning. "How long will you be away? Few months?"

"It could be a permanent move. I'm not sure yet." Leigh paused, then plunged on. "And I'm going to Massachusetts for Christmas ... in the States," Leigh said quietly. She wasn't sure how Eric would take the news and she didn't want any trouble. There were rumors that he had been seen with some men, men not from Pornic, maybe not even France.

Eric's jaw hardened. He hunched forward, the smoke curling up from the end of his cigarette as he studied her face. "Well, Leigh, I might just join you. I have friends. They've been urging me to follow them ... to Paris." He spit the words out through clenched teeth. "I can watch out for you. Make sure you're safe."

"I'm sure I'll be fine," she said with a little shoulder shrug. "I hear musicians are in high demand at some of the cafes. You're very talented, Eric. I hope you don't give up your music."

He sat back, his face softening. "As a matter of fact, these new friends of mine suggested the same thing. Maybe you can come have a drink with me, hear me play, hear our group. I'd like that."

"I'd like that, too." Leigh drank the last of her coffee and stood to leave.

Eric quickly did the same, reached out, putting his hand on her arm. "Wait. How will I know where you are, know where you live? Promise you'll tell me before you go so I'll know how to find you."

"I will. Au revoir."

———

Eric slumped down in his chair as Leigh stepped out of the café door into the sunshine. Watching her disappear down the block, he reached into his pocket for his cell phone, scrolled the directory of stored numbers, and tapped the one he was looking for. Listening to the ring on the other end, his mind spun. He wasn't about to lose Leigh to some damn American. He'll follow her. Draw her into his group ... *socially*. A beautiful woman could come in handy.

He stamped out his cigarette. His last. Smoking was forbidden by his new friends.

"Aalim Saleh?"

"Yes. Who's this?"

"Eric Duris. I've decided to come to Paris ... to join your group."

Part Four
Chapter 20

———

MADEMOISELLE JULIETTE BOUCHET, student counselor at the Academy of Chocolate Arts, had requested information from Leigh after her completion of the first chocolatier course. Juliette had three businesses in mind where Leigh might fit as an intern. The only thing missing was Leigh's personal profile, an electronic form to be returned as soon as possible.

Entering the final period with a tap of the key on her laptop computer, Leigh inched closer in her chair scrolling to the top of the document for one last spell check. Satisfied, she attached the form to her return email and clicked the send button, expelling a long breath of air. Staring at the computer monitor, the arrow pointing to the left of Juliette's message indicating a reply had been sent with an attachment, Leigh wondered about the three companies. Were they large, small, or just right? The internship would last three months but could be extended and might even turn into a part-time job.

She pulled the sleeves of her sweater over her knuckles, the thought of interning in Paris sending chills up her arm. A job in Paris! Was she ready?

The ring of her cell lying beside her laptop jerked her back from the daydream. It was Juliette, her counselor. Had she made a mistake in filling out the form?

"Bonjour, Juliette."

"Is this Mademoiselle Leigh Dobrev?" Juliette giggled into the phone.

"Oui, Juliette. Did you receive my profile? I just sent—"

"Oui. Received and scanned. In fact, your instructor just left my office. We were talking about you. Were your ears burning?"

Leigh suddenly felt alarmed, but Juliette was laughing so surely it couldn't be too bad. "No, my ears aren't burning. Is something missing from the profile?"

"Honestly, Leigh, we can't wait to meet you in person. Your instructor was telling me about all of your emails—questions, questions, questions. How do I do this? How do I do that? Is there a better tool? What is the best candy thermometer? She said you were the most conscientious student she's ever had and loved the pictures you sent of the candy as you completed each step, and the final product. In fact, because of your complete absorption, dedication to each project, she's making some alterations to the program. I had to call to tell you I'll be sending your profile out today to the businesses I have selected for you. As I receive their replies I will email you descriptions of their company and what they plan to include during your internship. I think you will be pleased."

"Merci, this is so exciting. Can you send me the names so I can begin my research of the kinds of candy they produce?"

"There you go—more questions," Juliette giggled again. "Patience, Mademoiselle. Patience. I want to be sure each comes back with the offer of the best training for your internship. If not, I'll send your profile to another. I promise, as soon as I hear from them I'll forward what they say … if I think there's a fit."

"Will I have to wait for all three to contact you?"

"No, no. I'll send them on as I hear, and approve them," Juliette chuckled again. "Don't be surprised if you start receiving correspondence from me very soon. Au revoir, Leigh."

Disconnecting the call, Leigh felt her blood surge. Clapping her hands, her lips curving up, she looked to the ceiling with a sigh closing her eyes.

It's happening. My dreams are taking flight. June … summer in Paris. Rawly … I have to let him know. No … I'll wait until I can tell him where I'll be interning. I'll soon be in a big city … big like Boston.

Her surging blood began to settle.

Paris. Boston.

So far apart.

Six more months.

Chapter 21

———

ANOTHER CUP OF TEA, pacing in and out of the cottage, periodic squeals and hugs as Leigh monitored the incoming emails from the Academy of Chocolate Arts. Her counselor Juliette Bouchet relayed via email the responses from companies inviting Leigh Dobrev to interview with the head of their candy factory.

Hearing the ding indicating another email had arrived, Leigh opened, read and immediately replied to each in turn. Tea was exchanged for a glass of wine as the sun began descending from its arc. Marie felt they both could use a little drink to settle the nerves and excitement.

Replying to Juliette's emails containing information about the three companies triggered another flurry of rapid-fire questions from Leigh asking for Juliette's rationale for each pick.

By the end of the day Leigh had highlighted the Parisian Candy & Gift Shoppe as her favorite. The shop boasted one of the finest chocolate factories in France—small but unique, their candy made from the very best chocolate.

Juliette asked if Leigh could travel to Paris for interviews on Monday. Leigh responded she would take the train to Paris on Sunday afternoon, ready to begin the interviews on Monday morning and to please reserve a bed for her in a woman's hostel. She also asked that the interview with the Parisian candy shop be scheduled last—Tuesday, if possible.

The following four days were hectic. Leigh, with Marie's help, laid out on her bed several outfits suitable for her interviews. This in turn precipitated more emails to Juliette asking for the counselors opinion on how to present herself, which in turn meant swapping some of the outfits she had pulled from her closet.

She settled on a dark chocolate-brown tailored suit—knee-length pencil skirt, brown one-inch heels, and a silk V-neck white blouse to soften the look. Marie flitted to her bedroom, hustled back with a perfect caramel-colored shoulder bag and long silk scarf of multi-hued caramel, black, and white to tuck under the collar floating down the front to the bottom edge of the suit jacket. The black in the scarf emphasized Leigh's long wavy hair. Her smoky-blue eyes sparkled in contrast.

Her interview wardrobe decided, Leigh strolled down the hill to the drugstore facing the little harbor to pick up fresh toiletries.

Feeling a tap on her shoulder, she turned, hardly recognizing Eric. His reddish beard was tidy, trimmed short, but his hair was tinted an orangey-red and grazed his shoulders instead of anchored in a ponytail.

"Going somewhere?" he asked with a grin.

"Oui, but how—"

"Travel toothbrush and toothpaste in your hand," he said with a smirk.

"I'm going to Paris on Monday to interview for my internship at three chocolate factories, and—"

Eric leaned back on a column at the end of the aisle, eyes narrowed as he interrupted her. "You'll be moving to Paris soon?"

"Not sure you'd call it moving although it may end up that way. My counselor told me that once I accept an intern position I should be ready to start within a week."

"Well … I guess I'd better finalize my plans. Don't want you to leave me behind."

"Really, Eric, it doesn't matter one way or another if you're in Paris. I'm going. If you're there … you're there. You mentioned before you were thinking of going to Paris … doesn't matter if I'm there or not. Sounds as if you have some plans. What are you going to do?"

"I have friends. They want me to join them."

"Friends … join? Musicians?"

"Yes and no. But I have to make some money so I'll probably join a band, a group, or be a fill-in between acts at a café. Where are you going to stay?"

Leigh looked away. She didn't want to lead Eric on, and she certainly didn't want to get involved with him. An image of her high school graduation night penetrated her thoughts. She shook her head, never wanting to think of that night. "I'm not sure. My counselor is making arrangements."

"Taking your cell phone?"

"Oui. I have to run. Good luck to you in Paris." Leigh turned abruptly, paid for the few items in her basket, and left Eric next to the post as she stepped out into the warm humid air—June the end of spring and beginning of summer.

———

Leaning on her bed's headboard, her computer propped up on her lap, Leigh logged into her email account.

> To: RawlyScott@yahoo.com
> Date: June 5, 2012
> Time: 4 p.m.
> From: LeighDobrev@gmail.com
> Subject: My Internship
>
> I'm taking the train to Paris tomorrow afternoon. Interviews scheduled at three chocolate factories on Monday and Tuesday. Rawly, it's really happening. I can't believe it. I'm sooo nervous. Not quite sure what to expect—the big city, the interviews. Maybe they won't want me.
>
> I bet your family was excited about your graduation and commissioning ceremonies. They must be proud of you. Send some pictures, Monsieur Lieutenant. When do you start the classes for your master's?
>
> You asked me about dates for Christmas. OMG are we really going to spend the holidays together? Anyway, how does arriving on December 23 and leaving on January 1 sound? Too long? Too much for Kathy? I don't want to impose.
>
> More kisses,
> Leigh :) :)

———

To: LeighDobrev@gmail.com
Date: June 5, 2012
Time: 5:10 p.m.
From: RawlyScott@yahoo.com
Subject: Re: My Internship

Paris! I'm excited for you. Wish I was there so we could have a coffee, so I could see the sparkle in your eyes, so you could fill me in on all the details.

A couple of pics are attached—not graduation but the commissioning. It really hit me—such a big step AND a big commitment. An officer, 2nd Lieutenant in the Air Force.

Master's classes start next week—still working on the timeline to complete the requirements by next June.

The dates are perfect. Classes are out that week. Nice, huh?

I'll be picturing you in Paris, Mademoiselle. Where are you going to stay? I don't like thinking of you alone in such a big city.

As you say in French,
Gros Bisous (Big kisses. Right? I'm trying!!)
Rawly

———

To: RawlyScott@yahoo.com
Date: June 5, 2012
Time: 6:11 p.m.
From: LeighDobrev@gmail.com
Subject: Re: Re: My Internship

My counselor, Juliette, is making reservations for me at a woman's hostel so I should be fine. I wish you were here too. Be prepared to receive tons of emails.

Bumped into Eric today. Strange. Very strange. He has the same short beard but colored his hair a bright orange-red. He said he's going to Paris too. Joining his new friends and plans to play his guitar in a café.

*Marie loaned me a purse and a scarf to jazz up my outfit.
Wish me luck.*
Gros Bisous, (very good)
Leigh :) :)

———

To: LeighDobrev@gmail.com
Date: June 5, 2012
Time: 6:46 p.m.
From: RawlyScott@yahoo.com
Subject: Re: Re: Re: My Internship
Good luck and be careful.
Bisous, bisous, bisous
Rawly

Hugging herself, Leigh gazed at Rawly's email, put her finger to her lips feeling the kisses he sent. She looked over at her dresser, at the stone shining in the subdued light of the bedside table lamp. Setting the computer to the side on the blanket, she tiptoed to the dresser. Opening the top drawer she rooted around and found the first stone he had given to her eight years ago and then pulled out a lacy silk handkerchief of her great grandmother's. Wrapping the two stones in the silk hanky, she tucked the little bundle in the zippered pocket inside her purse. They were going to Paris with her for good luck.

Chapter 22

Paris, France

A BEARDED MAN—olive skin, black trousers and T-shirt—sat across from Eric at a table marred with names chiseled into the surface. The man's large black eyes, pupils dilated in the dim light of the bar, seared into Eric's green eyes. His body tense as he sized up the man with bright red hair.

"Aalim, it's good to be with you at last," Eric said. "I'm eager to meet with your brothers. Now, if possible." He toyed with his mug of coffee. Looked around the bar—almost empty at this hour of the day except for a man flirting with the barmaid. She hiked up her short skirt, then bent over to pick up his tip displaying her ample cleavage. She was interested.

"Good. You will meet them shortly, and I've arranged for you to perform tonight. You won't be paid. You're new. Nobody knows of your talent, but they will. Bring a hat, guitar case, something for your tips. I've heard you, Eric. You're masterful and don't be timid about your arm. A little sympathy—big tips," Aalim said smiling. "Your music is far better than anything I've heard from others around here so you don't need their sympathy, but go ahead and pull a few heart strings of the lovers sitting at the tables. Stupid women."

"The last we talked you thought I might be able to join one of the groups. I have limited money, Aalim. I must work."

"I know. I know. There's a room just down the street. A room where new brothers joining our cause stay until jobs are found. I will take you there now and later to the café where you will pull those heartstrings I mentioned."

"Tell me about the café. Who comes? You mentioned couples. I presume it's a place they hang out … young?"

"Let's say, Eric, they will not be bringing their parents. Now come, let's drop that backpack and the rest of your gear at the room, meet the newest recruits ... like you."

"I want to hear, understand more about the cause. From what you've said so far, I'm in." Eric leaned forward, spitting out his next words. "I told you I want to avenge the deaths of my mother and father. The French military has their blood on their hands. If I can strike at them through your faction, so much the better."

Aalim threw a few bills on the table to cover their coffees and sandwiches as Eric hoisted his backpack around his shoulders as well as the strap of a duffle bag on one side and the strap of his guitar case over the other shoulder. He raked his fingers through his long orange-red hair hanging over his forehead. "Let's go. I'm eager to meet the other recruits."

The bright sun struck Eric in the eyes, blinding him for a second. Blinking, he quickly fell into stride with Aalim. Sweat began to discolor his shirt from the weight of his bags.

Rounding the corner onto a narrow, shadowy street lined with multi-storied buildings of ancient stone, weathered dark gray with age, Aalim stopped in front of a heavy oak door smeared with dark brown stains. He shoved the unlocked door open stepping into a small vestibule at the head of a hall lined with closed doors. A narrow staircase rose to the right crisscrossing several times between the four flights. Aalim jogged up the first and second flight of the creaky stairs, knocked on a door which was immediately opened by a clean-shaven twenty-something man. Eric was not as fast, stomping up the stairs with his bulky gear.

Introductions were made as they entered the room lined with mattresses, a room filled with a musty smell. An open door at the far end revealed a small bathroom. In the opposite corner was a kitchen setup—rusty sink, hotplate, small scratched and dented refrigerator beside a cupboard with shelves above. All the walls were painted in a faded lime green with graffiti drawn in black here and there by previous visitors.

Eric glanced around the room, shrugged. He didn't care where he stayed. He only cared about joining Aalim. He was shown a spot to deposit his bags and guitar at the foot of a mattress topped with a gray blanket and pillow in a clean, brown-cotton pillowcase.

"We pitch in for the daily room rent, Eric," Aalim said as he flopped down on a mattress in the center of the line of mattresses— five on each side facing each other leaving a narrow path to the bathroom. All but three mattresses were assigned.

"The brothers are like you, Eric—new to Paris, looking for work. Now, everyone, sit," Aalim said. "I want to fill you in on our cause and for Eric a quick history lesson so he understands, at least a little, about us."

Grumbles were heard from the five other roommates which were not lost on Aalim. "Hey. Stop it. Eric is a brother. We need help, and he can give us that help. He is French not Arab. Right, Eric?" Eric nodded but remained silent. He hadn't been informed of the dress code noting they all wore black trousers, black shoes, and T-shirts of various bright colors. *Well, I only have to spring for a pair of black trousers. Who cares. I'm not here to make a fashion statement.*

Aalim smiled at Eric. He knew very well the Frenchman could be valuable in the future.

"A little history, Eric. We Muslims, here in this room, are governed by Sharia Law. Sharia came into being with the creation of the Quran, Islam's most important holy book, immediately following the death of Muhammad."

"Muhammad ... when did he die?" Eric asked.

"Ah, you would never guess," Aalim said, looking around at the men. "He died in 632. I repeat, 632. Muhammad, like so many major religious figures, wrote nothing himself. What we know of him—his sayings, teachings, and dictates—come to us from his followers, later interpreters. Sharia is the entire body of Islamic law. Literally the term means *the way to the water source*.

"It is wide-ranging, personal rules regulating matters of hygiene, politics, business, banking, family, sexuality, diet, and society and legal philosophy. You can see it is all inclusive, meant to serve as the governing principle both within the Muslim world and for Muslims living outside it."

Aalim looked from face to face, each turned to him, serious, taking in his words. Each man sat on his mattress, legs crossed at bent knees. Eric, sitting at the head of his mattress, leaned against the wall, legs drawn up to his chest, arms to his side.

"We live by Sharia law. Some of its better known requirements are simple and easy to explain such as prohibiting the consumption of pork and alcohol, among other things. Sharia also requires the use of the right hand for eating and drinking." Aalim looked at Eric. "Unless you can't use your right hand."

Eric nodded with a slight wave of his right sleeve.

"Come on, Aalim," one of the men, with a clipped black beard under black eyes staring at Aalim, his arms across his chest, blurted out. "Enough. I didn't come here for a history lesson. Tell us what you're plotting. I came here to join the Muslim Brotherhood's Jihad, our struggle."

"Wait, Jamal. I'm coming to our Jihad." Aalim smiled as a father might on an unruly son. "You have all heard, some of you participated, of the protests sparked by an online film that mocked our holy prophet Muhammad. Demonstrators took to the streets in Egypt, Afghanistan, Indonesia, Pakistan, Yemen, Lebanon and Iraq. Thousands of protesters chanting, *'Death to America!'* We are joining them! We are joining this Muslim Brotherhood Jihad beginning with the American embassy here in Paris. We are part of a larger movement—do not forget that. You are now members of Jihad that will bring the world together, our world, under Sharia law. We belong to the Muslim Brotherhood, the largest political organization in many Arab—"

"Excuse me, Aalim, how big is this Brotherhood?" Eric asked.

"The Brotherhood had over two million members at the end of World War II. We have gained thousands of supporters since that time throughout the Arab world and influenced other Islamist groups with our model of political activism. The Brotherhood's credo: 'Allah is our objective; the Quran is our law, the Prophet is our leader; Jihad is our way; and death for the sake of Allah is the highest of our aspirations.' Our slogan, used worldwide: *Islam is the solution.* We wage Jihad to bring all countries under Sharia law."

The five new members of the Muslim Brotherhood stared at Aalim as if he was a prophet. Silently they stood following Aalim out the door, down the stairs to the street. He led them to a park where they sat under a large tree. Their leader began detailing their assignment: breach and burn the buildings of the American Embassy in Paris, taking hostages.

Chapter 23

———

THE PITTER-PATTER of a rain shower streaked the train's windows as the Eurostar jerked to a stop in the Paris station. Nervous excitement raced through Leigh as she exited the train with one hand gripping the handle of her rolling suitcase, the other on the strap of Marie's caramel shoulder bag.

Following the other passengers out of the train depot to the curb she was relieved to see a line of taxis—she didn't have to hail a cab like she'd seen in the movies. Assuming the nonchalance of a veteran traveler, in a strong voice she gave the driver the address for the Dunham Square Hostel as she settled in the backseat of his cab.

At the hostel, the driver held her door and wished her a pleasant visit in Paris as she calculated the tip placing the fare in his hand. She apparently hadn't fooled him. Her case bumping up the cement steps, she entered the hostel, eyes straight ahead glued to the window: se présentez à l'enregistrement et les informations. Checking in with the reservation Juliette had made for her, the attendant gave Mademoiselle Dobrev directions to her room and bed number.

Nerves under control, Leigh climbed the stairs to the first floor, found her room, and shoved her small case under the bed. Sitting on the green blanket, she called Juliette to let her know she was in the city and would arrive at the Academy and her office shortly.

Stepping out of the hostel the sun broke through the clouds producing a brilliant rainbow arching in the sky. *This is going to be a lucky day. The beginning of my new life in vivid color,* she thought grinning up at the picture-perfect sky.

Within twenty minutes she was standing in front of the woman she had been corresponding with for several weeks. Leigh immediately was taken by Juliette Bouchet's friendly greeting, a kiss on each cheek and cheerful smile, instantly knowing she was in good hands. Juliette took charge handing Leigh a typed interview schedule with contact names, addresses, and appointment times. Speaking in rapid French, she relayed her thumbnail impression of each company.

"Two interviews today and one tomorrow morning," Juliette added in a serious voice. "The third tomorrow at the Parisian Candy & Gift Shoppe as you requested. You'll see my notes at the bottom of the schedule. I suggest you take a cab to the two interviews today, but after the last interview ride the metro back to the hostel. Might as well learn the subway system—much cheaper than a cab."

With a quick hug and wishing her good luck, Juliette sent Leigh on her way calling after her, "Please call when you return to the hostel. I want to hear what you liked or didn't like at the first two factories."

Leigh waved, nodding that she understood.

A cab was waiting for a fare in front of the academy and Leigh climbed into the back seat reading off the address to the driver as he slid in behind the wheel. Nerves suddenly kicked up at the mass of vehicles darting from lane to lane grateful she that didn't have to flag down a taxi. The driver pulled away from the curb merging with the rest of Paris rushing to somewhere. Within minutes he shifted to the outside lane, pulling up in front of a large building—The Montmartre Candy Factory.

Settling up with the cab driver, Leigh saw him disappear into the heavy traffic as she checked her schedule for the name of the man she was to see. Entering the lobby, Marie's caramel shoulder bag secure and smoothing the scarf in place over her suit jacket, she identified herself. Leigh Dobrev had an appointment with the manager, Monsieur Cameron Lefèvre.

A short, forty-something trim man with a black brush mustache hustled up to her. "Mademoiselle Dobrev, so nice to meet you. So nice. Follow me, s'il vous plaît."

Lefèvre scooted her around the factory explaining the mass of large copper and stainless steel melting pots. Conveyor belts moved small buttons of chocolate through a chocolate fountain, then marching along through little tunnels cooling the chocolates, exiting the tunnel as bite-size chocolate truffles.

The operation was impressive and overwhelming.

A smiling Cameron Lefèvre was delighted with Leigh—her questions probing, intent on the process that was taking place in front of her eyes. At the end of the interview he offered her an internship. With an adrenalin rush at his offer, Leigh thanked him adding she would let him know her decision in the next few days as he continued pumping her hand.

The offer of an internship on the spot was not what she had expected. Floating out of the factory she stood on the sidewalk, dazed, her mind flitting from image to image of what she had just seen—a major chocolate factory. *Oh, my God, am I ready for this? Such a big operation. But he must not have thought I was some light-headed girl, or—*

A cab driver called to her through his open window. "Taxi, Mademoiselle?"

"Oui, merci, merci." Fumbling for the schedule, Leigh took a deep breath and in a clear voice gave him the address of the second chocolate factory. Driving across town, the driver let her out in front of a café. He was sorry, explaining that the address was two doors down, but it was a no-parking zone. Paying him, she thought it was just as well. She had twenty minutes to spare and time for a cup of coffee while she collected her thoughts was definitely a plus.

The second interview was at a very small factory, no more than a mom-and-pop operation, their equipment much like what Leigh had set up in Marie's kitchen. Their techniques were simple, straightforward, the entire process done by hand. No conveyor belts, no fountains applying layers of chocolate over soft centers. No cooling tunnels. Dipping, enrobing, was done by hand. The owners offered Leigh an internship and hoped she would give them due consideration. They had plans to expand and desperately needed help. They said goodbye with kisses on each cheek and directions to the metro.

Exhausted, Leigh looked longingly at the cab, the driver calling to her. She shook her head. She certainly didn't want to disappoint Juliette by not trying to navigate the metro system back to the hostel. It wasn't that confusing, and she was soon standing in front of the building where she started.

Pushing through the front door of the boarding house, she climbed the flight of stairs to her floor. Entering the room, glancing around for the first time, she counted six beds. She saw three of the beds had pieces of clothing, backpacks, and a few pairs of sneakers on top. The owners were out and the other two appeared to be unoccupied. She freshened up down the hall and decided to venture out to a little café for dinner. First, however, sitting again on the green blanket, she called Juliette to report on the interviews.

Juliette excitedly told her she had talked to the two contacts relating how much they each wanted her to intern with them. Both felt that she would fit right in and could potentially have a full-time job with them in the future. The near future.

Fatigue and aching feet forgotten, Leigh giggled with Juliette over what she had seen at the Montmartre Factory and how she wanted to dive in at the second interview—the couple obviously needing immediate help and very unnerved over their plans for expansion. Leigh promised Juliette she would check back with her before returning to Pornic after her interview at the Parisian Candy & Gift Shoppe.

Chapter 24

———

RAIN SPATTERED AGAINST the window waking Leigh from a deep sleep just as her travel alarm, muffled under her pillow, signaled it was time to rise and shine. Stretching her arms above her head, a smile spread across her face. She was going to the Parisian candy shop to interview today. Picking up her interview outfit, she quietly left the three snowy-haired senior women snoring softly in their beds. Hustling down the hall in her PJs to the community bathroom, she quickly showered and dressed at the same time thinking of questions primed with what she had seen the day before.

Leigh paused at the front door of the hostel checking if she needed an umbrella. *Thank you Marie,* she thought pulling a small, pop-up umbrella from a side pocket of her shoulder bag and stepping out the door into a warm rain. It wasn't a downpour. It was a happy shower, the sun trying to break through the clouds so she decided to brave the metro.

Misreading the signs, Leigh stepped off the metro two blocks early and quickly trotted to the Parisian candy shop, her umbrella jerking her arm with an occasional wind gust. Approaching the shop her pulse quickened at the sight of a bright red and white-striped awning covering the expanse of two picture windows separated by a plate-glass door, the name of the shop etched into the glass.

The windows were framed with lace curtains pulled to the side revealing a quaint interior—small bistro display tables with tiered risers, much like a wedding cake. Each tier held little boxes wrapped with ribbon. Some of the boxes were white shielding the delicate candy, others clear plastic giving the buyer a glimpse of the delicate chocolates inside. A wide-brimmed, yellow hat was prominent in the window to the left with plates and boxes of chocolates circling beneath. Leigh's hand covered her lips—the straw hat was exactly like hers from the souvenir shop, the hat she had dreamed of her mother wearing.

Stepping into the shop to the tinkle of a little brass bell mounted at the top of the door, Leigh was greeted by a woman of about her height and blonde hair piled high with curls. Her blue eyes twinkled above ruby-red lips drawn into a big smile. The woman immediately stopped fussing with the display, cocked her head, and stuck out her hand. "You just have to be Leigh Dobrev, but I have to tell you, chèrie, your picture doesn't do you justice. I'm Betsy Marceau, but you must call me Betsy."

Leigh shook the slightly rotund woman's hand and was quickly drawn into a tight hug and three quick kisses in the air almost landing on her cheeks.

"Now, don't you be fooled by what you see, chèrie. I have a very sophisticated operation through that swinging door. You just come with me." Betsy's ruby lips again drew into a toothsome smile, but she stopped short of the factory door as a man entered the shop.

"That's a lovely red rose on that yellow hat, Madame," he said to Betsy pointing to the straw hat on display in the window.

"Yes, it's fresh today," Betsy replied flashing her normal full smile as she lifted a tote from the shelf under the counter, handing it to man. He grasped the handle, gave Betsy a slight nod and turned to leave.

"Bye, Aalim," Betsy said returning to Leigh standing by the swinging doorway to the factory.

A woman, dressed smartly in a black skirt, white blouse, and black apron with *Parisian Candy & Gift Shoppe* embroidered in gold on the bib, smiled and stepped to assist a lady holding two boxes of candy at the cash register.

Leigh followed Betsy through the swinging door to the back of the shop beaming at Betsy as she chattered explaining what was going on in her mid-size factory. It looked much like the large factory she had seen the day before but on a smaller scale—chocolate melting in stainless steel pots, shorter conveyor belts, and a section dedicated to the soft centers which would eventually be coated with dark or white milk chocolate, then packaged to be sold out front or to be shipped to other specialty shops around Paris and other cities.

All of a sudden Betsy shouted at the man monitoring a conveyor belt—soft-centered chocolate buttons were heading for a stream of chocolate under which the buttons would be enrobed in melted chocolate flowing over the top of each soft center but just enough so as not to run onto the conveyor belt.

"Stop the belt," she shouted. "The chocolate has cooled. Too thick. Stop! You must return the chocolate to the tempering pot. Do you understand?" she barked at him.

With a look of chagrin he said nothing but nodded in agreement. He understood he should have seen that the chocolate was too thick, that it had cooled.

Betsy turned, her eyes wide, shaking her head in disbelief that such a thing could have happened in her shop. It was not acceptable. Watching Betsy in action, Leigh understood how much the woman cared about the quality of her product warming to her even more. Here was someone who could teach her the fine art of making chocolate candy. She dearly wanted to study under the watchful eye of Betsy Marceau.

Bringing her anger and rapid breathing under control, Betsy flashed another disdainful look at the man cleaning chocolate that had drizzled along the conveyor belt and dropped to the floor in thick globs.

Turning to Leigh, facing the stranger … Betsy remembered where she was, quickly letting go of the absurd incident, her red lips curving up. Threading her arm through Leigh's she led her out front to a white bistro table with two white-filigree iron chairs.

Madame Marceau wasted no time, could not hold back another minute, asking Leigh if she could start Monday. Her blue eyes seared into Leigh's smoky blue ones. There was only one answer she would accept. It was obvious to Betsy that the Parisian candy shop was the place Leigh should intern. There was no other offer. It was a fait accompli. Monday Leigh would report to begin her internship.

Leigh laughed, thanking Betsy profusely, and replying that she couldn't wait for next Monday. Betsy walked her to the door, again blew a kiss at each of the girl's cheeks with puckered ruby lips. Leigh said goodbye and walked out of the little shop into bright sunshine turning in the wrong direction for the metro. Realizing her mistake, she quickly reversed directions. A woman passing by gave the chuckling girl a startled look.

Stopping at the hostel for her suitcase, and reserving a bed for two weeks beginning the following Sunday, Leigh hopped on the metro to catch the Eurostar for the return trip home. At the train station, Leigh called Juliette, filled her in on her interview with Madame Betsy Marceau and that she was scheduled to show up on Monday.

Juliette, bubbling with excitement, responded that Madame Marceau had called her forbidding her to let Leigh interview with anyone else. It was obvious that the two had an immediate admiration for each other. Grinning from ear to ear, Leigh called Marie as she boarded the train. She was coming home with big, big news.

———

Marie was waiting at the front door as Leigh ran up the path her rolling suitcase hopping along behind her. Dropping the suitcase on the doorstep she fell into Marie's arms. Emotions released, she went limp—no tears, only a big smile and sparkling eyes.

Water boiled in the tea kettle, then poured over tea bags, as Leigh began filling Marie in on her adventure. Pausing, looking down into her teacup, Leigh lifted her eyes to Marie. "I'll be staying in Paris for the next several months … until I return from the holidays with Rawly."

"Speaking of Monsieur Rawly, there is a letter from him on your dresser," Marie said with a wide smile. "Go on up while I get our dinner ready."

Leigh hugged Marie, pulling back at arm's length. "I love you, Marie."

"I love you too, ma chérie. Now shoo, read your letter."

The tension drained from her body, Leigh picked up the handle on her suitcase, and slowly mounted the stairs to her bedroom. Rawly's letter was propped up against the small, white-porcelain lamp under a blue silk shade. The white envelope was the size of a card and Leigh eagerly tore open the flap. The beach scene on the front of the card was labeled, Plum Island, Newburyport, Massachusetts. There was an "**X**" where the sand met the water.

> *Dear Leigh,*
>
> *I always log in to my email account anticipating, no, hoping there will be a new message from you. I enjoy hearing from you. I want to know what's going on in your world but I can't touch it. I can't touch something that arrived on my computer, not from your hand to mine.*
>
> *So, I found this card and I'm writing to ask you to send me one in return. Something personal that I can put in my drawer with my socks, well, maybe with my handkerchiefs. Something with your perfume. Happy faces at the end of your emails are nice but not quite enough.*
>
> *Hugs,*
> *Rawly*

———

Leigh fished around in her desk drawer for the box of hand-painted note cards Marie had given her a couple of years go for her birthday. If she remembered right, one of the cards had a nosegay of jasmine. Finding it on the third try in the bottom drawer, she smiled as she quickly picked through the cards to find the one with the jasmine.

> *Dear Rawly,*
>
> *Your card will sit on top of my dresser where I can see it first thing when I come into my room. But it won't be there for long. You see, I accepted an internship today at the cutest little chocolate candy factory. So, I'll be living in Paris until my trip to be with you for Christmas. Your card will travel with me whenever and wherever I go.*
>
> *I put this sprig of jasmine from Marie's garden inside. The butter-yellow pinwheel blooms will infuse the paper with*

*their scent, the perfume I dabbed under my ears when you
were here.*
   Hugs,
   Leigh :) :)

Leigh closed the card on its fold line, closed her eyes pressing the card to her chest, then slipped it inside the envelope. Hurrying outside, she found the jasmine bush in full bloom and pinched off a cluster of yellow blossoms. Her eyes once again shut, she inhaled the sweet scent. Hustling back to her room, she tucked the sprig inside the card and sealed the envelope.

Skipping down the stairs, she stuck her head in the kitchen. "Marie, I'm going to run down to the post office. I'll be right back. Do you need anything?"

"Not at the moment, chèrie. Is that a letter to Rawly you have in your hand?"

"Yes, it is. You'll be happy to know that I found the note cards you gave me, and a perfect one with a spray of jasmine."

Marie smiled as she watched Leigh disappear down the path and out the gate below. *A girl falling in love is a lovely sight. But … so many changes, for ma chérie. A handsome man entering her life and … and she's going to work in beautiful Paris. I wonder how she will manage the two?*

Chapter 25

———

LEIGH SLIPPED INTO her ice-blue shorty nightgown, opened her bedroom window inhaling a whiff of jasmine floating on the night breeze. It had been a very long day. She looked over at Rawly's card propped up on her dresser.

Rawly was right. To have something to touch, something that he had held in his hand brought him closer. She felt nearer to him as she ran her finger slowly over the "**X**" he penned on the sandy beach. Sitting cross legged on her bed, she opened her laptop and logged into her Gmail account. She wanted to tell him about the internship she had accepted and about the flamboyant owner of the Parisian chocolate factory, Madame Betsy Marceau.

As her account displayed on the screen an email was deposited in her inbox.

To: LeighDobrev@gmail.com
Date: June 8, 2012 Tuesday
Time: 10:26 p.m.
From: RawlyScott@yahoo.com
Subject: How was the Parisian?
Anxious to hear if the last was the best. Write, write, write.

I'm registered for the Masters Program in Electrical Engineering. One more year of school. It means I have to research, write, present a thesis. My professor thinks I can do it.

The senatorial campaign I'm supporting is heating up. I'm learning a lot about what it takes to be a candidate—hard work and layers of thick skin when lies are written about you.

I've been looking for an email from you today. Hope it comes soon. You must be exhausted and ready to close those beautiful blue eyes. Maybe I'll have to wait until tomorrow.
    Hugs and a squeeze.
    Rawly

Leigh quickly hit the reply button.

To: RawlyScott@yahoo.com
Date: June 8, 2012 Tuesday
Time: 10:35 p.m.
From: LeighDobrev@gmail.com
Subject: Re: How was the Parisian?
    WOW! An advanced degree. You are going to have a very big year. An extremely busy year. If anyone can do it, you can. Can I read your thesis, what you have when I arrive? I won't understand any of it, but maybe a word here or there.
    My interview at the Parisian was amazing. To paraphrase Goldilocks, the Montmartre Chocolate Factory was too big, the mom-and-pop kitchen operation was too small, but the Parisian was just right. The owner, Madame Marceau, is going to be a tough taskmaster. I'm going to learn from the best—a woman who cares deeply about her chocolates. I want to be just like her—well, maybe not quite as crazy.
    It's late, so as you say, I'm closing my blue eyes which are very tired and blurry.
    Hugs,
    Leigh, :):)
    PS: I sent you a card today … a real card. :)

Chapter 26

———

A NEW TREND WAS sweeping Paris transforming many bars and cafes into impromptu, live music venues. They lured new musicians, groups, and bands eager to perform for audiences who usually got in free, or paying only for their drinks, dessert plates, or sometimes heavier fare. Music was as eclectic as the musicians and their audiences. Out for a night of entertainment, a person had a potpourri of music choices everything from songs, old and new with French lyrics, to an afrobeat, or salsa, jazz and blues, and punk rock.

On stage this Friday night musicians stomped, banged drums and strummed guitars singing raucous pop tunes to the delight of some and dismay of others in the café full of workers trying to get a jump on the weekend. Sometimes the so-called musicians received as much applause for ending their spot on the evening program as for their performance.

Eric followed Aalim from café to cafe, each offering a new experience, a new venue where he might play, might earn money, might land a permanent gig. The visual of each new café teased his senses. There were bawdy red decors, flashing neon, psychedelic flashing lights, but always offering dim corners designed for those looking to escape with a romantic date, and others who wanted to catch and listen to new artists playing their hearts out, hoping for their big chance.

Café managers looked at Eric's stump-arm with skepticism, but they had seen all types of musicians come through their doors. If an eager artist was booed, he or she was booted.

Eric kept his cool, and after stopping at five or so cafés on Aalim's list, he thought it best not to jump in at any of them, not to begin to play no matter how much he itched to do so, until he had visited the two that Aalim had starred. Get a lay of the land, so to speak, so he knew what to expect, how the audience interacted with the artists, but, more importantly, what was expected of him.

He also wanted to ask Aalim why he starred the two cafés. Did it mean the patrons, or the management, or both, supported their cause? Are they venues where he would meet like-minded men, men who were not satisfied to live under the present French government's so-called leaders who ruled the populace.

Eric surmised Aalim's choice of cafés also met the Muslin rules: no drugs, alcohol, or smoking. He found the two cafes did not have the stench of tobacco only the vibrant scent of rich coffee. However, they were not totally devoid of Western sins. Most served beer, wine, and liquor.

After spending several hours with Aalim, Eric decided to return to a cafe he had visited during the day. He didn't care what politics they espoused. He felt a strong urge to play at Autour de Midi located behind the Moulin Rouge in Montmartre. The basement of the café, Cave au jazz, was known for spontaneous jam sessions. The walls of grayed stone and mortar blocked the raucous sound from overzealous musicians.

Seizing an opportunity to join a group, Eric strolled up to the raised stage, pulled a stool to the side with his foot and sat slinging the strap of his guitar over his head and around the shoulders of his white poet's shirt tucked into tight black trousers. The shirt's full sleeves were tight at the wrist—left side displaying a hand, the right side not. Resting a foot on the lower rung of the stool, his knee raised to secure the instrument against his arm and knee, he began to finger the board with his left hand, picking at the strings.

The jam session continued with the new artist.

Eric increased the tempo, his fingers flying over the board and strings. One by one the other musicians stopped, stared, fascinated by Eric's dexterity, the tone, the vibrations—sometimes ear-piercing cords as he plucked, then suddenly soft, sweet notes floated over the audience, and just as suddenly the deafening notes with fast-paced fury.

Three couples sitting at a front-row table stood, clapped in rhythm to the accelerated tempo, then clapping at random not able to keep pace calling out, "Go red. Go hot pepper." Others joined them with additional cheers the music erupting from all the musicians on stage to the pandemonium from the audience—feet stomping, hands clapping, couples filling every space on the floorboards, swinging their partners in every nook and cranny of the cave.

An exhausted audience settled back onto their chairs as Eric, his face serious, played a few soft cords. Leigh's image filling his mind, his very being, he began to sing.

> *"You can flee from me but I will follow thee.*
> *You can run away, but I will follow thee.*
> *My heart is strong ... it will find thee.*
> *My eyes will search until they see thee.*
> *My voice will call until I can whisper to thee.*
> *My arms will not tire until they hold thee.*
> *You can flee, but I will follow, I will find thee. I will be with thee."*

Eric stared down at the strings, his body still. The cave fell silent as if empty of all souls. The souls realizing the artist wasn't going to sing another stanza sprang to their feet, whistled, shouted, "More, more." Several new musicians sensing the redhead was finished scrambled onto the stage, took their positions and swung into a lively, hot, Latin beat. A few couples jumped up, followed by others swinging partners to the thumping sound.

The cramped cave held the musicians, the dancers, the music in a frenzy of hot air, sweat, and absolute joy. It was a night they would not soon forget.

It was a night when the stage name *Redd Pepper* was coined. The fiery, orangey-red-haired artist, the son of an Irish mother and a French father, had found his calling.

Chapter 27

PULLING A LARGE SUITCASE on wheels and weighted down with a backpack, Leigh laughingly accepted the help of a fellow passenger as she struggled to exit the Eurostar train. Thanking the man for his assistance, she strode to the metro, Marie's caramel bag swinging from her shoulder. Adjusting the black sweater knotted around her neck over a white T-shirt, she stepped along in her jeans and black leather shoes with cushioned soles wearing the bulky items to save room in her suitcase.

She was glad she made the trip to Paris on a Sunday—fewer people to dodge. Yes, there were tourists but no worker-bees, and so far everyone had been very friendly and helpful. In spite of the load, Leigh's back was iron straight as she maintained a jaunty step.

She planned to check in at the hostel and then go to the café around the block to map out her first day at the Parisian tomorrow. Excitement filled every pore of her being.

Paris! The Parisian candy shop! Madame Marceau! What fun. Oh, sure, it's going to be hard work but I know I'm on the right path. I'll take my laptop to the café … send a note to Rawly.

The metro screeched to a stop. Leigh shepherded her rolling suitcase to the exit banging against each seat as she passed, her backpack slamming against passengers. "M'excuser, Madame, désolé. M'excuser, Monsieur, sorry." A young man jumped from the metro car, turned around and grabbed Leigh's big suitcase setting it beside her on the pavement.

"Merci, Monsieur." Struggling again with the heavy bag she looked up at the flight of stairs to the street level.

The young man, seeing her predicament, once again came to her rescue. He easily picked up the case and carried it out of the dark subway into the bright sunshine.

"Merci, merci," Leigh said smiling, grabbing the strap from the man's hand.

Laughing, he gave her a slight bow and raced off in the opposite direction.

She chuckled watching him scoot away. Probably thinks I'll need more assistance down the block.

The pesky suitcase seemed to have a mind of its own as she dragged it trying to keep its wheels pointed straight. Strolling up to the Dunham Square Hostel she paused, really looking at the building for the first time. The five-story hostel built of white stone with ornate white railings in front of tall windows on the third and fourth floors was impressive. Banging against the door she smiled at the bohemian décor—walls painted in orange, purple, and pink, like sherbet ice cream. Lights in the shape of frosted cones hung from fat black tubing curling at various angles. *So charming,* she thought. *Why didn't I notice this before? I guess I was too focused on meeting Juliette, and what I was going to say at the interviews.*

Stepping up to the woman behind the reservation window, Leigh let out a sigh, recognizing her from the week before. She'd made it to the hostel and it appeared none the worse for wear.

"Welcome back, Mademoiselle Dobrev," the clerk said in a high-pitched squeaky voice. Her lips drawn to a smile, she retrieved a key and a piece of paper folded in thirds. "I took this message for you not more than two hours ago. The caller insisted I write her message word for word. You have three roommates tonight. But, of course, our guests come and go, so this might change. Enjoy your stay and let me know if I can be of any assistance, s'il vous plaît."

"Merci," Leigh said picking up the folded paper. Setting her backpack on the floor next to her suitcase, she unfolded the note.

Leigh Dobrev.

Leigh I have slightly bad news. The Parisian candy shop closed its doors suddenly. Something about taxes. Madame Marceau is very upset and hopes to reopen in a month and would very much like you to finish your internship with her. I have arranged for you to start tomorrow morning as planned but at the Montmartre Candy Factory, the big factory, the

first one you visited. Very prestigious. Call when you get a chance. Don't worry, Leigh. It will work out.
   Juliette

Leigh's shoulders slumped, disappointment sapping her strength.

"Mademoiselle Dobrev, are you all right? Bad news?" the clerk asked straining to see around the corner of her window.

"Oui, bad news. I guess it could be worse. Merci."

Leigh looked up at the stairs and then down at her suitcase now as big as a refrigerator in her eyes. Not up to the struggle she dragged her bags to the elevator, then into her room on the second floor. Thankfully the three women she was sharing the room with were out. Several pieces of clothing were scattered on two of the bunk beds. Leigh released her backpack to the floor by her bed number, a bottom bunk, wedging her pesky rolling suitcase underneath. Thankfully, the bunks were designed to provide the handy storage space.

Dropping down on the firm, thin, mattress, she leaned back against the wall. "Okay, Mademoiselle Dobrev," she said mimicking the high-pitched voice of the reservation clerk, "the Parisian's closing is very disappointing, but you're still in Paris, and best of all you're still beginning your internship in the morning. The factory is only a few blocks away so you don't have to take the metro … saving money."

She sucked up a deep breath letting it out slowly as she gazed around. The floor-to-ceiling narrow window was covered with a sheer white curtain and raspberry side drapes. One wall was papered with a large flocked pattern—purples, shades of raspberry and dark blue—large squares, each with a pattern that appeared like needlepoint. The other three walls were painted a delicate pink.

Slowly getting to her feet she went to the communal bathroom to freshen up then back to the room to retrieve her laptop from her large suitcase under the bed. Leigh hoisted the strap of the computer's carrying case over her shoulder and headed downstairs. Passing by the clerk, her squeaky voice speaking into the telephone, Leigh paused at the empty dining room painted a deep yellow where breakfast was served cafeteria style—included in the price of a nightly stay.

Taking a peek into the busy bar, which she had been told was a fantastic bargain with cheap beer, she opted to continue on to the café around the corner. Sunshine and fresh air were what she needed to lift her spirits.

A latte and a quick note to Rawly and Marie settled her nerves. But not for long. As she paid for her coffee and croissant she felt the pinch of her sparse funds. She had to ask Juliette about the possibility of sharing a small apartment with some of the Academy's students.

The hostel was limited to a two-week stay, which could be extended depending on availability. She had joked with the manager, when she spent two nights previously, about helping in the kitchen … maybe he could bend the rules, not only on the length of stay but the price of a bed in the dorm. Twenty-eight dollars a night for a room shared with five other people was more than she could afford. The man had replied that one of his cooks was going on vacation and it was possible he could use her help—provided she could cook. She smiled thinking back on her bravado. "Of course I can cook, Monsieur," she had said taking a small box of four chocolates from her tote and handing it to the man. His eyes lit up as the creamy chocolate melted in his mouth.

"I have no samples for him this time. I can only hope he remembers," she mumbled shutting down her laptop.

Remember!

She had to forget.

Forget about working with Madame Marceau. Instead she was going to be gobbled up in the mammoth candy factory three blocks away.

Chapter 28

———

SLEEP WAS ELUSIVE. Leigh tried to push Madame Marceau and the Parisian from her mind, tried to replace her disappointment with a smile, tried to replace apprehension with a fierce determination to learn everything she could from Monsieur Cameron Lefèvre.

Forcing deep, controlled breaths, she dressed, slung the strap of her purse over her shoulder and strode out of the hostel entrance without a thought of eating breakfast. She was too nervous to eat fearing she would lose the contents of her stomach.

Juliette told Monsieur Lefèvre about Leigh accepting an internship at the Parisian only to have the shop close. He remembered Leigh and was more than happy to be her second choice.

Lefèvre greeted Leigh with a hearty handshake and immediately introduced her to Blair Durance, an expert in tempering chocolate. He was sure Madame Durance could teach Leigh the proper method of tempering, the method whereby the heating process did not crystallize the cocoa butter. With a grin, Lefèvre made a quick U-turn, leaving Leigh standing in front of the tempering authority staring down at her.

"The first thing you have to do is stuff that mass of black hair in a net," Blair Durance snapped slapping a hairnet into Leigh's hand. Durance, a plain woman in her forties, had taken an instant dislike to the newcomer.

Leigh decided she'd better be careful around the woman, and she was also determined that as soon as she returned to the hostel she would try to secure a job as a cook. She prayed that the person scheduled to take a vacation had done so, and prayed the person would make it an extended vacation. If Durance was hell-bent to make this internship impossible, she sure wasn't going to run back to Pornic. No, she would find another position, but she needed money and a place to stay, and she needed both fast.

By the end of the day, Leigh didn't know if thick chocolate was good and thin was bad or the other way around. Was the correct temperature for melted milk chocolate 88 degrees or 86 degrees, or was that dark chocolate? She wearily exited the factory dragging her body back to the hostel.

Entering the front door she bumped smack into Gerard Depardieu, the hostel's manager. Depardieu grasped her shoulders, then shook her hand, then grabbed her by the elbow propelling her into his office. Wringing his hands, he paced back and forth in the tiny space telling her that she was an angel in disguise, that his weekend cook who, by the way, baked most of the muffins, croissants, and pastries for the following morning, and every morning as stated on the hostel's brochure, had called to tell him she had run away with her Spanish boyfriend and was not returning.

"Mademoiselle Dobrev, tell me you will step into her position, s'il vous plaît. You must. I will not charge you for your bed if only you will agree." The plump, little man came to an abrupt halt in front of Leigh daring her to answer, yes.

Shrugging her shoulders, a shake of her head, Leigh looked him in the eye. "Well, I see you are in a horrible situation, Monsieur Depardieu. But, I am in an untenable situation myself and require not only a place to stay but wages as well. I suppose I might work overtime at the chocolate factory ... but ...

"Oui, Mademoiselle Dobrev ...?

"If you come up with a better offer ... well—"

"But of course, Mademoiselle. I agree to your bed and well ... I will match whatever the chocolate factory offers you as long as it is a beginning wage. You must understand that I—"

"Oui, I understand, Monsieur Depardieu. When shall I start ... tomorrow evening ... the pastries?"

"Oui, ... no, tonight, s'il vous plaît?" Depardieu's brows shot to his forehead, his lips parting in a plea.

"What hours? What days?" Leigh asked wide eyed, taking a seat primly on the chair beside the door, hands folded in her lap, her brows raised back at him.

"Well, three hours every other night, and three hours on Saturday and Sunday … s'il vous plaît? No evenings on the weekend."

"And payday is when, Monsieur Depardieu?"

"Friday," Depardeiu said nodding, accepting the arrangement for her.

"I accept your offer as a part-time cook, Monsieur Depardieu. But I must have an hour before reporting to work this evening," Leigh said smiling sweetly at her savior.

"Of course, Mademoiselle," he said squeezing her hands between his. "Of course, an hour."

Chapter 29

—

JULY'S SUMMER HEAT and humidity enveloped Paris. Tourists swelled in the streets. Cranky children were let loose in the numerous parks while their weary parents slumped on benches gazing at the bountiful flowerbeds. Cafés overflowed morning to night with patrons sipping espressos over decadent pastries. Lovers, under the spell of the city of lights, kissed as they strolled along the River Seine.

Leigh loved being part of milieu as she attacked her days, keeping to the stringent schedule as intern and pastry cook while managing to stay out of Blair Durance's line of fire at the chocolate factory. It was Saturday which meant a reprieve from the woman's strident voice.

The morning baking almost complete in the hostel's stifling kitchen, Leigh looked forward to a relaxing afternoon browsing in the nearby shops. Removing two trays of croissants from the oven, placing them on the cooling racks, Leigh took the opportunity for a fifteen-minute break—a chance to check her email.

Propping her pillow against the wall she leaned back in her bunk and turned on her laptop. Nothing from Rawly but there was an email from Eric asking if she could possibly get away for coffee, and maybe even a bite to eat tonight. He was playing with a group in the basement of a café behind the Moulin Rouge, a room called The Cave. They could meet at the café a few doors down from the Moulin Rouge. He suggested eight o'clock and asked again where she was staying.

She had put him off for so long she felt she owed it to him to at least have a cup of coffee. She smiled typing her reply—*it would be good to see a friend from home*—yes, she knew the café he suggested and eight was good. She added she was staying in a hostel in the Montmartre area but would have no trouble finding her way to the café on the Champs-Elysées.

On the way back to the kitchen she poked her head into Depardieu's office to ask if she could borrow one of the bicycles. The hostel was on a side street leading to a main avenue and the larger boulevard. The streetlights were bright and having taken a bike ride in early evening, as well as nighttime, she felt safe.

Depardieu immediately said yes. If truth be told, he would agree to almost anything she requested. Mademoiselle Dobrev was proving to be an asset, a valuable asset as the word was spreading that the woman's Dunham Square Hostel was the place to stay because of the yummy pastries that were included with their breakfast.

Dressed in sandals, a short black skirt and a white tank top, the evening air felt glorious on Leigh's skin as she skillfully cruised along the side street. At the boulevard she hopped off the bike steering it through the crowds of people out for the evening, thankful for the cooler air. Spotting Eric sitting at a red umbrella table, she chained the bike in the bicycle rack and joined him. He saw her approach and jumped up greeting her with a bear hug and signaling to the waitress.

Over a cappuccino and a shrimp salad, Eric told her about his initial success playing for money. "Can you believe it? I'm actually getting paid to do what I love. I'm sharing a room with some buddies. We pitch in for the rent. Some weeks are good, others I barely scrape by."

"Will your friends be playing with you tonight?" she asked licking the coffee's froth from her upper lip.

"Oh, they aren't musicians. One is a man I met in Pornic. After I joined him here in Paris he recruited others, and I think there are more staying in different places. Aalim Saleh, that's my friend's name, is out of town for a few days. Sometimes he comes to hear me play but not very often. He prefers another café where he and the guys hang out."

"That's nice. Is he Muslim?"

"Yes. They all are. It's great, Leigh, to meet, hang out, and plan with like-minded men."

"What do you mean like-minded?" Leigh asked watching Eric as his demeanor changed from a relaxed friend to a man with a scowl crossing his face. His breathing seemed to quicken, his voice deeper.

Even sinister. *Sinister? Come on, you're imagining things*, she thought. *At least he's not drinking ... here anyway.*

As suddenly as Eric's face turned dark, he leaned back, grinning. "Come on, it's playtime. Unlock your bike and we'll walk around the block. There's a rack at the end of the parking lot. And, I'll ride my bike with you at my break to be sure you get home safe."

———

The Cave was beginning to fill up as Eric guided Leigh to a little table to the right of the stage where he introduced her to a couple he had seen several times sitting in the front row. They were delighted to take charge of the musician's girlfriend.

A group of four, including Eric, ambled onto the stage and began playing a set of lively music guaranteed to get the evening started, to rev up the crowd. Polite applause followed the group as they left the stage to Redd Pepper, the one-handed guitarist.

Eric nudged his stool, sliding it to the center of the stage. A spotlight followed him, remained on him as he hitched up on the stool. Placing the guitar strap around his shoulder, his foot on the top rung of the stool, he wedged the instrument between his knee and arm. He looked like a Parisian artist—black trousers, white poet's shirt, the full sleeves buttoned at his wrist and at the end of his stump arm.

He plucked a few strings, made an adjustment, and then looked up at Leigh as he began a slow French ballad, singing as he caressed the board, fingering the strings. Swinging into a hot Latin piece, he banged the instrument faster and faster with his stump arm—sometimes hard, sometimes soft producing a variation of musical sounds. Suddenly he stopped playing, paused, his hand motionless over the strings as he stared down at the board, transported to another world. Slowly he raised his eyes to the audience holding their breath. Was he all right?

With a slight bow, Eric slid off the stool and left the stage. The crowd jumped to their feet yelling, "More, more."

Chapter 30

———

THERE WAS A LET UP in the summer's heat wave as July became August. Summer felt endless to Leigh but the days flew by as she fell into bed late each night exhausted from the intense hours at the chocolate factory and then baking in the hostel kitchen. Roommates came and went. Ages? She didn't know. They were bodies in the beds when she crept into the dorm at night. In the morning, she dressed and was gone before the bodies rose for their day of sightseeing, travel, or perhaps searching for a job. She didn't know and was too busy, or tired, to care.

Now settled into a daily routine, Leigh itched to get back to studying, to advance her dream of not only becoming a professional chocolatier, but to have her own chocolate shop in the vibrant city of Paris. The curriculum offered by the Academy of Chocolate Arts listed the follow-on course to the Professional Chocolatier: Mastering the Cocoa Bean. $498 plus another $195 for supplies. How could she afford that? The answer was simple— she couldn't. She was building her savings but not enough.

Watching the chocolate buttons slowly move along on the conveyor belt, a proposal began percolating in Leigh's mind. She had to think big. *Wasn't that what Marie said—THINK BIG!* Maybe, just maybe Gerard Depardieu would back her. By the time she stepped into the hostel's kitchen, she had a plan.

Leaving the kitchen she knocked on Depardieu's office door. Hearing him call to come in, she entered the office and was surprised to see his wife Shelby sitting across from her husband's desk.

"Excuse me, Monsieur, I didn't mean to interrupt—"

"Come in, Leigh. Come in. We were discussing, well, discussing hostel business," he said with a half smile.

"Those croissants you baked last night with that creamy chocolate filling were out of this world," Shelby said raising her brows nodding to her husband.

Leigh had warmed to Shelby when they first met. Madame Depardieu had hustled into the kitchen one Saturday morning exclaiming over the muffins Leigh had baked with bits of chocolate.

Think big. Go ahead. Ask. "Well ... I guess what I wanted to say has to do with business, a business proposal."

"Sounds interesting," Depardieu said leaning back in his chair. "Go on. What kind of proposal?"

"It has to do with Madame's comment about the muffins ... with chocolate bits." Unable to contain to herself, Leigh began spouting out her plan in rapid fire. "Monsieur, when I suggested working for you in the kitchen I told you about my desire to be a chocolatier. That I had begun to study ... taking courses. But I was home at the time and had the luxury of a kitchen to prepare the projects. My next course is about the cocoa bean—"

"A whole course on the bean?" Depardieu asked perplexed.

"Oui, that little cocoa bean is magic. But the projects in the course require a kitchen and costs $498 and I don't have the money, but I wondered if you could loan me the money and I would make chocolates for you to sell and the profits would pay off the loan and—"

"Whoa. I don't see how—"

"Gerry, let the girl talk," Shelby said leaning forward in her chair.

"I will complete the projects, creating delicacies as part of my job in the kitchen. I'll pay for the ingredients required for the course, estimated at $195. If you like the product, then you will buy the ingredients, I'll create the product and you will keep all the profit ... to ... to pay off the loan and then to keep. Monsieur, you could also sell the product to shops or cafés ... or not. And—"

"Gerry, we were just talking about ... business. I believe Leigh's proposal fits nicely into that subject."

"Oh, no. Not that twinkle," Gerry said closing his eyes.

"Twinkle, Monsieur?"

"Oui. When Madame gets that twinkle in her eyes there's no use talking. I simply agree with her. Saves me a headache. Go ahead, Shelby, let's have it." Depardieu smiled lovingly at his wife.

"Excuse me, Madame, Monsieur, I don't mean to be disrespectful, but do you think the owners of the hostel will go along with my proposal?"

"But, my dear the owners do agree," Depardieu said. "We *are* the owners, so you see—"

"You are the—"

"It just seems to me, Gerry, that Leigh has given us a solution to my desire to help with the business. Here's a perfect opportunity to learn from this ambitious woman. I'll work alongside her in the kitchen as she learns about that magic little bean, maybe she'll even give me some instructions on what she learned from her first classes—making chocolate candy. You, my dear husband, luuuve chocolate. Do you not?"

Depardieu looked from his wife to Leigh.

"Well, the bean … " Leigh said, now pacing in the cramped office—two steps, turning, two more steps. "Learning about sourcing of the bean, to … well, chocolate-making equipment and suppliers, the flavor and taste from various beans, finding the best for the finest candy, then the process to turn dried cocoa beans into chocolate, and planning for production has more to do with the business of candy production. I will be more than happy to repeat my first courses for Madame where I produced the candy from scratch—the tempering, crystallization, and—"

"Stop," Madame laughed, holding up her hand. "My head is spinning with excitement. The first order of business is that you must call us Shelby and Gerry … I mean, if we're going to be business partners in the kitchen. Don't you agree, Gerry?"

"Oui, ma chèrie, I agree," he said rolling his eyes.

Chapter 31

———

BYPASSING THE ELEVATOR, Leigh took the stairs two at a time racing to her dorm room. She pulled her laptop out from under her bunk, scrunched on the covers and leaned against the wall.

> *To: RawlyScott@yahoo.com*
> *Date: August 29, 2012*
> *Time: 7:32 p.m.*
> *From: LeighDobrev@gmail.com*
> *Subject: Amazing Agreement*
> *I don't believe it. Gerry and Shelby Depardieu just agreed to pay my tuition for the cocoa-bean course AND I can use the kitchen AND I'm going to teach Shelby how to make truffles. And, get this, they will be SELLING the truffles to their guests and maybe even to some of the little shops down the street. All of that was my proposal, well, teaching Shelby was a negotiating point. How's that, Monsieur President?*
> *How's your thesis going? Any BIG electrical breakthroughs?*
> *Have to run. Dough rising for bread. How's that for dedication?*
> *Seriously, how is your thesis coming along?*
> *Gros Bisous,*
> *Leigh*

Shoving her laptop back under her bunk, Leigh returned to the kitchen, punched the dough, slipping the bowl into the refrigerator for the morning shift.

———

Leigh fished the alarm from under her pillow punching the button before it went off. Excitement over the deal with Shelby and Gerry still buzzing through her body, she dashed to the shower, then dressed, grabbing her shoulder bag, and raced to the Montmartre Chocolate Factory. Too happy to care, she took Blair's hostile remarks in stride about the chocolate being too thick for sluicing over the orange-cream centers as they moved along the conveyor belt.

Her mind sparked with ideas on how she was going to incorporate the cocoa-bean course with the previous chocolatier class she had perfected in Marie's kitchen. Out of the corner of her eye Leigh noticed Blair, hands on her hips, staring at her. *That witch has me in her sights. Don't goof up, Leigh Dobrev. You have to keep this internship. If not … it would be a big black mark on your resume.*

The bell rang, signaling the end of the shift and Leigh queued up to punch out on her timecard. On aching feet she shuffled back to the hostel, contemplating a quick nap before going to the kitchen. When she emailed Rawly last night she noticed there was an email from the Academy of Chocolate Arts with an attachment. She'd been on the lookout for the guide which contained instructions on beginning the online coca bean course.

Relieved that the dorm was empty, she plunked down on her bunk, slapping around underneath for her laptop she had stashed under a towel. She felt the towel but nothing was underneath. Flapping her hand around again, she still felt nothing.

Dropping to the floor she peered on hands and knees under the bunk shoving her suitcase to the side, plus two pairs of shoes and a few boxes.

No laptop.

Her body seized, panic pumping through her veins.

Someone had stolen her computer.

Again bypassing the elevator, she raced down the stairs, gripping the railing as she ran. The reservation attendant was about to remind her that no one was allowed in her space but Leigh dodged her searching in the lost and found bins.

Her computer wasn't there.

Looking down at the bins, arms hanging limply at her sides, she felt a lurch in her stomach, a gut punch. Her class notes, papers requested by the instructors, recipes were stored on her laptop—everything she had worked on for the past two years. Closing her eyes, looking to the ceiling, she tried to comprehend what she had lost. Forcing herself to breathe, she turned and shuffled down the hall to Depardieu's office. The door was open. She stepped in, slumping in the chair facing him. He looked up over his glasses from the paper in front of him, raised his brows with a nod.

"Someone stole my laptop."

"Are you sure? Maybe you just misplaced it," he said offering a reasonable solution.

"No. It's gone. I can't stay in the dorm any more. All those women. I'm lucky no one stole it before this. I should have—"

Shelby walked in taking note of the slumped figure facing her husband. "What's going on?"

"Someone stole Leigh's laptop."

Shelby knelt in front of Leigh, took her hand. "Wait a minute, young lady. Knowing you, you printed everything of importance?" She raised her brows, questioning. "Well?"

Leigh focused on Shelby. Her mind reconstructing the hours, days, months she had sat in front of her computer. Her eyes widened. "Almost all."

Shelby patted her hand, stood up and looked to Gerry for his help.

"Unfortunately I know everyone who stayed in that dorm last night has checked out," Gerry said looking at his wife. "Leigh feels she can't remain in the dorm any longer. In a way it would be better if we had someplace else for her to stay. There've been several times I could have sold her bunk. I thought I'd show her the room in the basement—"

"Gerry, no. The attic would be more suitable."

Turning to Leigh, he said, "Well, I'll show you the basement first. It's twice—"

"And perfect for growing mushrooms," Shelby said glaring at her husband.

With a sigh, Gerry stood. "Come on, Leigh. I'll show you both rooms—your choice," he said picking up a set of keys.

The basement room, while large, gave Leigh the creeps, literally sending shivers up her arms. Getting on the elevator, Gerry explained that the car didn't go to the attic floor so she would have to climb a flight of stairs once they got off.

As opposed to the basement room, the attic was delightful. Leigh loved it and immediately said this was the room she wanted. Gerry explained that he and Shelby had camped out in the attic while they were renovating the hostel.

Struck with nostalgia as he saw how much Leigh liked the space, he told her the history of the hostel. Saying that not long after he and Shelby were married they had toured Europe and America. Both found the accommodations lacking especially where young people were concerned—traveling on limited funds, trying to find inexpensive places to eat, and trying to find a safe place to sleep before they moved on.

After numerous fiascos on that trip, they spent many months checking out the hostel business—what worked, what didn't work. Paris was exceptionally hard for young travelers and, of course, so many had Paris on the top of their itineraries.

Leigh listened to his story with a new appreciation for Gerry and his wife. They had an idea for a business that became a dream and had struggled to bring their dream to a reality. It was no wonder they understood and appreciated her plight, and were willing to give her a hand. She wondered if along the way someone had done the same for them.

Glancing around, taking inventory of the space, she saw a kitchenette of sorts—hot plate, small sink, and a counter refrigerator, and two TV trays to hold their dishes. There was a small bathroom with a tiny shower, and a standing clothes rack, abandoned from some store display, served as a closet—at least a place to hang her clothes.

Standing at the window, Leigh ran a tissue around the middle of the dusty glass, squinting through the small circle. "Gerry, is that the Seine way over there?" Leigh asked. She turned to look at Gerry who was smiling in the doorway. She smiled back at him.

"Hey, what's this?" Leigh asked spotting a laptop computer on the counter next to the refrigerator.

Out of breath from hiking up the stairs, Shelby staggered into the room. "My *old* laptop. As you know, we have a wifi internet connection in the building. I checked while you were in that God-awful basement to see if the computer worked from here. It does."

"Your *old* computer?" Gerry asked noting that twinkle again.

"Well ... I guess I'll have to go buy a new one today. Can't very well keep track of the business without a computer now can I," she said moving to her husband as his arms circled around her.

Chapter 32

———

WITHIN TEN MINUTES Leigh had packed her toiletries, stuffed her pajamas and a few pieces of loose clothing tucked under the bunk into her suitcase. Setting the suitcase by the elevator, she scooted back to the dorm retrieving two boxes. Everything removed from under the bunk, she pushed the elevator button. When the door slid open she quickly transferred her possessions into the elevator and rode to the top floor.

Wiping the sweat from her forehead, tucking her hair behind her ears, she grabbed the suitcase handle and climbed the short flight of stairs, the suitcase bumping against each step. After two more trips, she pushed everything inside the attic room. Standing straight, rubbing her back, she grinned and trotted to the window cranking it open.

A soft breeze greeted her as she closed her eyes, raising her face to the sunshine. Opening her eyes, she saw Paris lying out in front of her. Maybe not the best view but a view—the Seine was visible between two tall buildings. She hadn't realized how much she disliked the dorm, the constant invasion of her privacy.

Life is good.

The bed wasn't really a bed. It was a cot. It didn't matter that the mattress was thin. No more cracking her head on the bunk above. Shelby had piled a few sheets, a pillow, a pillow case, and a couple of blankets on top of the mattress. Twirling around, she spotted Shelby's laptop. Leigh hugged the down pillow. A real, soft, plump pillow. Propping the pillow against the wall, she grabbed the laptop, flopped on the cot, and leaned against the wall buffered by the pillow. She had to tell Rawly about her new room.

Within seconds of sending her email his reply pinged her inbox.

To: LeighDobrev@gmail.com

Date: August 30, 2012
Time: 5:30 p.m.
From: RawlyScott@yahoo.com
Subject: Miss you – room sounds great
Much better than a dorm.
Holidays—only three plus months to go!
If you're going to be selling your candies you need to reserve a website for when you go big time!! Yahoo has a nice setup for a small business.
How about DobrevChocolates.com?
Or   LeighDobrevFineChocolates.com?   or BeautifulGirlFineChocolates.com?
Let me know what you think. If you like, I can register a web name for you.
Christmas—still seems like a long time away.
Kisses,
Rawly

———

To: RawlyScott@yahoo.com
Date: August 30, 2012
Time: 5:45 p.m.
From: LeighDobrev@gmail.com
Subject: Re: Miss you – room sounds great
Please reserve: RawleighDobrevChocolates.com.
Have to run. Still have to bake the muffins for morning.
Three months? Hope it flies by.
Gros bisous,
Leigh

———

In spite of Blair's critical eyes questioning everything, Leigh was learning new methods and techniques, and learning about the latest advances in equipment. Baking in the hostel's kitchen was easy—she could whip up dozens of croissants in her sleep. Sleep? What was that? Her feet hurt as she traded one pair of shoes for another trying to find a shoe that could support her and provide some kind of comfort.

But even with all the stress Leigh was staying even with her expenses, always keeping in the front of her mind Christmas in New England with Rawly. Hugging her pillow, closing her eyes … Rawly! She bolted upright in bed, glanced at the clock. It was 2:30 a.m. and panic crept into her chest. Christmas meant presents—Marie and Rawly and the Scott family.

The Scotts brought gifts when they came to Pornic eight, almost nine years ago.

She had to reciprocate.

Marie had mentioned she was going to buy her a new dress, a dress she could wear on New Year's Eve. Marie's excuse for such an extravagant gift was that surely the American would take her out to a fancy place on such a special evening, an anniversary of sorts, two days after he threw the bottle into the ocean some thirteen years ago.

———

The pace was frenetic at the chocolate factory. Orders for Christmas boxes packed with a variety of chocolate candy were pouring in from shops around Paris, other cities and countries. Blair was her usual witchy self, but Leigh paid close attention to her piece of the production.

She watched the soft centers—cherry, coconut, orange-cream and caramel—as they slowly received the bottom coating of chocolate, continuing along on the conveyor belt to the chocolate fountain enrobing them with shiny, thick chocolate, and then into the cooling tunnel. Leigh asked the young man who had been assigned to help her on the production line if he would stand watch for two minutes. She had to take a quick break.

He nodded, grinning, rubbing his elbow against her arm. Ignoring his advance, she hurried to the restroom.

Hustling back, Leigh checked up and down the moving soft buttons. All seemed in order when suddenly the conveyor belt jammed. The creamy centers with their bottom coating of chocolate began bunching up. Began tumbling to the floor. More and more bunching and tumbling. The hose feeding the chocolate enrobing fountain uncoupled. Chocolate streamed out of the piping onto the floor and down the aisle.

Leigh's fist shot out to the emergency switch to stop the conveyor belt but she couldn't find it. The emergency switch was hidden under flowing chocolate.

Leigh yelled for help as Blair scrambled across the room, pulled a backup emergency lever mounted on the wall cutting power to the entire factory.

The factory looked like it had been hit with a chocolate bomb.

Melted chocolate gushed from under the conveyor belt flooding aisles and pathways leading to bags of sugar, to boxes of chopped chocolate waiting to be melted, to the final staging area where the chocolates were boxed for shipment.

Blair ran screaming up to Leigh staring down at the oozing chocolate. "How could you be so negligent? How could you let this … this disaster happen?"

Cameron Lefèvre yelling, bug-eyed, red faced, jogged slipping and sliding toward Leigh wagging his finger at her.

Leigh stepped back wiping her hand on her blouse smearing chocolate, then up to her face leaving a smudge of chocolate along her cheek. Lefèvre stepped forward, chocolate oozing up over the toes of his shoes. He continued to yell. "The line will be down for hours, maybe days to fix, clean up the goo, the equipment. Orders delayed. Money lost." Lefèvre's nose was an inch from Leigh's.

"Mademoiselle Dobrev, you are fired. Leave now and don't come back."

Chapter 33

Pornic, France

THE GENTLE SWAY of the train did nothing to alleviate Leigh's feeling of failure. A tear puddled in her eye as she stared out the window at the golden fields sweeping by, the clicking of the iron wheels running over the tracks sending a gentle hum through the silver bullet's cars speeding south from Paris to Nantes, home to Marie.

Leigh mulled over and over in her mind the mayhem that broke out at the chocolate factory. Did she really cause the conveyor belt to jam? Was she responsible for the uncoupling of the tubing carrying the melted chocolate to the trough that released the precise amount of chocolate onto each soft center?

Again and again she played over her actions—leaving the line of slowly moving soft centers for a brief break, no more than a few minutes. The young man standing beside her said he'd watch the conveyor belt while she was gone.

What was she missing? She was sure before taking the break that everything was running smoothly, not even a tremor on the belt, not even a quiver in the tubing.

Well, something happened.

Who did she think she was anyway? Going to Paris. Working in a chocolate factory with no experience. She could hardly equate Marie's kitchen with conveyor belts, pots of melting chocolate, over fifty pounds at a time were way more than the pound she tempered on the stove in the little French cottage.

She didn't send an email to Rawly. How could she possibly accept a ticket from him? Christmas holiday in New England? Hardly. How would he introduce her? *I'd like you to meet my friend from Paris. She was just fired from a chocolate factory.*

The Depardieus told her not to worry about the hostel's baked goods. They would hire temporary help. It would not be the same as her muffins with chocolate bits but they would cope.

The train jerked, dragging Leigh from the images of oozing chocolate dropping to the floor on top of a pile of syrupy cherry centers. Slowly the train came to a full stop. Conductors opened doors and let down the steps for passengers to disembark onto the cement platform.

Dragging her rolling suitcase, Leigh spotted Marie waving from the back of the crowded platform. She hurried into the woman's open arms and the warmth of her love. Love given no matter what calamity had befallen her, no matter if she was to blame or not, her love and greeting were unconditional.

Without saying a word, Marie threaded her arm through Leigh's guiding her to the car. They exchanged only a few words during the forty-five-minute drive to Pornic, both waiting for the comfort of the cottage away from prying eyes in the event tears were shed, or strangled words catching in Leigh's throat as she tried to explain why she was fired.

"Meatloaf is ready to be popped into the oven along with a couple of baked potatoes," Marie said as she turned up the hill away from the little harbor, parking by her gate.

"Wine?" Leigh asked.

"Oui, before, during, and after if we want," Marie said patting Leigh's hand then climbed out of the car. Standing at the gate, Leigh closed her eyes, breathing in the salty air of the ocean breeze. Marie watched as the tension seemed to drain away from the young woman. Opening the gate, Leigh's steps quickened up the path to the cottage made of rectangular blocks of weathered stone, the windows punctuated with frames of dark brown stone of various lengths under the orangey-brown tiles covering the roof.

Home!

The aroma of baking potatoes and meatloaf soon began circling the kitchen. Candles were lit as the sun called it a day. Mellow red wine was poured into goblets.

After several sips of wine, a sigh, Leigh began talking about the chocolate factory, the hostel and how great Shelby and Gerry Depardieu are to her. Talking about her little room in the attic and how wonderful it is to open a window, to feel the stimulating Paris air. Leigh paced the kitchen's worn wooden floorboards with excitement about the crazy cocoa beans—their flavors very different depending on where they were grown.

Marie retrieved the meatloaf, served slices with mushroom gravy along with the potatoes as Leigh topped off their wine.

Leigh related how she came to have the attic room—her laptop stolen most likely by one of the women spending the night in the dorm. She would check the boxes of papers in her bedroom in the morning to see what she had or hadn't lost, information gone with the computer.

Then came the story of what happened yesterday, the day she was fired. Pouring the last drop of wine in their glasses, Leigh sat staring into the flickering flame.

"Marie, I've gone over every minute of my shift, every second before I took a quick break only to come back and find mounds of sticky chocolate flowing over the floor, Blair Durance screaming at me, screaming how could I leave the conveyor belt unattended, how … wait … wait … Blair screamed I had left the conveyor belt unattended."

Leigh pushed back her chair, stood, wrapped her arms around her body, head down she paced the floor.

"What?" Marie asked watching her. Leigh was remembering something, seeing something in her mind that was amiss.

Leigh whirled around. "I didn't leave the conveyor belt unattended. I asked Blair's assistant, she told him to help me, I asked him to watch, that I'd be back in a few minutes. Marie, he wasn't there when I returned from my break, when Blair started screaming at me, accusing me. Monsieur Lefèvre, the owner, ran up to us. Blair continued to yell, pointing at me, that I had caused the destruction."

Leigh shook her head, turned to Marie, stared into her eyes. "Marie, I would bet my life that Blair sent her assistant away and sabotaged the belt, pulled the tubing off the fountain of chocolate. Blair set me up. I know it."

Plopping down on the chair she locked eyes with Marie, both women understanding that Leigh did nothing wrong, except that she would never leave equipment in someone else's hands unless she was certain they would stay and watch as promised.

Marie ran around the table, pulled Leigh up into her arms into a fierce hug. Grasping her shoulders Marie pulled Leigh's eyes to her. "You will finish your dinner, a cup of hot tea, and then get a good night sleep in your own bed, ma chérie.

"And, in the morning I'm taking you back to the train station. You are returning to Paris and that wonderful Depardieu couple. They are counting on you, you know. Then you call Juliette at the Academy, tell her what happened and that you have to finish your internship someplace else. Now, off to bed with you while I tend to the kitchen. We have to get up early so you can catch the morning train back to Paris."

Chapter 34

Paris, France

THE OFFICE DOOR BANGED OPEN.

"I didn't do it. I'm sure of it," Leigh screeched throwing her arms around Shelby.

"Didn't do what, chèrie?" Shelby asked returning Leigh's hug.

Gerry looked up from the stack of papers on his desk into Leigh's beaming face. "Welcome back," he said bemused at Leigh's startling appearance. Last he knew she was ready to move back to Pornic and the shelter of home.

"The chocolate factory—I was set up. Sabotaged." Leigh stood, eyebrows hitched, staring at the Depardieu's blank faces. Not waiting for their response, she smiled and took a deep breath. "How's everything here? I'll go to the kitchen. Bake the muffins for tomorrow. Oh, and another thing. I called my counselor at the Academy. I still can't believe what she said. The Parisian candy shop has reopened and Betsy Marceau insisted I complete my internship with her. Isn't it wonderful? See you later." Leigh hugged Gerry, hugged Shelby again and danced out the door.

———

Jumping onto the metro car Leigh grinned from ear to ear. She had rejoined the morning commuters. She was one of them. Going off to work. How great was that?

Hopping off the metro her shoulder bag wagging in rhythm with her jaunty steps, she strode up the street for her first day back at the Parisian. She stopped in front of the candy shop, stood gleefully gazing through the display window at the wide-brimmed yellow hat banded with a black grosgrain ribbon atop a pedestal circled with various sizes of wrapped boxed chocolates, lovely old-fashioned gift cards, and a pair of rhinestone encrusted glasses. So pretty. So inviting.

Betsy dashed to Leigh as she entered the shop, squeezing her in a warm embrace, kissing her cheeks. "Ma chérie, you're back where you belong." Grabbing Leigh's hand, she pulled her to the cozy back room, pushed her into a chair laughing as she filled two demitasse cups with espresso over a cube of sugar. She chattered all the way saying how happy she was to see Leigh, how much she missed her, how dreadful she felt when her shop was closed.

Finally, taking a breath, she sighed. "You look wonderful, chèrie," Betsy whispered her eyes twinkling. "I'm excited about my plan to complete your internship requirements. But first, tell me all about what you learned at that horrible chocolate factory. New tricks for me?"

"You know I was fired," Leigh said in a soft voice, hoping Madame Marceau wasn't going to be upset. She certainly didn't seem upset.

"Fiddle-faddle. I don't believe a word of it. You're much too responsible, too careful." Betsy leaned forward, circling her hand over Leigh's. "Here's what I have to say … good morning, mademoiselle. Welcome to my candy shop." An ear-to-ear smile spread over her face.

"Thank you, Madame Marceau—"

"No, no, no. You must call me Betsy. Now tell me about Monsieur Lefèvre and that Blair Durance."

"You know Blair?"

"Notorious. You aren't the first employee to fall under her evil eye."

Leigh relayed her suspicions to Betsy, also inside information on the supplier of his cocoa beans and what regions he felt grew the best beans.

"The little sneak. Any tricks to keep the cocoa butter from crystallizing?'

"Oh, my, yes. Monsieur Lefèvre went on and on how important it was to watch the temperature of the chocolate so it didn't crystallize. He didn't trust thermometers. Said some were faulty and insisted the best way to check the temperature when melting chocolate was to pull on a pair of latex gloves. There were always pairs in the cabinet underneath the melting pots. He put his hands right in the melting chocolate. It was amazing. After a few times I began to feel the difference in what was too hot, too cool and just right."

"Oui. Priceless. I will get the gloves and you will show me. I've heard of this … the Goldilocks' method—too hot, too cold, just right. I'll institute the test immediately. And, your classes, chèrie. What have you completed?"

"Two: Professional Chocolatier Program and Chocolate Making from the Bean. Both online but both required projects in the kitchen, and now the course on putting together a business plan. I'm sure you had to develop a plan—the marketing, financing, and, of course, the products. I'm interested in how you decided to incorporate a gift shop along with your love for chocolate."

"Oh, Leigh, it took me over two years and more to obtain the financing. I made lists of the equipment required for my factory, then the recipes … really hard. Had to winnow the recipes down from several I liked to the very best. And then there was the sourcing of the ingredients for each recipe, keeping in mind the high quality I wanted to achieve, wanted to become known for. Chérie, there were many times I threw up my hands—I can't do this— wanted to give up."

"But you didn't give up."

"No, I didn't. And now, I have this wonderful shop, and a wonderful intern who will teach me all the latest she has learned … like dipping my hands into my velvety chocolate."

"I've been working part-time in the hostel kitchen—for my room and board. The Depardieu's have been wonderful."

"Oh, you don't have to tell me that. I talked with them, while you were in Pornic. They sang your praises."

"But I was only home for a day. You mean—"

"Oui. I've been keeping tabs on you. When I reopened I called the Academy and they told me you were still interning at the chocolate factory and staying at the hostel. But that lovely woman, Juliette, let me know immediately when you left Montmartre and that you were fleeing home to your mother—"

"Oh, Marie isn't my mother, more like a Godmother in every sense of the word. She's been wonderful—"

Betsy held her palms up, shaking her head. "No more, chèrie, no more. Everyone believes you walk on water. You're causing me to have an inferiority spasm. Just wait until Monsieur Lefèvre realizes what he's lost. He'll be after you again. Now, let's get down to work."

Flitting from her chair, Betsy opened a cabinet retrieving a white shirt box tied with a gold ribbon. "This is for you. I hope you will wear it with pride."

Leigh pulled the end of the ribbon and lifted the lid. Smiling, she shook out an embroidered, black bib apron: *The Parisian Candy & Gift Shoppe, Leigh Dobrev.*

Leigh blew kisses to Betsy's cheeks and then slipped the apron over her head.

"I like a uniform look for everyone working for me, so a white blouse, short sleeves in summer, long sleeves in winter, tucked into chocolate brown slacks," Betsy said, all business as she tied the new apron around Leigh. "Wear black shoes with crepe soles because you will be on your feet all day. A hairnet is required when working in my factory. When you are out front you can let loose your beautiful hair. You are so pretty I expect there will be many young men, and old geezers, who will come to the shop just to take a look at the new girl. That will be you, chèrie."

———

To: RawlyScott@yahoo.com
Date: September 15, 2012
Time: 8 a.m.
From: LeighDobrev@gmail.com
Subject: The Parisian Candy & Gift Shoppe

Dear Rawly, I'm now interning at the Parisian. A dreadful incident happened at the Montmartre Chocolate Factory and I was fired. They said I was responsible for the disaster. I believe I was framed but have no way to prove it. Oh, it was awful, Rawly—chocolate everywhere.

I'll tell you more when I see you … see you. Two beautiful words.

I'm sorry I didn't tell you when it happened. I just couldn't. I felt like such a failure.

How is everything in your world? Your thesis research? The election is coming up. November I think you said. First week?

I've made sure that Madame Marceau, she insists I call her Betsy, and the Depardieus have the dates I'll be away. The timing is bad. The holidays are a busy time for them both. Both said they'd manage and that they were excited for me—the States, Christmas in New England.

Lucky me, everything has worked out considering how shattered I was when Monsieur Lefèvre screamed at me: You're fired!

Please write soon.

Bisous,

Leigh

———

To: LeighDobrev@ gmail.com
Date: September 18, 2012
Time: 10 p.m.
From: RawlyScott@yahoo.com
Subject: Re: The Parisian Candy & Gift Shoppe
That Monsieur what's-his-name is a knucklehead for firing you. It just proves that you were meant to intern at the Parisian—your first choice.

My thesis, 120 pages and counting, and classes are demanding—lots of hard work. The election: I think my candidate is going to win but the polls show it's too close to call. Not sure I have the stomach to be a candidate.

I understand what Betsy and the hostel people are saying—the holidays are a busy time for retail and hotel services. I'm just glad I'll have a breather from my classes.

I'm meeting constantly with my professor, thesis advisor. Just when I think I have the majority of research covered he comes up with another angle and I'm off delving into more research and lab work. Lots to juggle. It's a good and bad time for a vacation.

Enjoy the Parisian.

Rawly

Leigh stared at Rawly's email. Re-read it. The word vacation stung. She wasn't going on a vacation. She wanted to be with him. It had taken him three whole days to reply. *Lots to juggle? What's he saying, or more important what isn't he saying? Maybe he doesn't want me to come to the States. Oh, God, maybe he doesn't want to see me. I'm inconveniencing him ... I'm just another thing he has to juggle. Maybe he doesn't care about me. He didn't even send a kiss.*

Chapter 35

December 2012

IT WAS ALMOST MIDNIGHT when Leigh stepped off the elevator and stumbled up the stairs to her room in the turret. Removing her shoes, she flopped down on the narrow bed massaging her right foot. No strength to undress, she curled into a ball closing her eyes. But sleep was elusive as her mind took flight. It was December first. A little more than three weeks and she would be flying over the ocean to Rawly for the holidays. Meeting his family.

She had asked him if she should cancel her visit with all he was juggling. He had reassured her that this was precisely the right time and the whole family was eager to see her. She sensed, right or wrong, that some of his excitement had cooled, but pushed the thought away.

December. Where had the weeks gone?

Now that the Business Plan course was completed she had come away with a good grasp on how to start a business, all of the required pieces that had to be assembled before presenting the plan to a potential investor, or to a bank for a loan. But, the thought of starting a business scared her. She wasn't ready.

Working at the hostel plus putting in the hours to fulfill her internship was killing her. Thank God she would be done soon. The thought of working at one job looked like a vacation. But where? Betsy hadn't mentioned anything beyond January tenth. Every time she got up the courage to say something she swallowed the words. Shelby Depardieu had hinted more than once that she was welcome to stay on at the hostel, more than welcome, urging her to consider taking over the hostel kitchen.

But serving up breakfasts and dinners were not her passion.

Her breathing gradually slowed, each breath deeper, sleep finally releasing her mind.

———

Flipping the page of the calendar tacked to her wall before rushing out to ride the metro, she saw December twenty-second circled in red. The date she had been waiting for. Rawly's emails were shorter and shorter and she had responded in kind—without kisses when signing off. She half thought he had forgotten his invitation to visit. The other half shouted back, "Don't be absurd. The tickets will come soon. If they don't, well …"

Then what?

Pushing a stray lock under the hairnet, Leigh fished around in the closet next to the doorway into the shop for fresh brushes and gold paint to gild the molded chocolate holly-leaf candies. She looked up at the jingle of the brass bell as a bearded, olive-skinned man walked in.

Betsy hustled from behind the counter to the man. Carrying a tote, she slipped in a box of chocolates as she closed the short distance. Leigh thought she had seen the stranger before but couldn't think of where.

"That's a lovely red rose on the yellow hat, Madame," he said.

"Yes, it's fresh today," Betsy said with a full smile as she handed him the tote. Grasping the handle, he gave Betsy a slight nod and turned to leave.

"Bye, Aalim," Betsy said returning to the counter.

Completing the task of gilding the chocolate holly leaves, Leigh cleaned the brushes and put the painting supplies back in the closet. She shook her hair free of the net fluffing the waves with her fingers and then sought out Betsy. She wanted to go over the final weeks in December, making sure her trip departure and return dates were on the calendar and to once again try to talk to Betsy about the end of her internship and a possible job.

Betsy was helping two ladies picking out hostess gifts for a party they were attending on Saturday night. Leigh took the opportunity to saunter through the displays admiring how clever Betsy was showing her products in delightful pick-me-up arrangements. Pausing at the front window display, a particular favorite of hers, she gazed at the yellow wide-brimmed hat, a frown slowly crossing her lips. *A red rose? There was no red rose. The man must have been mistaken. But Betsy had replied as if there was a rose.*

Hearing the cha-ching of the cash register, Leigh turned away from the hat instantly thinking of the dates she wanted to check on the calendar.

"Betsy, my trip schedule … do you have the dates?"

"Of course," Betsy said reaching for the December chart. "You're leaving on December twenty-second returning on January second. Is that right?"

"Oui. I will also have completed my internship on January tenth."

"What are your plans, Leigh, after your formal training? Any more courses?"

Courses? I don't want to talk about courses. I want a full-time job. "As a matter of fact, there is one more. Master Chocolatier, but I'm thinking a little more experience, job experience, would be beneficial before taking the course. Juliette says it's quite advanced."

"I see. In the meantime, I'd like you to put a date on your calendar—the American Embassy party on January eighth. They have placed a very large order for our little four-piece candy gift boxes. They plan to arrange them by the champagne flute and place cards for each guest. I'll need your help in putting the boxes together, over fifty, and to deliver them the morning of the eighth. The Ambassador also asked if I had any young ladies who might help serve at the party. It's going to be a very elegant affair. If he asks again, would you like to help? It will pay handsomely."

"Of course. What do I wear?"

"Hair tied at the nape of your neck with a wide black ribbon in a bow, white long-sleeved collared shirt tucked into a knee-length black skirt, black hose, black flat shoes. I think I've seen you in that outfit. Do you have all those pieces?"

"I do, but I think I'll buy a new blouse."

The brass bell jingled breaking up their conference and the day passed with no resolution on Leigh's future at the Parisian Candy & Gift Shoppe.

———

As the days had melted from October to November and now to December, she thought her desire to see Rawly would fade, but instead of fading, a longing to see him had grown stronger. However, the twinge that her interest in him was not reciprocated remained. Perhaps she had mistaken his interest in her all along.

Betsy was right when she said men of all ages would make return trips to the shop asking if she could take a break for coffee, or dinner, or maybe a drink after work. None interested her, not even a little tickle of curiosity. Her ready smile and attentiveness were directed at serving the customer not a possible date.

She found her love for the business grew everyday—joking with repeat customers, finding them just the right item, and tallying up the daily sales. She wanted to learn the expense side, see how all the chocolate, sugar, flavorings, packaging related to profits.

With all of that, why did she gaze out the metro window at the end of the day, her mind returning to Rawly? A feeling of longing replaced any thrill she had experienced during the hours at the Parisian. *I'm being ridiculous. He's probably thinking as I am: I live in France. He's an American. An American who is losing interest.*

With a jerk the metro screeched to a halt at her stop. She smiled at a gray-haired woman struggling to rise from her seat jostling several bundles.

"Let me help you, Madame," Leigh offered taking the woman's elbow to steady her as they stepped off the car.

"Merci, chérie, merci." With her arm in a tight grip around her bundles, the woman turned off in the opposite direction, her heavy-soled shoes moving in quick short steps.

Watching the woman until she rounded the corner, Leigh repositioned her shoulder bag, and ambled down to the street to the hostel and another three hours of baking muffins with either chocolate bits or grated orange peel and flavoring. Looking at her reflection in the shop windows as she passed she saw Rawly looking back at her.

Chapter 36

———

A COLD, WINTER WIND licked at Leigh's face as she hustled down the Champs-Elysées to meet Eric at the café next to the Moulin Rouge. Wrapping her coat close to her body, she blinked several times, against the sting of the air. Shuddering, she pushed open the door stepping inside the café with a whoosh of icy air.

Glancing around the tables she spotted Eric's orangey-red hair as a man stood, slapped him on the shoulder and turned to leave jostling against her as he stepped out into the frigid air. Leigh stared after him—the man Betsy called Aalim. He seemed to be a friend of Eric's.

Her eyes turned, focused on Eric sitting with his back to her. Snaking between the occupied tables, Leigh slid into the chair across from Eric. "Bonjour. Who was that man tapping you on the shoulder? A friend?" she asked as she shook her arms free of her coat sleeves.

"I don't know who you mean. I don't have any friends."

"The man with the beard. He just left."

"Don't know. All I do is play my guitar—people come up to me all the time. I'm a novelty you know—one handed musician." His green eyes fastened on her as she finally extricated herself from her coat, laying it over the back of her chair.

"Okay, okay. Don't bite my head off." She reached back into the pocket of her coat. "Here … I brought you some chocolates. A little Christmas treat."

"Early isn't it? Five days yet," he said eyeing the small box, leaving it on the table beside his coffee.

"I won't be here. Remember? I'm flying to Boston for the holidays."

"Oh, that's right, the big man. Rawly."

"If you're going to be nasty, Eric—

"Redd. Redd Pepper."

"Excuuuse me—Monsieur Redd Pepper. Sorry for the faux pas. Now, be nice. Tell me where, what café, you're playing at this week—The Cave?"

"And, the Cafe de Paris. My friends meet there."

"You said you had no friends," Leigh said mocking him.

"Are you cross examining me? Giving up chocolates to become a prosecutor?"

"Eric, excuse me, Redd," she said rolling her eyes. "What's the matter with you? Are you going home ... to Pornic, for Christmas?"

Redd laughed. Leaned forward. "What a joker. You know I have no home, besides the money's here. Hand or no hand my music pays."

"I don't know why you're so surly, but I'm not staying to find out. I came to wish you a Merry Christmas. So, Merry Christmas." Grabbing her coat, she shoved her arms through the sleeves, and strutted out of the café.

———

Getting off the elevator, Leigh stomped up the stairs to her room, throwing her purse on the bed as she slammed the door. Eric, Pepper, Redd, or whatever he called himself these days, was so irritating. Picking up her laptop she slumped onto the bed, leaned against the wall, and waited for the white arrow to appear on the screen and then began typing.

> To: RawlyScott@yahoo.com
> Date: December 20, 2012
> Time: 9:52 p.m.
> From: LeighDobrev@gmail.com
> Subject: Three more days
> The tickets arrived yesterday. Can't believe I'll be seeing you, your family, and a new country. I'm sooo excited. Nine months—will I recognize you? Ha-ha. Are you still awake?
> Leigh

Almost immediately, a reply from Rawly pinged her inbox.

To: LeighDobrev@gmail.com
Date: December 20, 2012
Time: 9:58 p.m.
From: RawlyScott@yahoo.com
Subject: Re: Three more days
Yes, I'm awake. Thank God you received the tickets. After mailing, I thought maybe I should have sent them FedEx.

You'll recognize me. I'll be the one with 4 people screaming hello—Tyler, mom, Grammy Kathy, and yours truly.

Be sure to pack warm clothes but no need for extra. You're about my mom's size. She has boots, hats, gloves, etc. etc. for the snow.
Rawly

———

To: RawlyScott@yahoo.com
Date: December 20, 2012
Time: 10:14 p.m.
From: LeighDobrev@gmail.com
Subject: Re: Re: Three more days
SNOW??
Leigh

———

To: LeighDobrev@gmail.com
Date: December 20, 2012
Time: 10:22 p.m.
From: RawlyScott@yahoo.com
Subject: Re: Re: Re: Three more days

It's predicted—can't beat snowflakes on your eyelashes and tongue on Christmas Eve. Three inches fell last night. You should have seen Goldy dashing around in it. First time she's been in the snow.

Rawly

———

To: RawlyScott@yahoo.com
Date: December 20, 2012
Time: 10:28 p.m.
From: LeighDobrev@gmail.com
Subject: Re: Re: Re: Re: Three more days
GOLDY??
Leigh

———

To: LeighDobrev@gmail.com
Date: December 20, 2012
Time: 10:35 p.m.
From: RawlyScott@yahoo.com
Subject: Re: Re: Re: Re: Three more days
I gave GK a Golden Retriever puppy for Christmas. She's a real clown. The puppy, not GK. Although the way she's preparing for your visit, she is a bit of a clown as well.

Rawly

———

To: RawlyScott@yahoo.com
Date: December 20, 2012
Time: 10:46 p.m.
From: LeighDobrev@gmail.com

Subject: Re: Re: Re: Re: Re: Three more days
When I wake up it will two days.
Night :)
Leigh

———

To: LeighDobrev@gmail.com
Date: December 20, 2012
Time: 10:51 p.m.
From: RawlyScott@yahoo.com
Subject: Re: Re: Re: Re: Re: Re: Three more days
Sweet dreams. See you soon!
Rawly

"Umm, sweet dreams. I'll take it, Monsieur," Leigh whispered as she pulled Shelby's quilt up around her ears.

———

Part Five

Chapter 37

Newburyport, Massachusetts, U.S.A.
Christmas Holiday – 2012

THE PLANE LIFTED OFF the tarmac at Charles de Gaulle Airport quickly banking west over the Atlantic Ocean. Leigh was captivated with the vast body of water, a slight shake of her head in disbelief. How did that tiny wine bottle ever travel all those miles to the beach where she discovered it thirteen years ago—evading storms, dodging ship traffic. She was nine when Rawly tossed it in the surf, and, now, at twenty-two she was traveling to the spot where their story began.

Her lips drawing to a smile, she pulled the lever reclining the seat several inches. Closing her eyes, Rawly filled her thoughts. She wondered if he would kiss her, or, as she sensed from his emails, was he withdrawing? Her fingers ran across her lips. Would she feel his lips soon?

———

Grasping the handle of her rolling carry-on case, Leigh followed the line of passengers snaking their way up the jetway into the terminal. Her heart was pounding as she strained to find Rawly.

Hearing her name, she turned and there he was waving, straining against the rope. Sprinting around the airport attendant, he swooped her into his arms, planting a hungry kiss on each cheek and her lips. Setting her back on her feet, he took hold of her suitcase guiding her to a smiling group and Kathy's arms. Then it was

Tyler's turn to give her a hug, and Meg, and a man she presumed was Rawly's father, and another young woman.

Rawly hastily introduced her to his dad, Michael Scott, who hugged her again. Then Tyler stepped forward with his girlfriend Sandy, who gave her a second hug. Michael took command of her carry-on while Rawly, not letting go, guided her to the carousel to pick up her bigger suitcase. Michael excused himself to get the van that Rawly had borrowed so they could all travel to Newburyport together.

Leigh pointed out her bag with a red piece of heavy yarn tied to the handle. Rawly dragged it off the carousel, giving her another quick kiss. He whispered in her ear, "I've missed you Rawleigh Dobrev."

Finally, he said something, and oooh, the kisses.

"I've missed you Rawleigh Scott," she whispered back as Tyler relieved his brother of the suitcase. Leigh's eyes suddenly puddled. Rawly's greeting was warm, tender, affectionate. He hadn't withdrawn, quite the reverse.

Seeing her smoky-blue eyes misting, Rawly abruptly stopped. "Hey, baby, what's the matter?" he whispered gently dabbing her eyes with the end of his scarf.

Calling her baby pushed the puddles over her lids. "Nothing. I'm just happy to see you. I wasn't sure—

"Don't say it. I was an idiot," he said softly. The tears mopped away, they continued to walk to the exit.

Kathy threaded her hand through Leigh's arm. "You certainly have changed, my dear—a young girl to a beautiful woman. We are all so happy you'll be with us for Christmas."

"No more so than I, Kathy," Leigh said hugging Kathy's arm to her body.

Laughing, they exited to the cacophony of cars honking, veering in and out of line in the pick-up area. Michael squeezed around a van and pulled alongside the curb. Tyler deposited Leigh's suitcase in the back as everyone piled into the van, Michael remaining at the wheel. Surmising his son wasn't going to leave the pretty French girl alone, he had already told Rawly he would act as chauffeur. He didn't trust Rawly to keep his eyes on the highway for the forty-mile drive to Newburyport.

Driving north on Interstate 95 everyone jabbered, laughed, asked Leigh about her flight, pointed out places of interest, and gave suggestions on what she should absolutely must see while in the Boston area.

"Just wait until you see Newburyport," Sandy said. "It looks like a little European town, well, how I envision a little town. You tell me." Kathy, mindful that Leigh might be overwhelmed with all the Scott's had maneuvered Sandy to sit next to Leigh in the van.

Turning off the highway into Newburyport, Michael drove to the Merrimack River's waterfront slowing to a crawl after turning right onto Water Street. "Okay, Leigh, here's what Sandy was talking about—a typical New England seaport."

Rawly, still gripping Leigh's hand, raised it to his lips for a quick kiss. The car was quiet for a few seconds, then, unable to remain silent, erupting with chatter as everyone pointed out the quaint shops and favorite restaurants. Rawly explained that the river led to the ocean where he launched the bottle. Squeezing her fingers he added he would take her to the beach, the exact spot, tomorrow.

Michael turned into a narrow side street and parked in the first spot he saw declaring he was lucky to find a place. Piling out of the van, Tyler laughed that it was about time they stopped for a bite to eat. He was starving. Meg added that this was one of the Scott's favorite restaurants.

Leigh stood facing an old building constructed of red brick around many tall windows on the ground floor with whitewashed stone covering the floor above. Green and white striped awnings covered each of the street-level windows. A black sign, *Grog,* in gold letters spanned the entrance.

Stepping inside, Kathy was immediately greeted by a young man. "Mrs. Scott, hello. The table you reserved is ready for your party. I made sure there was a fire in the fireplace as you requested," he said to Kathy, grinning at the group in front of him. "This way, please."

Leigh felt the warmth of the wide, very worn floorboards under her feet, the dim lighting, and a bar much like the little pub in Pornic. The party of seven settled into the mellow pine captain's chairs positioned around a long tavern table in front of a large fireplace, the low flames licking the logs. The wine Kathy ordered was delivered to the table, poured, and a toast welcoming Leigh was proposed. The waiter placed a menu in front of each of his guests warmed by the flickering fire.

The soft sounds of clinking glasses, the soft voices of others in the pub, the crackling sap of the logs, enveloped the table as the party made their dinner selections.

"So, Leigh, do you feel at home in this little pub?" Sandy asked looking across the table at her new friend.

"Perfectly, merci."

Sandy closed her eyes, then popped them open. "I love your accent. The French words. No wonder Rawly can't stop talking about you."

Leigh's eyes twinkled as she sought Rawly's eyes. He gave her hand a squeeze under the table, his lips in a sheepish grin. Sandy had outed him. Yes, he had talked about Leigh all the time. His emails hadn't reflected that. He was an idiot. He would have to explain, if he could, sometime in the next few days.

Leaving the Grog, Michael once again took the wheel. All their cars, including Rawly's, were parked at Kathy's townhouse. The townhouse was to serve as home base for the balance of Leigh's holiday visit.

In the van, Michael navigated the narrow Newburyport streets, Sandy hunching over the back-row seat laying her hand on Leigh's shoulder. "You have another treat in store. Wait till you see Kathy's townhouse—built in 1850, red brick, three stories, four fireplaces. And if that isn't enough, the cutest little black picket fence. Oh, gee, is GK's townhouse more English than French, Tyler? What do you think?"

"Maybe English," Tyler replied. "New England," he added chuckling

Kathy chuckled along with her grandson.

After dropping everyone off, Michael headed to his condo in Portsmouth, and Meg to her condo in Nashua, both cities in New Hampshire. Both planned to return for Christmas dinner. Tyler and Sandy were spending the night and Christmas Eve with Kathy—Tyler and Rawly sharing a bedroom, and Sandy and Leigh sharing a bedroom.

"Leigh, you must be tired," Kathy said. "I think we should all go to bed. I'll show you around the house in the morning. Rawly, if you and Tyler could stay up a little, fill me in on the plans for tomorrow and Christmas day. I have a turkey—not sure when I should stick it in the oven."

———

Letting out a contented sigh Leigh pulled the quilt up under her chin.

"You have to be exhausted," Sandy whispered from the small closet. "You've been up for, what, almost twenty-four hours?"

"It does feel good to lay my head down on a pillow."

"All set?" Sandy asked. "I'll turn out the light?"

"All set."

The glow of the street light shadowed the little third-floor attic bedroom, the curtain filtering a lacy pattern on the far wall.

Leigh squirmed around onto her side facing Sandy in the opposite twin bed. "Where do you work, Sandy?"

"At a graphics company not too far from the Hancock Tower where Tyler's company is located. Actually, not far from Rawly's dorm at MIT. The three of us get together a lot. Our friends call us the three Musketeers."

"Are you and Tyler going to get married?"

"That's the plan. We moved in together about a year ago. Found the cutest studio apartment. I wish you could see it. There's a Murphy bed so when it's up, it looks like we have a big living room. There's an alcove which conceals a galley kitchen, more of a kitchenette. Perfect for the two of us. We talk about getting married in another two years. We have student loans we're trying to pay off. Starting salaries don't go far, but Tyler's had a couple of raises as have I. Of course, Rawly's ROTC scholarship pays for all of his education." Sandy snuggled under her quilt, head propped up on her pillow. "Leigh, are you a virgin?"

Leigh's eyes shot wide open. "Sandy ... what kind of a question is that?" she whispered over a nervous giggle.

"Well, are you?"

"Why?"

"Are you or are you not?"

"Not," Leigh replied in a barely audible voice. *Why was Sandy asking such a question?*

"That's good," Sandy said turning on her back, looking up at the ceiling. "Rawly changed after he visited you last spring. Changed like if he was walking in one direction, he suddenly turned and walked in the opposite direction."

"I don't understand what you're saying, Sandy. When I said *not*, I didn't mean that—

"Well, before last spring he was very much a playboy—dates with different girls every weekend. It was like he was looking for something ... or someone. He had many conquests."

"Conquests?"

"Sex. His biggest conquest since he returned from that trip to France is a double-decker, hot-fudge sundae with whipped cream and chocolate sprinkles."

"Sandy, how do you know that ... the conquests?" Leigh rested her head on her arm. "Did he tell you ... Tyler?"

"Oh, no. The girls. The women. They were crazy for him and thought that by talking to me they could find out if he liked them. A few of them went so far as to say they had sex. But that's not exactly why I'm telling you this. I'm telling you because when he came back from Europe he was a different man. I don't think he's been out on a date since then, not one that I know of anyway. I asked Tyler and he said that he even asked Rawly why he stopped dating."

"What did Tyler say? Err, what did he say that Rawly said?"

"Only that he wasn't interested. Wanted to work hard on his Masters, his thesis. But, and this is what I want you to know, he began talking about you. Just a comment here and there ... at first ... until about three weeks ago. He's been talking about you non-stop since the beginning of December. What he wanted to show you, where he wanted to take you. Leigh, I know he's hoping you'll move here."

Leigh sat up in bed, her legs dangling over the edge, staring across at Sandy. "How do you know that?"

"Does he hold your hand?"

"Yes, but—

"Does he put his arm around your shoulders?"

"Yes, but—

"I saw him greet you at the airport. That was some kiss he planted on your mouth. And, from where I was standing, you didn't exactly hold back. Did you have sex when he visited in France?'

"Really, Sandy."

"I take that as a no. I doubt any woman ever said no to Rawly Scott."

"That may not be a good thing—maybe he has expectations. I'm not ready."

"Well, I sense he's hopeful that you'll move. You'd be safer here—all those terrorists in Europe."

"Oh, that's the Middle East area. Not Paris."

"What about the train bombings—London, Madrid?"

Slipping back to the warmth of the bed, Leigh pulled her legs up under the quilt, curling into a ball. "I'm okay. Feel safe."

Sandy curled in a ball under her blanket, looked over at Leigh. Her mouth was slightly ajar, her breathing slow and rhythmic. Rawleigh Dobrev was fast asleep.

Chapter 38

Christmas Eve

THE SCENT OF COFFEE BREWING, muffins baking, and bacon crisping circled Leigh's nose. Snuggling deeper under the quilt her mind warmed to the aromas remembering where she was.

New England.

Christmas Eve.

Rawly ... his kisses.

Miraculous!

"Sandy? You awake?" she whispered.

No answer.

Holding the quilt under her chin, she sat up. Sandy's bed was empty. Peeking over the edge of the quilt she saw a sunny day through the curtain, a new day in Newburyport with Rawly.

Raising her arms over her head, touching the slant ceiling of the attic turned bedroom, she pushed her toes down to a delicious stretch, tip to toe.

Flinging off the covers, Leigh dressed, trotted down a flight of stairs to the second-floor bathroom, and then down another flight of stairs following the tantalizing whiff of breakfast.

Rawly intercepted her in the wide doorway between the living room and the kitchen, folded her in his arms, kissed the top of her silky black hair, looked into her smoky-blue eyes. "Good morning, did you sleep well?"

"Oui. Et vous?"

"Scary. I think I know what you asked ... yes, I slept well, too."

"Sit, you two. Here's your coffee, dear," Kathy said grinning at Leigh. "Help yourself to the muffins, butter and jam. Bacon and scrambled eggs coming up. Long day ahead of us."

Sandy watched Rawly and Leigh. "Gotta love that French stuff," she giggled.

"What, no wine bottles with messages this morning, GK?" Tyler asked laughing as he topped off Sandy's coffee from the black carafe and then helped himself to a cranberry-orange muffin from the basket Leigh passed to him.

"No need, Tyler. We couldn't top the last time even if we tried," Kathy said with a chuckle. "Now eat up everyone. You sleepyheads almost missed morning. I'm going with you to the beach, and then I have to come back to begin preparing for Christmas dinner tomorrow." She smiled at the happy faces eating breakfast at the five-foot round kitchen table. It was just large enough to seat her growing family thanks to the eight antique ice-cream chairs.

The cozy kitchen served as the gathering place for all meals. Seeing the red brick fireplace rising to the ceiling, the hearth with a black iron pot hanging from a crane, one could easily drift back in time to when a woman, a hundred years ago, placed pans in the beehive oven behind the black-iron door and latch for slow cooking, or to keep dishes warm, or a warm place for bread dough to rise.

"Kathy, you're not chopping, dicing, toasting, etcetera, etcetera, all by yourself. I'm coming back with you," Sandy said taking her empty coffee cup to the sink.

"Me too, Kathy. I'm sure you can show me how to handle all the etcetera jobs," Leigh giggled removing her empty coffee cup, nodding to Tyler if he was finished, then picked up his plate.

"Not today, dear. Rawly has your day mapped out and it doesn't include slicing and dicing."

"Get your coats on, everyone," Rawly said. "I'll go warm up the van." Tying a red scarf around his neck, stuffing it under his parka, he gave Leigh a peck on the cheek and was out the door.

"Meg left a quilted coat for you, Leigh," Kathy said.

"And … how do you say my dear in French?" Sandy asked, her head in the hall closet.

"Ma chérie."

"And, ma chérie, Meg brought you this knitted cap. Looks very French don't you think—French beret like? And, these gloves. No need for boots but snow is predicted tomorrow. Tyler, do you think we'll have a white Christmas?" Sandy asked wrapping her arms around her lover, her eyes seeking an affirmative answer.

"There's a chance," he said with a wink and a kiss on the tip of her nose.

Sandy smiled, releasing him. "Good answer, ma chérie."

"Come on, GK, let's go," Tyler said pulling his grandmother's coat up around her neck.

———

Blue sky and beams of bright sun bouncing off crashing waves greeted the group piling out of the van, and stepping onto pristine white sand. Leigh's eyes sparkled in anticipation of walking to the spot where nine-year-old Rawly had thrown the bottle into the ocean launching it on its way with a message to her: *Call me!*

Rawly put his arm around her shoulders; Leigh put her arm around his waist as they ambled over the sand to the water.

Tyler, holding Kathy's hand on one side and Sandy's on the other, pulled them to a stop midway to gaze at the large waves sweeping over the sand. Tyler and Kathy said nothing, reliving the scene thirteen years ago, a scene which Sandy could only imagine.

Leigh and Rawly sauntered a little closer to the crashing waves, stopped, stared. Squeezing Leigh's hand, Rawly squinted out over the horizon. "How could that bottle have possibly made it to your beach, your eyes, your hands?"

Leigh leaned into Rawly, her head against his shoulder.

Tyler watched the couple. "What do you think about them … as a couple?"

"All I know is I wouldn't deny the magnetism that brought them together," Sandy replied.

"Nor would I, Sandy. Nor would I," Kathy chimed in.

Rawly stooped, picked up an open clamshell—barnacles on the outside but shiny, pearl-white inside. Turning Leigh's hand over, he slowly pulled off her mitten and placed the shell in her palm. "Merry Christmas," he whispered, his eyes warm and tender.

Leigh looked around, spotted a small conch shell no bigger than the end of her thumb. Picking it up, she placed the creamy shell in the palm of Rawly's hand. "And, Merry Christmas to you."

All of a sudden a wave crashed in front of them spewing water over their shoes. Laughing, they ran back to join the others.

Chapter 39

———

SANDY HAD HER WISH. Five inches of snow had fallen during the night and light flurries were predicted throughout the day.

The Christmas feast finished, coffee served, and with hugs, kisses, and wishes given to Leigh for a safe trip home, Meg headed to Nashua, Michael to Portsmouth, and Tyler and Sandy left for Boston to return the van before the drive in the snow became treacherous. After the final wave goodbye Kathy closed the door, and leaned back with a smile on her face. She was tired but it had been a wonderful day, a family day.

Leigh excused herself thanking Kathy with a hug, a quick kiss for Rawly, and wearily climbed the two-flights of stairs to her third-floor bedroom. Mimicking Kathy's response to her family leaving, Leigh leaned back against the closed door, hugging herself with a contented sigh.

It had been a wonderful Christmas. Very different than any she had experienced before. Such a big gathering—all family, all warm and friendly, jokes shooting back and forth between the brothers. Stepping to the small bench in the window, she sat on the blue-velvet pad and gazed out through the lace curtain at the snowflakes sparkling in the light of the streetlamp.

Is this how it would feel if I lived here? Of course, every day can't be like Christmas, but this family, so kind, so accepting, making me feel welcome. I hope Marie had a nice day with her mom and dad. She didn't answer the phone. Must have gone to their home to celebrate. Home. Celebration. Different country. So far away, yet somehow close together. No, it's not close. No. Stop. No bad thoughts tonight. Watch the snowflakes. Enjoy these days with Rawly ... the Scotts.

Leigh slipped into the yellow fleece pajamas Sandy had given to her so she wouldn't freeze. "The heat is a bit tepid by the time it reaches the attic," she had laughed. Snuggling under the quilt, Leigh looked at the empty bed. She missed Sandy. She had become a dear friend.

————

Over the next few days Rawly took charge of Leigh's indoctrination into life in Newburyport. He wouldn't admit to an ulterior motive but it was there in his eyes, his grasp of her hand, the quick kisses on her cheeks.

He wanted her here.

He wanted her.

By mid week, he pulled out what he hoped would be the trick to win her over—the Chocolate Delight candy shop. The owners, Mr. and Mrs. Becker, were ready to retire. They met in Boston as children, immigrants from Germany with their parents. They saw nothing beautiful in the falling snow.

It had snowed the four days since Christmas leaving almost a foot. The sun was finally shining, and Mr. Becker, a portly man, was half-heartedly pushing the shovel, another dusting of white stuff to the curb, when Rawly stepped up, took the shovel from Becker's hands finishing the job in short order.

Grinning, Rawly handed the shovel back to Mr. Becker and joined Leigh inside the shop. She was in an animated conversation with Mrs. Becker, explaining something about crystallization of cocoa butter. Mrs. Becker was nodding sharply in agreement to whatever it was that Leigh had said.

A lady entered the shop jingling the little brass bell. Leigh looked up, smiled, seeing the little bell on the Parisian candy shop door. A clerk immediately went to help the lady perusing the chocolate display.

Mr. Becker stomped the snow off of his shoes and invited Rawly to join him for a cup of hot chocolate. "I've earned it and so has this young man," he said to his wife. "Finished the job for me. You too, miss," he said to Leigh smiling.

"Oh, yes, you must sample my cocoa," Mrs. Becker said to Leigh as she led the way through a curtain.

The back of the shop was cozy with two chairs set at a white bistro table. Mr. Becker quickly produced two more chairs. Pink-flowered chintz tieback curtains framed a small window and a tiny window in the back door. A space heater turned on low warmed the little nook. Mrs. Becker, a stocky woman, white hair pulled back in a bun, poured steamed milk over a chocolate mixture she had placed in four china cups.

"Here, Rawly, and …

"Mr. and Mrs. Becker let me present Miss Rawleigh Dobrev, a professional chocolatier straight from Paris," Rawly said kissing Leigh's crimson cheek.

"How wonderful. No wonder you're so well versed on the vagaries of chocolate." Mrs. Becker said beaming. "And here Mr. Becker and I are planning to retire, looking to sell our shop or to find a manager—

"Miss Dobrev is interested in a shop of her own …

Leigh threw Rawly an icy stare.

"… someday …" Oh, oh. This isn't going well, he thought.

Another icy glare under raised brows.

"… maybe." Now I've done it.

The Beckers were exchanging glances of their own and missed the shards of ice darting from Leigh to Rawly daring him to continue.

Pushing their wire-rimmed glasses up on their noses, they looked from Rawly to Leigh. Mr. Becker stepped to a small oak desk, picked up a business card, and handed it to Leigh. "Here's our number if you'd like to discuss a business arrangement. Just write, or call," he said his eyes pleading to take him up on his suggestion.

Leigh stood accepting the card. "Thank you, Mr. and Mrs. Becker, but we've taken up too much of your time. The chocolate was wonderful." She blew a kiss onto each of Mrs. Becker's rosy cheeks. Shaking Mr. Becker's hand, she stepped out of the cozy nook into the shop and out the front door stopping on the wet pavement not sure which way to turn.

Rawly came up behind her. "What's the matter?" He knew full well what had ticked her off. He had pushed too hard.

Leigh spun around. "What was that back there? My own shop?" She glared and in rapid French, continued, "Tu essayez de réarranger ma vie. Arrêt, s'il vous plaît!"

"What did you just say?"

"I said … you are trying to rearrange my life. Stop, please!"

"Look, I'm sorry. I only wanted to show you a candy shop, show *you* in the shop, in this town, in my life. I was only trying to open your eyes to see your life here, the possibility—

"Rawly, my life is in Paris, not here. I am NOT moving here. You misled the Beckers." Leigh jammed her fists into the pockets of Meg's quilted jacket.

———

Kathy noticed a change in the couple's body language the minute they stepped in the front door. Dinner was cordial but the gaiety, the warmth between Leigh and Rawly had chilled.

Leigh went to bed early and Rawly went out for a walk.

Chapter 40

STROLLING ARM IN ARM, heads down watching for ice patches, Leigh held Kathy's elbow tight to prevent either of them from slipping, occasionally pausing in front of a shop window framed with garlands of pine boughs.

"How about a cup of coffee at the Grog? I bet they have a fire going," Kathy said. "Maybe a sandwich?" She had hoped a little shopping in the fresh air for trinkets to take back to Paris might return the sparkle to the smoky-blue eyes. If only the young woman would confide in her, tell her what was bothering her, maybe she could help.

"A cup of coffee would be nice, Kathy. Then I think I'd like to stop back at that cute Christmas tree shop around the corner. They had some beautiful ornaments—lacy, sparkly—perfect gifts."

The outing did produce a smile, a few laughs, but the smile was pained, the laugh hollow. Only two more days—maybe that was why she seemed sad. Kathy was going to miss her. Both had delighted in each other's company, an easy companionship had formed.

Tonight would be their last night alone and Rawly fervently hoped to put Leigh's visit back on track. He had made reservations at Ceia, a small restaurant endowed with romantic ambiance in the soft flicker of candlelight.

He hoped the charm of the seaport's antique red-brick buildings under the glow of old streetlamps along State Street would give her a feeling of home, a new home similar to the old.

Pulling into a parking lot carved out of the center of the downtown section, Rawly helped Leigh from the van keeping a strong grip on her arm as they skirted the banks of snow. The night air was crisp, each breath a puff of white mist.

"The Ceia's specialty is fresh salmon," Rawly said his foot sliding on a chip of ice.

What did he say … fresh salmon? Leigh's mind was wondering—the stars, a moon and the lingering upset with the Beckers.

Holding the door for her, they stepped inside and, as Rawly had requested, the hostess settled the couple on the plush, red cushions in the bay window. Rawly helped her out of her coat as Leigh gazed out at picturesque New England stippled with snow.

Turning to Rawly, she caught a look of sadness in his eyes. Her heart lurched. She didn't want to be the reason for his sadness. Her feelings were one of confusion—happy, sad. How could she leave him in two days? When would she see him again? Should she see him again?

Rawly ordered a carafe of white wine and two appetizers to share—Tuna Tartar with Pickled Green Tomato and Melon relish, and a peach with honey crostini. For the entrée he proposed the wild salmon with cranberry-almond sauce. Leigh smiled nodding in agreement with his choices, as he looked for her okay.

The waiter returned promptly with the chilled carafe of wine, pouring a little into Rawly's glass for his approval. Receiving his customer's okay, he poured a portion into the goblets sparkling in the candlelight. Pushing the melancholy away, Leigh smiled brightly raising her goblet to his. "Here's to a wonderful new year."

Rawly sipped the wine, his eyes never leaving Leigh's. Reaching across the table, laying his hand over hers. "I'm sorry about yesterday. I realize now I put you in a very awkward position which was the last thing I wanted to do."

She looked down, traced the knuckles of his hand on hers. "Rawly, this visit has been wonderful, beyond my wildest dreams. Kathy, your brother, Sandy … we became so close so quickly. How naive I was. I never thought about after … never asked the question—then what? That's not quite true. I did ask myself once. But I pushed it out of my mind. It was a question I couldn't answer."

Looking outside at the passersby—couples, a man or a woman, or a family with a small child, people bundled in boots, mufflers, caps, mittens—all were smiling, laughing. "It's as if I stepped into a beautiful Currier and Ives painting that Kathy and I saw in one of the shops this afternoon. It never occurred to me … other than a glimpse … that I might be part of that picture … I have to go home, Rawly. Back to Paris … my life. My internship ends in a few days—

"And then what?" Rawly leaned back as the waiter set the appetizers in the center of the table, moving the candle sheltered by a crystal hurricane shade to one side, pouring a little more wine into the goblets, asking if there was anything else he could bring them.

Rawly shook his head. "No, this is fine, thank you," he said nudging the crostini to Leigh to try the first piece, then cutting the tuna tartar into bite-size pieces. "Here, try the tuna," Rawly said offering to feed her a tiny piece of tuna on the tines of his fork.

"Umm," Leigh closed her eyes. "So good."

"So, what now?" Rawly asked leaning forward, not giving up, his expression intent on receiving an answer.

The sound of drums preceded a marching band in bright red uniforms, trimmed with gold buttons and braid on their billed hats. Brass instruments gleamed in the light of the streetlamps, and colored lights in store windows: trumpets, trombones and a piccolo. The strutting drum major in front of his band vigorously pumped his baton. All of a sudden a very tall Uncle Sam on stilts walked in front of the bay window, waved to Leigh and continued on down the sidewalk.

Laughing, Leigh glanced at Rawly, eyes wide.

"The holidays. You never know what or who will wander down the street. The beginning of the New Year's Eve celebration, but we'll be in Boston tomorrow night with Tyler and Sandy."

"I know and I'm excited about seeing the city. Marie bought me a dress just in case we went out." The marching band out of earshot, Leigh ran her finger down the stem of her goblet, then looked up into Rawly's eyes. "At the airport when I started to ask you a question you cut me off, told me not to say more, that you were an idiot. You knew what I was going to say. Rawly, I sensed something was wrong. I honestly didn't know if you still wanted me to visit. But then your greeting … well—

"I missed you, Leigh. I missed you so much yet I was consumed with my classes, the research for my thesis … and my ROTC commitment, and definitely caught up in the excitement of the Massachusetts' senate election which my candidate won by the way. All I can say is that it all disappeared when I saw you walking toward me. I was an idiot not to pay more attention to a very important person in my life. I'm sorry. Believe me it won't happen again. But—"

"It's been, what, nine months since this past spring when you came to visit me in Pornic for a day … you stayed a week. You invited me to come here, to spend the Christmas holidays with you and your family. But like you, that's not all I've been thinking about … for months … my continuing courses through the Academy, moving to Paris, where was I going to stay, was I going to survive the internship? All those things and yet this visit … you … were always in the front of my mind when I closed my eyes at the end of the day. I didn't let myself think about when I was going to see you after … after I left here … left you." She turned the stem of her goblet in her fingers.

Rawly watched her then reverted his eyes to the stem of his wine glass.

"The Depardieus said I will always have a job in their kitchen." Leigh said glancing up at Rawly. "I didn't train to be a chocolatier to cook bacon and eggs in a hostel. Madame Marceau hasn't said a word about my staying on at the Parisian when my internship is up. Her chocolate factory is amazing. You should see it."

See it? What Rawly saw was the excitement in Leigh's eyes, hear the excitement in her voice as she talked about the chocolate shop. He was losing her.

The waiter cleared the appetizer plates and set the entrées on the table, again asking if there was anything else as he poured the last of the wine.

Rawly looked up at the man, a white towel draped over the sleeve of his white shirt, a very professional waiter, but he couldn't give Rawly what he really wanted. "Another small carafe of wine, please," he said softly.

The waiter quickly returned with the wine and left the couple to their conversation.

Leigh took a small bite of salmon, set her fork down on the plate and looked out the window. A light snow had begun to fall dusting the street and sidewalk with tiny diamonds. She sighed. *What am I going to do? You're going to return to Paris, Leigh Dobrev. You are but a visitor in this fairyland, this fairytale. What did Rawly just say?*

"What?"

A party of ten hustled into the restaurant with a whoosh of cold air, laughing as they stomped snow off their shoes.

"I said that Tyler and Sandy think it's our destiny … to be together. Leigh, we need a chance to get to know each other and we can't do it if we're so far apart … at least, it will be difficult if we remain this far apart," he continued in a whisper. "That's why I said what I did to the Beckers. Can you envision becoming a chocolatier in Newburyport? For a year?"

Leave Marie, leave Paris, Madame Marceau for a year? Still leaves the question—then what? I have to be ready from now on, no matter what I do, to have some idea for what follows.

"Rawly, have you asked yourself the same question—moving to Paris?"

"I did. I can't now. I have to serve four years with the Air Force." Rawly raked his fingers through his thick brown hair, brushing a stray lock out of his eyes. "I'm not saying never, but …

"Ah, that word again … but what? Leaving, even contemplating leaving your home country is difficult. Just the thought of it makes me cry." Leigh's eyes sought Rawly's—*how does one leave one's country.* "I don't think that's possible. Plus you'll probably leave, be deployed elsewhere," she whispered. "France is my country. A visit to the States is one thing, but moving … I just don't think so."

After several minutes of silence, Leigh's words hanging in the air—*I don't think so*—they talked about Kathy's turkey dinner, and his plans for New Year's Eve—a ball, dancing at the Ritz, and then spending the night with Tyler and Sandy in their studio apartment. Tyler had borrowed two cots and he and Sandy were planning to drive Leigh and Rawly to the airport.

They finished dinner with small talk over a cup of espresso. Never one to give up, Rawly took Leigh's hand as they left the restaurant leading her slowly down to the boardwalk along the Merrimack River.

"You don't play fair, Monsieur Scott. Did you order the snow to fall, the lights to shimmer on the water, the—

Stopping mid-sentence, she looked up at Rawly who turned her into his arms, brushed the crystal snowflakes from her hair, and then softly placed his lips on hers, lingering, holding her close to his heart inhaling her scent of jasmine. "I've never felt this way, Leigh. It's hard to handle. I don't know what to do," he whispered.

Chapter 41

Paris, France
January 2013

THE PLANE BANKED to the east out over the Atlantic Ocean. The long flight would land in Paris on the morning of January second, but Leigh knew more than a day was slipping away. Pressing her forehead to the plane's window, she stared at the water below—gray melting to black as the plane flew deeper into the night sky. A tear trickled down her cheek, dropped to her fingers clutching the seam of the plane's window frame.

Rawly, how can I leave you? A year? You asked me for a year. Why not? I can always return to Paris if it doesn't work out. Like you said … one year … get to know each other. There's more to life than being a chocolatier for God's sake. But that's all I've dreamed of, all I really know. If it's so right, why am I filled with so much doubt? Pain?

Leigh fished in her purse for a tissue, wiped her eyes, and leaned back in the seat. She knew she should try to sleep. It will be a new day when she lands. Dosing fitfully, images of Marie, Shelby and Gerry Depardieu, Betsy Marceau, flitted through her subconscious. And then there was Eric. What was it he wanted to be called? Oh, yes, Redd Pepper.

Someone tapped her on the shoulder.

The flight attendant smiled at her. "We're preparing to land, Mademoiselle. Bring your seat into the upright position, s'il vous plaît."

What? I slept all the way?

Leigh glanced at the passengers around her—taking a last trip to the restroom, removing items from seat pockets, stuffing books into totes and cases. She was disoriented. She hadn't made arrangements with anyone to meet her, preferring to take a taxi to the hostel. All so different than when she landed in Boston—the Scotts lined up, waving, calling her name. She gulped, blinking furiously to hold back the tears.

Get a grip on yourself, Rawleigh Dobrev. You're home. You have people who love you, depend on you. You have work to do.

Setting down on the Charles de Gaulle tarmac, the plane turned, slowly taxied to the gate. Passengers jostled against each other, lifting down carry-on cases, and then queued for the tedious process of deplaning.

It seemed forever before she exited the jetway into the bright lights of the terminal, shuffling along with the other passengers to baggage claim. Leigh kept her eyes like a zombie on the back of the purple suit in front of her, with no clue where she was going only that she couldn't move anywhere but with the purple suit.

"Leigh."

She thought she heard her name but that was absurd. The only person she had given her arrival schedule to was Marie knowing she wouldn't travel to Paris to meet her. She had decided she couldn't bear to see anyone welcoming her home with smiles. She certainly didn't feel like smiling.

"Leigh."

Her head snapped to the right. Marie was waving a hanky at her, squeezing in front of people, straining against the rope.

To hell with keeping a grip. Leigh burst into tears as she yanked her rolling case leaving the purple suit, stepping on toes to get to Marie, falling into her open embrace.

———

At the café down the street from the hostel, Leigh poured out her heart to Marie—the Scotts, Sandy, Newburyport … Rawly. In a side pocket of her purse, she retrieved the tiny clamshell Rawly had given to her. She showed it to Marie, unable to explain, words catching in her throat. But Marie knew exactly what the little shell represented. The poor girl sitting beside her … her heart was breaking.

"Well, it's very clear to me, chèrie. You are going to finish your internship, fulfill your obligations to Betsy Marceau and the Depardieus, and then you're going back to Newburyport. I will go with you on my spring break at school. April in New England should be lovely. Then I'll return to Pornic once I know you're settled. *You* …" Marie gently lifted Leigh's chin so the young woman looked into her eyes. "You are going to accept Rawly's invitation to live in the States for one year. Then, I either fly to a beautiful wedding in Newburyport, or you will return to Paris to start your own chocolate shop. It's simple really."

Leigh stood, grasped Marie into a standing position and gave her a fierce hug. "*You* … are right!" Leigh stammered, a smile spreading from ear to ear. "It is simple. *But* … I'll sleep on it for two days and then, if it's still *simple*, I'll call Rawly."

———

Chapter 42

IN AN ABANDONED stone warehouse on the outskirts of Paris sixty-three men sat cross legged on mats in a semi-circle. They listened intently to their leader's briefing, going over for the last time, the plans to torch the American Embassy and to breach the Embassy's residence. The mission: snatch the ambassador and eight others as hostages.

Aalim stood to the left of a large screen facing the men. He tapped the remote control button advancing the images stored on his computer—images of the driveways, the grounds around the embassy building, and the ambassador's residence in the Hotel de Pontalba. The images included details of the residence, schematics of the floors, specifically the entrances, the grand hall to the dining room and access to and from the kitchen. The residence, surrounded by lush bushes and flower gardens, was a hotel in name only.

A major function had been arranged by the Ambassador's staff at the request of the American's Secretary of State who would not attend the meetings but had furnished the guest list. The Secretary's counterparts from various countries including Russia, Mexico, and Brazil, were in town to discuss the turmoil erupting in the Middle East and were to be briefed by the Ambassador on the United State's plans for the near future. Each planning session was to be capped by a gala dinner party for the diplomats and their spouses.

The U.S. Ambassador was given the task of hosting the dinner, of leading the discussions in hopes that the various diplomats would better understand the constraints each was working under.

The American Secretary also hoped that a joint communiqué might be issued as a result of the meetings and could foresee that a dinner, bringing the diplomats together in a less stressful venue, might facilitate a positive communiqué to begin the year on a more congenial footing between the countries. The President of the United States would then call a meeting of the leaders in the future to drive home the hope that by working together they would be better able to smooth the progress of peace in the region.

Aalim closed the slideshow file, turned off the computer, and ambled to the center of the group. "I was ordered to build a group ready to strike at the moment the word is given.

"You men are that group.

"You are ready.

"The word has been given.

"We strike tomorrow night.

"Never forget the reason behind our mission. Never forget our brothers who are imprisoned. The hostages we take in the attack will cause the infidels to exchange our brothers for them. Many countries will pressure the Americans and their allies to give up our brothers in such an exchange."

"Aalim, who ordered you to build the group?" a bearded man in the back, left-hand side, asked.

Aalim's head snapped in his direction. *How dare he ask such a question.* "This is not information you need to know. However, if we are successful … we will be successful … you will meet him."

Turning his attention back to the full group, Aalim continued his briefing. "Remember, when the assault begins you are to say nothing, stay focused on your mission. There will be chaos … if you are threatened you are to shoot but only if you are attacked. Dead bodies are not what we are after. Live hostages are."

Aalim paused striking home his point, scanning the group, making eye contact with several he knew would be leading the others.

"Are the vans equipped to handle the hostages?" he asked.

"Yes," shouted three men sitting in different places amongst the group.

"Is your black clothing ready: jackets, pants, shoes, black latex gloves, black-knit full-head masks?"

"Yes," they shouted in unison.

"They had better be. There are a few of you who could be recognized if not covered with the mask." He smiled at Redd Pepper staring at him from the back row.

"Are your weapons and ammunition checked and ready?"

"Yes," they yelled again.

"Are your assignments and targets seared into your brains?"

"Yes," they screamed.

"Are the rocket-propelled grenades distributed and ready to fire?"

"RPGs, IEDs, fire bombs distributed, checked and ready," a voice from the center of the group yelled.

"Communication equipment assembled, distributed, and tested?" Aalim yelled at the group.

"Yes," they screamed.

"There can be no mistakes, no second chances. The world will be watching within seconds after the embassy is set ablaze and word that the residence is breached. Are you ready to attack in the name of Allah?"

"Yes," they screamed again.

"I can't hear you," Aalim yelled.

"Yes," they yelled louder.

"I STILL CAN'T HEAR YOU," Aalim screamed.

"YES!"

———

Aalim entered the Parisian Candy & Gift Shoppe to the jingle of the brass bell. He looked at Madame Marceau standing behind the counter. "That's a lovely red rose on the yellow hat, Madame," he said. "The hat would be lovely with two triumphant red roses, I believe."

"Yes, it's fresh today and two would be especially nice," Betsy said with her normal full smile as she handed the man a tote. He grasped the handle, gave Betsy a slight nod and turned to leave.

"Bye, Aalim," Betsy said softly returning to the counter.

An hour later, a man with bright red hair and only one hand entered the shop.

"Bonjour, Monsieur," Madame Marceau said. "Looking for a box of chocolates for a girlfriend?"

"No. I was told that a Mademoiselle Dobrev works here. I would like a word with her, s'il vous plaît."

"Oui, désolé. Mademoiselle is working at the American Embassy all day. Can I give her a message—

Madame Marceau did not finish her sentence. The brass bell banged against the door as the man hastily exited the shop.

Chapter 43

———

FLOWERS AND MORE FLOWERS were delivered to the American Ambassador's residence—large and small bouquets, along with numerous standing plants to soften and warm the grand hall leading from the front entrance to the dining room. Maids vacuumed, dusted, polished: tables, chairs, mirrors. The marble and tile floors were given a special treatment bringing out their luster. Chandeliers were lowered, prisms removed, washed, reattached, the chandeliers then raised to their original height sparkling with renewed brilliance.

Leaving the Parisian Leigh was bundled in the Boston Celtic's jacket Rawly had given her at the airport, wrapping it around her shoulders with one last kiss. She arrived at the Ambassador's residence with cartons of tiny boxed chocolates, all tied with narrow gold ribbon.

Henrietta Steuben, the woman in charge of overseeing the gala dinner party for the Ambassador, had commandeered Leigh's help in setting the banquet table. Steuben ordered a maid to hustle Leigh into the dining room and to assist the temporary helper in setting the boxes at each place setting. Then Leigh and the maid began the arduous task of adding the china, silverware, and glassware. Leigh was instructed to begin with the china charger. "Think of it as an elegant tray that is placed under the dinner plate. The Ambassador's wife prefers the charger to be the same china. It is slightly larger framing the dinnerware. The charger enhances the setting creating an even more elegant table don't you think?" the maid asked.

"Oui, beau," Leigh replied. "Beautiful, indeed."

The maid snapped her fingers at a younger staff member, ordering the trays of silverware be brought to the dining room. Leigh began setting the table following the placement guide the maid had given to her. Leigh was instructed to follow the diagram precisely—silverware for the bread and butter plate as well as each course: appetizer, fish, main, salad, cheese plate, sweet dessert. Four crystal goblets were then added to the table in the proper order. And always, always the maids checked each piece of the place setting for a spot or speck of dust that, if found, was immediately replaced or buffed clean.

Preparations reached a fevered pace. With only an hour before the first guest was to arrive the Ambassador and his wife were due any minute to inspect the dining room. The place cards had yet to be set out on the table according to the meticulous diagram the Ambassador's wife had given them.

Madame Steuben pulled Leigh to the side ordering her to remain. Not only were they behind schedule but two of her servers had called in sick. Steuben suspected they suffered from a case of state-dinner nerves. She had noticed Leigh remained calm, took direction without a fuss, even under her sharp commands.

When Leigh said she would be glad to help Steuben grasped her shoulders, turned her around, around again, scrutinizing her outfit. "Your clothes will have to do, but ask one of the girls to pull your hair into a bun."

Leigh did as she was told jogging to the staff restroom located in back of the kitchen. She pulled her phone from her slack's pocket. She should let Madame Marceau know she was staying and that she would see her tomorrow at the shop. There was a message from Eric on the cell. Without taking the time to read his message she hurriedly sent a text to Betsy and then slapped it shut as one of the maids pushed her onto a bench and began pinning her hair back. An order came that they were all to line up in the dining room for inspection by the Ambassador's wife.

———

It was a glittering affair—the crème de la crème of Paris mingled with the foreign diplomats. Leigh marveled at the beauty of the diplomats' wives and their beautiful gowns. European countries were well represented: Germany, Italy, and Spain. Most of the diplomatic posts were assigned to men. The wives accompanying their husbands from Russia and Brazil caught Leigh's eye for their exceptional beauty.

Once the guests were seated the American Ambassador rose and proposed a short toast welcoming his guests.

The wait staff sprang into action and the service began. Leigh marveled at the brilliance of the scene as she carefully placed the appetizer plate in the center of the charger plate. Soft chatter and the clinking of silverware, china, and crystal filled the room as guests engaged their dinner partners, to their right and left, in conversation as servers removed and added dishes.

Suddenly, there was a loud explosion.

Another and another burst of explosives in rapid succession.

Not the residence.

Somewhere down the street.

Guards scrambled from the dining room. Left the residence.

Guests rose from their gilded chairs only to be shoved back down by a swarm of masked men, or yanked to their feet, their noses covered with a cloth then falling unconscious, dragged into the kitchen, out the servant's entrance, and thrown unconscious onto mats into three waiting vans. The black vans careened out of the driveway onto the street. At the first intersection the three vans squealed in opposite directions—one straight, one to the right, one to the left.

Within seconds after the unconscious guests were dragged away the Ambassador's residence went dark. A guard charged one of the masked men and was immediately shot dead. Women screamed as they were pushed under the table by their husband or dinner partner.

Electricity was cut.

Emergency lights did not snap on.

Wave after wave of explosives was heard in the distance. Rocket propelled grenades were shot at the residence but clear of the windows creating a deafening noise.

In the cover of darkness black-suited terrorists disappeared— some melting into the bushes, others hopping onto trucks as they roared by, slowing only long enough to allow the terrorists running alongside to grab a hand, to leap aboard.

Within a few minutes of the first wave of masked men entering the glittering dining room they were gone, vanishing with their prey.

The distraction of the explosives fired at the embassy building had worked, triggering the withdrawal of many security guards from the residence to the embassy.

Sirens from fire engines screamed through Paris streets racing to the flames licking up the walls of the embassy.

Police cruisers filled the driveway and up and down the street of the Ambassador's residence. Officers raced in the front, side, kitchen and service entrances. Temporary spotlights were set up. In the shadowy light, terrified guests began emerging from under the banquet table, their chairs picked up from the floor for them to sit on. It was then that the officers and guards learned some of the guests had been dragged away.

Who was missing?

An ashen-faced Madame Steuben stepped up to an officer handing him a piece of paper, shaking so badly she dropped it. The officer picked up the sheet, looked at Steuben. "It's the guest list … a seating diagram," she stammered.

It took some time, but with the help of the guests it was determined nine of the guests, then fifteen, then up to twenty were taken hostage. Within the hour the number of hostages was back to the original nine, all diplomats, three with their wives: diplomat and his wife from Italy, diplomat from Spain, the American Ambassador and his wife, diplomat and his wife from Greece, diplomat and his wife from Brazil.

An officer reported to Inspector Andrew Boileau that the security lights were disconnected to the emergency power source. Another officer said that five of the terrorists had been killed by the security detail who had remained at the residence while the others raced to the embassy.

Police swarmed the grounds and found over twenty-three black-knit masks in the gardens, pathways, and bushes.

Madame Steuben strode to Inspector Boileau, pulled on his sleeve. She said one of her servers was missing—Mademoiselle Leigh Dobrev.

The hostage toll went up to ten.

Chapter 44

———

ON THE OUTSKIRTS of Giverny, a village north of Paris, three black vans turned onto a dirt road bumping over ruts and stones to an abandoned farmhouse. Aalim had picked the little village, population of five-hundred, as a perfect hideout. Hundreds of tourists swelled the population daily, tourists visiting the home of the impressionist Claude Monet—the hideout a mere needle in one of Monet's famous haystacks.

The pungent, sweet smell of chloroform lingered in Leigh's nose and throat. Tape around her head covering her eyes, mouth taped, and wrists taped behind her back, she fell against a body on her right, then against another on her left as the vehicle came to an abrupt stop. The van doors slid open and several men with raspy voices spoke rapidly in a strange tongue. She was yanked to her feet, hauled out of the van, stumbled forward with a man on either side roughly digging their fingers into her arms forcing, dragging her forward, tripping up steps into a building.

Shoved into a room, Leigh fell forward on her knees, her head banging down on the floor. She heard the thump of two or three others falling into the room. Not able to see she inched forward instinctively trying to get away from the male voices. As she hit her head against a wall the door was slammed shut behind her.

Nudging around on her bottom she wiggled her fingers. Was someone close? Using her heels to nudge backward again, wiggling her fingers she felt skin. An arm? A leg? She swiftly pulled her fingers into her palm. Was the person dead?

Slowly opening her fingers again, she felt a hand moving in jerky spurts. Their fingers locked. The hand was small, smooth. A woman's? Still clinging Leigh made a quiet moan in her throat. The person responded with a quiet, throaty grunt.

Her fingers gripping the fingers of the person behind, Leigh leaned her head to the side touching, resting against a wall. Think. Think. Think, Leigh Dobrev. Who are these creeps? That's easy. Terrorists. But why didn't they kill me … her, him? But they will. You know they will. Cell phone. I don't remember being frisked. Could've been. Could've fallen out of my pocket. So what. I can't reach it. So … is this it? Now I understand what Rawly meant by doing something big, meaningful with his life. He's working for his country. So … I can't join the air force. Work for my country? Work for France like the Resistance fighters? What capacity? Spy?

The door banged open. A raspy voice hissed something. The body with fingers was jerked away. Raspy voice. Tape ripped. Tinkle of water. Shuffling footsteps. A body fell against her.

The sounds repeated.

Then Leigh was jerked upright, pushed forward, tape ripped from her wrists, shoved onto a toilet. The raspy voice turned away. Footsteps.

Did she dare try for her cell?

She had to take a chance, maybe her only chance, to send a message for help. Without thinking she felt in her pants pocket. Her head throbbing from hitting the floor, she fumbled withdrawing her cell. There was only one button on the keypad that she knew in the dark, the number *one*. The number that would trigger Rawly's txt address.

Quickly prying up the lid, visualizing the keypad, she pressed the letters. Saying a prayer, she pressed the send button, sending a text message to Rawly with one word: *hlp*.

Footsteps.

She was jerked to her feet the cell sliding to the floor as she was dragged, stumbling forward. The raspy voice hissed, jerked her wrists behind her back, tied them together, and pushed her down.

Did he see the cell?

Footsteps.

The door slammed shut.

Dark silence.

Chapter 45

IT HAD BEEN FIVE DAYS. Five days since he had held Leigh in his arms and the anxieties of separation were not going away. The hours had ticked by slowly during the night, his sleep fitful, thrashing in a losing battle with the covers. Giving up the idea of sleep, Rawly rolled out of bed, flicked on the television as he passed, and entered the bathroom.

Looking in the mirror he ran his fingers through his disheveled hair. Grasping the edge of the sink, he leaned closer for a better look at his bloodshot eyes and reached for his shaving cream.

He was conscious of a man speaking with a French accent reporting the morning news as he pumped some cream into his hand. Smearing the shaving lotion on his stubble he turned to the doorway to hear the broadcast.

> "...as you can see by the pictures transmitted from this morning's television crew, the American Embassy in Paris has suffered extensive damage with blown out windows and only the charred shell of what were the first-floor offices. The Ambassador's residence—formal dining room, grand hall, and front entrance of the building, received minor damage.
>
> The Ambassador was hosting a dinner party for diplomats from several European countries at the time the attack occurred. It is not known exactly but upward to fifteen or more guests were taken hostage including the Ambassador.
>
> As I bring you this bulletin the police, under the direction of Inspector Andrew Boileau, are trying to identify the hostages. No communiqué, no demand has been received

from the perpetrators of this heinous act—who they are, where they have taken the hostages, or why. Because the damage was miniscule at the residence, it appears the attackers were looking for hostages not a fire storm.

We will bring you more as it is received from Inspector Boileau."

With four quick strides to his bedside table, Rawly snatched his cell phone lying next to the table lamp, flipped it open. A text message from Leigh popped on the screen: "hlp."

He instantly tapped her cell code: "It's a beautiful day in Paris. Please leave a message."

Rawly thumbed through his phone's directory. It had been nine months since he had talked to Marie, the last time his visit to Pornic in April. Did he save her number? He couldn't even come up with her last name.

There it is—Marie Binoche. He selected the entry as he calculated the time difference—plus six hours—one-thirty Saturday afternoon in Pornic.

"Bonjour?"

"Marie? Are you Marie Binoche?"

"Oui, Monsieur."

"Marie, it's Rawly. Rawly Scott. Do you know where Leigh is?"

"Monsieur Scott, how nice. I presume she's at work. The Parisian candy shop. Why?"

"She isn't answering her phone. Can you give me the telephone number for the hostel where she's living, and for the candy shop?"

"Oui, Rawly."

Marie relayed the telephone number for the hostel and added that the owners, who love Leigh like a daughter, are Shelby and Gerry Depardieu. A moment later she gave him Madame Betsy Marceau's number, the correct name of the shop, and the spelling of Betsy's last name.

"Thank you, Marie. Have you seen the news out of Paris this morning?"

"Oui, the American Embassy? The hostages?"

"Yes. I can't find Leigh. I'm hoping she wasn't at the embassy. Before she left Boston she told me about a party that was to be held at the embassy in the next few days. I don't remember the date. I don't know if she was doing anything more than delivering gift boxes of chocolates from the Parisian. If you hear from Leigh, will you ask her to call me, or will you call me?"

"Certainement. I'm sure she's all right. But, yes, I will call."

"Rawly disconnected and quickly punched in the numbers for the hostel.

"Bonjour, Dunham Square Hostel."

"Hello, I'm trying to reach Leigh Dobrev or one of the owners, a Mr. or Mrs. Depardieu, I believe."

"One moment, Monsieur, I will connect you to Madame Depardieu."

"Bonjour."

"Madame Depardieu?"

"Oui."

"My name is Rawly Scott. I'm a friend, close friend of Leigh Dobrev. Is she at the hostel? Gone to work? Have you seen her?"

"Monsieur Scott, nice to talk with you. Leigh has mentioned you. I imagine she is at the Parisian candy shop. You know she works there, and, no, I haven't seen her, but then that's not unusual—she generally leaves for work early in the morning."

"Madame, can I ask a huge favor? Can you check her room?"

Rawly could hear Madame Depardieu talking to someone, asking whoever it was to see if Leigh was in her room. "Do you mind waiting, Monsieur Scott? My husband is going up to her room. He has his cell phone so he can call me from there."

"I'll wait. Have you heard the news … the embassy?" Rawly could not bring himself to say the word hostage. He tried to breathe normally but a knot was forming in his stomach.

"The American Embassy? Oui, I heard there was some kind of an attack. Oh, wait there's my cell."

Rawly waited for Madame Depardieu to come back on the line. The same reporter he saw minutes ago was back on the television. It was a rerun of his earlier remarks.

"Monsieur Rawly, are you there?"

"Yes, I'm here."

"My husband said Leigh is not in her room so he presumes, as I do, that she left for work much earlier—the time difference you know."

"Yes, I know. Thank you, Madame Depardieu. If you see or hear from Leigh will you ask her to call me?"

Rawly disconnected and immediately punched in the numbers for the Parisian. Counting the rings he closed his eyes, prayed that Leigh was there.

"Bonjour."

"Madame Marceau?"

"Oui."

"I'm Rawly Scott—"

"Leigh Dobrev's friend? That Rawly Scott?"

"Yes. I'm looking for Leigh, do you—"

"I'm looking for her, too. I don't mind telling you I'm getting worried. She hasn't answered her cell."

"When was the last time you talked with her?"

"She went to the Ambassador's residence—they were having a dinner party. Oh, Monsieur Scott, it's awful what happened there last night. Guards, officers were killed. Leigh left me a text message around six-thirty saying she had been asked to help finish setting the table and was going straight home when she was done. She said she expected to be finished within the half hour but didn't want me to hold the shop open."

"Madame Marceau, I can't find her. If she calls you or you see her, please, please ask her to call me."

Chapter 46

SLUMPING ON HIS BED Rawly closed his cell. The knot in his stomach tightened sending shock waves through his system.

He snapped to his feet.

He had to go to Paris. His gut was telling him that Leigh needed him.

Reaching for the phone book, he opened it to the Yellow Pages, AIRLINES, his finger tracing down to US Airways, the airline he flew on to Paris last spring. He placed the call and asked what flights were scheduled today from Boston to Paris. Waiting, his eyes went to the television screen.

A woman, tape around her head over her eyes, tape across her mouth, wrists tied in back, was sitting on a chair. The reporter's words cut into Rawly's heart.

> "The following demand was received by Police Inspector Andrew Boileau with this video stating that the hostages taken from the Ambassador's dinner party would be released unharmed in exchange for all the prisoners unlawfully held at the American Guantanamo Bay prison, The swap must include Sheikh Omar Abdel-Rahman, known in the States as the blind Sheikh, an Egyptian Muslim leader currently serving a life sentence at the Butner Federal Correctional Institution, North Carolina, for the 1993 World Trade Center bombing.
>
> The communiqué states that verbal agreement to their demands must be received by the producer at TF1, the French national TV channel, within two days, and that the exchange must happen two days after that. The communiqué goes on to say that if verbal agreement is not received as demanded, the woman in the video will be shot. Thereafter a

hostage will be shot every day until the swap is completed. The American Ambassador will be saved for last."

A voice from the video shouted, "Stand."

The woman, her legs shaking, slowly rose to her feet swaying as she tried to keep her balance.

A man walked behind the women ripping the tape from her hair and eyes. The woman screamed in pain, her eyes staring wide in terror back at the camera, her long black hair falling forward. A black blindfold immediately replaced the tape over her eyes.

The voice shouted again, "Sit."

Blindfolded she was unsure of the chair as she slowly lowered her body. Losing her balance she fell to the floor, her body shaking.

The video ended.

Rawly stared at the television, unable to move, unable to speak into the phone.

The woman in the video was Leigh.

"Sir. Sir, are you there? There is a flight leaving in two hours."

"Book me on that flight, Lt. Rawleigh Scott. I'll be there in thirty minutes."

Rawly retrieved his passport from the desk, checked his wallet for his U.S. Air Force officer identification, and threw a change of clothes into his onboard case, along with toiletries. Glancing at the top of his dresser he grabbed the tiny conch shell, stuffing it into his pocket. Racing down the stairs of the apartment building, down the street to the corner, he looked for a taxi. None in sight, he darted to the subway, the Blue Line bound for South Station.

Staring out the window at the skyscrapers gleaming in the sunlight, the subway car swaying on the tracks, he stood, grabbed the bar overhead for support by the exit door as the car came to a halt. Jumping to the platform, he raced to the shuttle that would take him to the international terminal at Logan Airport.

At the US Airways terminal he ran to Customs. An official checked his passport and carry-on bag with time to spare before the plane's scheduled departure. At the gate the attendant confirmed his reservation and printed his boarding pass. Boarding would commence in five minutes.

Rawly paced to the side of the counter. Staring out the floor-to-ceiling windows watching his plane being serviced and baggage loaded from the conveyor belt into its belly, he called Tyler. Filling Tyler in on what he had seen on the television, that he was about to board a flight to Paris, and asking him to call their mom and dad, and GK.

Without saying goodbye, he disconnected, pressed 411 and asked for information, Paris, France, the police department. He placed the call: "Connect me to Inspector Andrew Boileau, the man in charge of the American Embassy attack. I have information. I know the woman in the video that ran on television within the hour."

After a few minutes of rapid French interspersed with clicking on the line from staff members transferring him up the chain of command, Rawly had his party.

"Inspector Boileau. Your name, s'il vous plaît?"

"Lt. Rawleigh Scott. I'm at Logan Airport, Boston, Massachusetts. I will be departing for Paris in thirty minutes. The woman in the video is a dear friend, Mademoiselle Rawleigh Dobrev. I received a text message from her, 1:23 a.m. Paris time."

"What did this message say, Lieutenant?"

"Help—spelled h-l-p."

"Do you have that cell phone with you?"

"Yes."

"I am putting an officer on the line who will take your name, your cell number, your flight number, and the time of expected arrival. She will meet you at the gate and escort you to my office. I ask that you speak to no one regarding why you are traveling to Paris. Do not use your cell phone until my officers check what is stored and if we can use it to locate where the woman placed the call. Do you understand? Your friend, Mademoiselle Dobrev, her life may depend on it. Also, tell my officer where Mademoiselle lives. In Paris?"

"Yes."

"Works in Paris?"

"Yes. Give my assistant the address, phone number of where she lives and works, now, before you board the plane. Do you understand, Lieutenant?"

"Put on your assistant."

Rawly's head dropped as he ran his fingers through his hair. Giving the information the Inspector requested, he noticed that passengers were beginning to board the plane. His eyes glazed over as he stood, stepped in line to board, looked out at the plane that would take him to Paris. The image of the plane faded as Leigh's face appeared so close he thought he could reach out and touch her cheek, her soft pouty pink lips. Loved swelled in his heart, his eyes misted. *Leigh, my beautiful Leigh, I love you. I'm coming. Somehow, some way, I'll find you.*

Chapter 47

Giverny, France

THE SUN WARMED the morning air over Giverny. The little town sat on the right-bank of the River Seine, fifty miles west and slightly north of Paris in the old province of Normandy. Little had changed over the decades in the village of five-hundred residents.

Stepping out the door of the abandoned farmhouse Eric sat on the step and breathed in the fresh smell of the wild hay growing in the field as he sipped his coffee. He gazed at the coned haystacks, fifteen to twenty feet tall, harvested by a farmer off in the distance. He imagined Claude Monet sitting on this very step back in 1890 painting the coned haystacks in all seasons at different times of day, the same images that now filled his eyes.

Eric's love of music extended to the arts and especially the impressionists—Monet his favorite. He wondered if he could walk to Monet's property. Arriving in the dark he didn't see any signs on the road indicating where to turn to the Monet homestead, a favorite tourist destination.

Couldn't be far. *If I'm given the opportunity, I'll go find the property, and the ponds that inspired the Lily Pond series. It must be...*

"Redd, come in here," Aalim shouted.

Eric sighed as he stood turning to the front door. He was filled with guilt, then terror, when he realized that Leigh had been taken hostage with the others at the Ambassador's dinner party. *What the hell am I doing here? How did I let my life drift into the mud?* He ambled into the kitchen now in disarray, nobody cleaning up their dirty dishes.

Redd looked around at the men standing, some sitting, as Aalim gave them new instructions. "Jamal, I want you to bring the same woman to us as before. Sit her at the table. I will remove her blindfold—

"But, Aalim," Jamal interrupted. "I don't think that's a good idea. When this is over we don't want her to be able to identify any of us."

"That's right, Jamal. Of course, she has to be alive to identify you," he said chuckling. "You didn't give me a chance to finish my words. Before you bring her to us, we will put on our black knit masks. Go everyone. Get your masks and come back here. Hurry up."

Twenty-one men tromped out after Jamal as Aalim and Redd removed the masks tucked in their waistbands, pulling them over their heads. Aalim shoved the table to the back wall with enough room behind for a chair, the chair where the girl would sit, would do what she was told if she wanted to live.

The men reassembled in the large country kitchen as Jamal pushed Leigh along in front of him, elbowing her onto the chair, her wrists still tied in back causing her to lean forward. Aalim stepped behind her removing the blindfold.

Her eyes shut, then blinking rapidly as they adapted to the bright sunlight filling the room, light that had not penetrated her eyes for hours, or was it now days? How many?

Men peering at her through holes in black caps stood in front of her in a semicircle. She glanced around, stopping briefly on each one, then jerked back to one in the back, a wisp of bright red hair poking out on his left side. She looked away, then back. The hair. The color. She focused on the eyes. Green.

She began to open her mouth. Green-eyes turned his body away. She clamped her mouth shut eyes darting to another man on the far right side. He had stepped forward. Her breathing quickened. She couldn't stop her eyes from seeking the man in the back—red hair, green eyes. It was Eric. She was sure of it.

The green-eyed man moved slightly ... backward. Said nothing.

Another man stepped forward, laid a newspaper on the table with the headline: *Hostages, Day 3*.

"You have a chance, girl, a chance to save your life and the lives of others ... if you cooperate. My brother here," Jamal stepped forward, "is going to take a video of you. We have written what you will say as you look into the camera." Aalim, smoothed out a sheet of white paper on the table, pushing it in front of Leigh. "Read it."

Leigh did as she was told, then looked up at the masked man.

"Now, read it out loud so all my brothers can hear you. Read it slowly. Add nothing. Read only the words you see on the paper. Do you understand?"

Leigh nodded.

"I can't hear you. DO YOU UNDERSTAND!"

"Yes, I understand," she whispered. Her eyes again scanned the array of men pausing briefly on the wisp of red hair. She couldn't see his hands. One? Two?

"No, you don't understand. You must speak up so we can all hear you. Now, read it again. Start with your name and then read the words in front of you," Aalim ordered.

"My name is Rawleigh Scott. I am a French citizen and I plead for the lives of the men and women held hostage with me. Our situation is unbearable as it must be for those held at Guantanamo Bay by the evil west, the United States. I plead with you, America, to exchange the lives of your prisoners and also the prisoner wrongly accused, Sheikh Omar Abdel-Rahman. My captors will kill me and the other hostages if you do not carry out their demands."

Redd walked out—out of the room, the house—hearing Leigh give her name as Rawleigh Scott. *Who was she trying to kid. He wanted a cigarette. What dumb rules—no smoking. No drinking.*

"Not bad, Mademoiselle, or is it Madame," Aalim laughed. "Now, read again, slower. We will capture you on video for the world to see and hear." Aalim laughed again as he nodded to Jamal.

Leigh repeated the words, her voice gaining strength with each word, trying to reassure those she loved when they saw the video that she was strong. As she said the last word a man to her side slapped tape over her mouth.

Jamal raised the camera to the ceiling. Aalim drew his gun and fired at the same time that Jamal stopped the camera. Several men rushed forward.

"Give me that flash drive, Jamal," Aalim ordered.

Jamal did as he was told and Aalim ran out of the house, looked around, saw Redd standing in the road.

"Redd, Redd, here, take this envelope. The video is inside. Go to Mantes-La-Jolie—fourteen miles. Use one of the bikes in the barn. Too risky to take the van in the daylight. Go to the newspaper Courrier de Mantes and ask for Hugo. Give the envelope to Hugo. Only Hugo. He will see to it that it is delivered within the hour to TF1 National News in Paris. Go now. Pedal fast. Do not stop until you meet Hugo. Do you understand?"

"Aalim. I heard a gunshot!"

"Yes, my friend. I was showing Jamal what a good marksman I am. Now go. And hurry back. We must be ready to act once the video hits the airwaves."

Redd ran to the barn, grabbed a ten-speed bicycle and started pedaling down the dirt road, eyes riveted so the wheels didn't catch in a rut. Out on the paved street he weaved in and out of the tour buses lined up at a corner. He read the sign as he rolled by: Claude Monet Visitor Center. *I'm going to be one of those visitors tomorrow,* he thought. *Leigh, I wish you could come with me. You would appreciate Monet's paintings. Leigh—Aalim's going to kill her. The gun shot—maybe he already did. There's no way the Americans will agree to such an exchange. They will try to call our bluff at least once.*

Now away from the congestion in the town, and on a flat paved road with occasional rolling hills, Eric's torment grew. "This is not what friends do to each other—lead them into danger. She obviously didn't read, or ignored my text message warning her not to go to the embassy, the party at the Ambassador's residence," he mumbled into the wind.

Chapter 48

———

TRAFFIC WHIZZED SOUTH veering wide to avoid a bicyclist coasting down a hill. Half-way down he began pedaling furiously again.

There was a road sign ahead: Mantes-La-Jolie, 1.6 Kilometers. Redd pedaled faster. He was almost there. Gulping air as his legs pumped faster. Faster. Faster. Fatigue was not an option.

A plan was formulating in his mind. If he executed the plan, he would be marked for death, hunted down the rest of his life. His life? What about Leigh's life?

Streaking into town down the main road Redd spotted the newspaper building: Courrier de Mantes. Stomping on the brakes, he jumped off the bicycle sticking the front tire into the bike rack. Running inside up to the receptionist, he breathlessly asked for Hugo. "I'm a courier. I have a package for Hugo. He's expecting it."

The clerk opened her mouth to speak.

"No," Redd said holding up his hand. "I am to give the package to Monsieur Hugo, only Hugo."

A skinny man in shirtsleeves hustled into the reception area, identified himself as Hugo in a strident voice, his hand outstretched. "I've been waiting."

Redd ignored the outstretched hand slapping the envelope into Hugo's chest, turned and ran outside feeling he was going to vomit. Bending over, hands on his knees, head down, he gasped inhaling gulps of cool air. Breathing under control he straightened up, yanked the bike from the rack and rode around the corner out of Hugo's line of vision. Bumping the bike up the curb onto the sidewalk he leaned against an old stone wall. Slowly his vision focused on the shops across the street.

A bar.

"To hell with the rules," Eric whispered.

Entering the bar he glanced about for a secluded booth, or table, or ... he saw the bar curved away from the entrance, away from the windows. An empty barstool was just at the bend. He would not be seen.

Hitching up onto the stool, a barmaid nodded, set a napkin down in front of him.

"Puis-je vous aider?"

"Oui, bière, s'il vous plaît. Giselle?"

"Oui, Monsieur. Vous parlez l'anglais ?"

"Yes, I speak English."

The pretty, dark-haired young woman, Giselle embroidered on her blouse pocket, stepped away, returning with a dazzling smile and set the bottle of beer on the counter in front of Eric. He hadn't talked to a woman in months, much less noticed a woman with such a warm smile looking at him, looking at him as if she was really noticing him. Him, Eric Duris.

"First time I've been in this town. Do you live here, Giselle?"

"No, I'm substituting for a friend today. I work at a bar in Giverny."

"Oh, I have business in Giverny. Maybe I'll see you there. What bar, if you don't mind my asking?"

"I don't mind, Monsieur. The Le Saint-laurent."

Eric nodded. "Okay if I drink my beer in that booth back there? I have to make a phone call. Noisy here," he said with a grin.

With another warm smile, Giselle nodded in the direction of the booth ... go ahead.

His decision was made with her first smile. He was going to put his plan into action and deal with the consequences.

Sliding into the booth, he took a long drag on his beer and fished his cell phone from his pants pocket. He opened it staring at the display. Did he dare squeal on Aalim? If he did he knew he was a walking dead man. He could hardly hide—might dye his hair again, but a missing hand was rather obvious. He would need protection, unless ... unless he went back to Giverny. Pray that Aalim didn't guess that he had tipped the police. And, he might be able to help the police from the inside. Might be able to protect Leigh, if they hadn't killed her already.

In a hushed voice he asked for the Paris Police telephone number, writing it on the cocktail napkin. Pausing, looking at the keypad, taking a deep breath, he tapped in the number. "Give me Police Inspector Andrew Boileau. It's urgent I speak with him about the American Embassy hostages."

Chapter 49

——

SHADOWS FELL ACROSS the worn oak floor of the cozy bar as the mid-day sun began its descent taking the chill from the January air. Eric's eyes followed Giselle as she waited on customers stopping for a beer, unwinding from their busy day. She smiled at everyone but Eric didn't see the warmth for them that she had bestowed when serving him.

Waiting for Inspector Boileau to come on the line, Eric watched Giselle saunter toward him. Seeing the cell phone to his ear, she nodded at his empty glass with her megawatt smile. He nodded, yes, wondering why she smiled at him that way and not the others.

Hearing the phone pick up Eric turned to the wall of the booth.

"Inspector Boileau here. I'm told you have information about the American Embassy hostages?"

"I know where they are," Eric whispered his head bent down.

"I see. Your name please."

Eric hesitated. Which name. The gang knew him as Redd Pepper. If he gave that name it was possible it would find its way into the newspapers, radio, or television. His stomach twisted.

"Your name, Monsieur?"

"Eric Duris."

"And where do you believe the hostages are being held?"

"Giverny. A farmhouse on the western edge of town. Dirt road."

"And how do you know this, Monsieur?"

"I was part of the group."

"I see." Boileau expelled a loud breath of air. "And, if, as you say, you were a member of the terrorist group, where are you now, and why am I supposed to believe you?" Boileau hissed.

"I was sent to Mantes-La-Jolie with a video of one of the hostages. You have to believe me because I'm terrified they killed the woman in the video."

Eric heard Boileau bark commands to someone near him. "Monsieur Eric Duris, an officer has joined us on the line. Give us a description of this farmhouse, the exact location, and a description of the interior where the hostages are being held. How many of the attackers are in the house, the perimeter? Also tell us what is on the land around the house. In other words, Monsieur Duris, everything you know. While you are giving this information to my officer, I'm arranging for you to be picked up ... where in Mantes-La-Jolie are—

"No, no," Eric spat into the phone. "I have to return to the farmhouse or they'll know I was the one who tipped you off. They are expecting me. I can help from the inside. I have to protect the woman if she's still alive ... the other hostages ... if I can."

"Monsieur, how many hostages are there?"

"Ten."

"Again I ask you, Monsieur, why should I believe you—we get many tips?"

"My name ... verify that I know the woman in the video. She's from Pornic. Call her guardian Madame Marie Binoche."

"Very well. Give me your description, Monsieur Duris, so my men don't shoot you."

Eric chuckled. "I'm the only one-handed guy with bright red hair."

Chapter 50

Paris, France

RAWLY CHARGED INTO Boileau's office jerking out of the grip of the officer trying to stop him. "Let me go. I'm the guy with the cell phone, the message from a hostage."

"Let him in," Boileau snapped. "You're Lt. Rawleigh Scott?"

Rawly didn't reply as a bulletin suddenly filled the television screen mounted on the wall across from the Inspector's desk.

> *"My name is Rawleigh Scott. I am a French citizen and I plead for the lives of the men and women held hostage with me. Our situation is unbearable as it must be for those held at Guantanamo Bay by the evil west, the United States. I plead with you, America, to exchange the lives of your prisoners and also the prisoner wrongly accused, Sheikh Omar Abdel-Rahman. My captors will kill me and the other hostages if you do not carry out their demands."*

As the woman spoke the last word she continued to stare resolutely into the camera lens.

The camera swept to the ceiling.

A gun was fired.

A commotion was heard as the screen went black.

"Nooooo!" Rawly yelled rushing forward, slamming his hands on the TV screen as the reporter droned on about just receiving ..."

Boileau stepped forward snapping off the television.

Breathing rapidly, his faced filled with hate, Rawly whirled around, hands on his hips, he stared grimly at the inspector.

"Lt. Scott, you told me the message left on your phone was from your friend Leigh Dobrev. The woman in the video said her name was Rawleigh Scott. Why did she give your name? Is she a relative?"

"No, no. I don't know why she said that. We have the same first name—Rawleigh. Your plans. What are you doing to rescue the hostages?" The lieutenant's voice was strong, in control, demanding, his hands balled into fists, his eyes ready to cut through any excuses the inspector might offer.

Boileau ignored the lieutenant who was towering over him. "The girl has chutzpah to lie about her name. Lieutenant, do you know a man by the name of Eric Duris?"

"What ... what did you say? What does Eric have to do with this?"

"I take it you do know an Eric Duris. I received a tip from this Duris fellow, not more than twenty minutes ago. He says he knows where the hostages are."

Rawly stepped closer to the inspector, his eyes burning into Boileau's. "Yes, yes. He's a childhood friend of Leigh's. He also goes by a stage name, Redd Pepper. He plays the guitar."

"Leigh?" Boileau said glancing up at a group of officers gathering in his office.

"Rawleigh ... she goes by the nickname of Leigh." Rawly looked at the blank screen. *She can't be dead ... it's a trick. Must be a trick.*

"Is there anything unusual about Monsieur Duris? Something that is different, recognizable?" the inspector asked.

Rawly's brows scrunched together. "Yes. His right hand was severed a long time ago. An accident."

Corroboration. Maybe the tip was real. Boileau's body snapped away from the lieutenant. He began barking orders to his men, orders to prepare a team to fly helicopters to the outskirts of Giverny but under no circumstances should they come close to the airspace over the farmhouse described by Monsieur Duris. The image of the American Embassy on fire had given him an idea from the tipster's description of the hideout—the farmhouse and barn.

Duris said the black vans used to whisk away the hostages were parked in the barn close by the farmhouse. He also said there were no men guarding the vans. There were guards at the farmhouse— two in front and two in back. Boileau planned to torch the barn as a diversion. He grinned as he described how his special weapons and tactics team—SWAT—would take down the terrorists at midnight.

Ignoring Lieutenant Scott, the officers scrambled out the door to alert SWAT of the meeting in the briefing room for their orders. Boileau followed the officers out the door.

Rawly grabbed Boileau's arm as he tried to pass, turning the smaller man to face him, glaring down at the inspector. "I'm coming with you and I want you to assign me a weapon."

"Oh, Lieutenant, I can't do that. This is a French detail."

"Assign me a weapon—as an interpreter, a negotiator … I don't care what you call me but give me a weapon."

Boileau had urgent matters to attend to, and arguing with an American Air Force officer was not on the list. He agreed to Rawly's request instructing an officer to assign a weapon and ammunition to the lieutenant, as well as black clothing and face paint.

Chapter 51

Giverny, France

CLOUDS ROLLED OVER the village and surrounding countryside as thirty-eight of Boileau's elite SWAT team, dressed in black, faces covered with black paint, boarded four helicopters for the hayfields of Giverny. Twenty-three minutes later they set down in a field three miles from the hideout. The pilots stayed with the aircraft as the SWAT team quickly traversed the distance to the abandoned farm and dispersed around the haystack cones. From there they crept through the cover of tall, uncut hay closing the distance to within yards of the barn and the farmhouse forming a wide perimeter around the hideout.

Boileau, Lt. Scott by his side, crept a few feet behind the team and stopped, listening to the rapid radio communications between his men, waiting for the word that they had taken their positions. Boileau didn't want an explosion which might scare the attackers away. The plan was to ignite a slow burn thereby sucking the terrorists into thinking they could extinguish the fire. He wanted as many terrorists as possible to run out of the house.

Boileau waited.

The fields were dark under the cloud-filled sky.

A night owl cried to his mate—a loud deep pitch. Crickets strummed then fell silent as intruders crept near. Wisps of chilly air floated over the field, around the stacks of hay, around the men dressed in black, their bodies ready to spring when given the command.

All were in place.

All was ready.

The word came.

Boileau whispered the command. "Torch it."

Four members of the team approached the barn from the blind side of the farmhouse. Quickly, efficiently, they poured accelerant around the old wooden structure.

Lit a spark.

A flicker of fire licked at the bottom of the weathered boards and then hungrily advanced up the walls. Flames raced across the hay-strewn floor to the first van, the second, the third. Hay dust was set ablaze shooting flames into the starless sky.

The guards at the front and back of the house began to run yelling, "FIRE!"

Men erupted from the farmhouse screaming at each other as they raced toward the firestorm.

Aalim shouted at Redd and Jamal to remain with him in the house. Ordered them to shoot at anyone trying to rescue the hostages.

In the barn a gas tank exploded fueling the inferno, sending sparks up to more dry hay in the loft.

The men in black crept closer waiting for the order to swarm the farmhouse.

Boileau and Lt. Scott counted as best they could the number of terrorists running to the barn—Boileau eleven, Scott twelve.

Boileau gave the order. "Go in."

Teargas grenades were tossed through doors left open by the fleeing men. Men in gas masks raced in. Aalim ran choking to the back door yelling to Redd and Jamal to kill the hostages. He was stopped in the doorway, swiftly rendered unconscious, bound, gagged, dragged into the bushes, left lying on the ground.

Jamal was hit in the arm but kept moving forward to the room with the Ambassador and the other male hostages. Redd ran into the room with the women, began yanking off blindfolds. A man wearing a gas mask ran in behind Redd. Jamal staggered through after them.

A gun fired.

Jamal went down, his gun falling to the floor.

The man with the gas mask scooped Leigh into his arms, raced to the back door holding her close. "Baby, I thought you were dead," he whispered.

Leigh didn't recognize the face covered with the gas mask, but she knew the voice. Her arms around him, she held tight, tears streaming down her face.

Redd grasped the hand of a woman. He yelled at the other two women to grab hold, creating a chain, as he dragged them out of the room, through the teargas sputtering and coughing, down the hall, out the back door into the fresh air of the night.

Rawly dropped to the ground wedging into the bushes, holding Leigh in his arms. He spotted Redd dragging a terrified string of women out of the house. He scrambled to help as the women stumbled to the ground beside Leigh, terrified, mumbling. Were they being captured by yet another group of terrorists?

The women safe with Rawly, Redd sprinted from the group but was immediately surrounded by three black-faced men. With a great show of force, the men screamed that they had found another terrorist. Two more officers rushed up and bound Redd's wrists, then his ankles. Lt. Scott joined the men, his weapon aimed at Redd's back as the black faces dragged the redhead away.

The lieutenant removed his gas mask, throwing it to the side as he rejoined the women. He began checking them for lacerations, blood, or signs of torture. All three were hyperventilating.

Leigh, her throat burning from the gas, whispered as loud as she could to the women. "You can trust this man. He's a friend."

Unable to speak, their eyes and throat burning, the women nodded that they understood, and let the man check for cuts. No one was bleeding, but they flinched when he touched an arm, a leg, or an ankle. Rawly couldn't see in the dark but he determined nothing seemed to be life threatening. "We wait. The officers know where we are," he whispered.

"My husband?" one woman asked with a heavy Spanish accent.

"We'll hear soon. I'm staying with you."

With the women huddled together, Rawly crawled next to Leigh, picked up her hand, held it to his heart. "Are you okay, babe?" he whispered.

She nodded, yes, moving their clasped hands to her heart.

Chapter 52

———

FIRE ENGINES ROARED down the dirt road to the barn, hoses pulled from the tanker, but it was too late. The barn was leveled. The charred skeletons of three black vans smoldered as smoke continued to billow up into the sky. The only action the firemen could take was to douse the embers, soaking them so no sparks could be picked up by the breeze threatening the farmhouse and nearby dry fields.

"Lt. Scott. Lt. Scott, where are you?"

Rawly nudged away from Leigh, leaned into the women whispering to them to stay quiet until he identified who was calling his name. They nodded.

Rawly saw the black face paint, and called out to the SWAT officers.

"Here, the women are here," he said moving forward.

SWAT members saw the movement, heard the call and swarmed into the bushes. They encircled the women, helping them to their feet. Rawly, his arm around Leigh, waved them off. He didn't need their help.

As they emerged from hiding, the diplomats rushed to their wives, none speaking except the universal language of hugs and kisses, all suffering from one degree to another from the effects of the teargas. Rawly understood the hand jesters—the meaning was obvious. They were more than happy to be reunited. More than grateful their ordeal was over.

Rawly turned Leigh into his arms, pressed her head to his chest, smoothing her long silky hair. "Can you walk?"

She nodded, yes, signaling with her hand that she couldn't talk, mouthing the word, *burns*.

The helicopters that had carried the SWAT team appeared overhead, hovered, and landed softly in a line on the dirt road. Their new passengers filed slowly out of the vegetation in back of the house—clothing and hair fluttering in the breeze of the rotor blades.

Boileau's men took charge of the freed group, helping them into the choppers for the short flight back to Paris. The Inspector nodded to Rawly that he and Leigh should board with him.

———

All the hostages had survived unharmed. They were told that an official from the Directorate, the French CIA, would be in touch to debrief them in the afternoon after they had a chance to clean up, and change clothes, giving them an opportunity to rest.

Boileau thanked the Lieutenant for his cooperation and that he would personally conduct Mademoiselle Dobrev's briefing. The initial conversation to be short but another would follow the next day.

Marie was waiting for Rawly and Leigh in Inspector Boileau's office. She had made reservations for two hotel rooms, an adjoining suite, so Leigh could rest for a few days. She handed the inspector a card with the address and phone number to facilitate his visit.

Boileau said goodbye, shut his office door and picked up his desk phone. "Bring Eric Duris to my office immediately along with the two SWAT members who brought him in." The Inspector shuffled the papers on his desk as he waited. He had a plan for Duris, actually two plans. Which plan he would offer depended on how Duris handled himself. One was extended jail time, the other a way for the Inspector to monitor terrorist activities from the inside.

A knock on the door preceded Duris accompanied by two officers.

"Please, take a seat Monsieur Duris. I want you to understand that while I appreciate your coming forward with the information on the hostages, it does not erase the crimes you participated in, namely terrorism, which could be called treason by some in the court. You are potentially looking at eighteen to twenty-two years in prison. Do you understand the severity of your actions?"

The redhead squirmed in his seat but said nothing as he stared into the Inspector's eyes.

"I take that as a, yes. While you participated in the terrorist act, your call did save lives, and your actions at the farmhouse also took courage. As I see it, Monsieur, you're looking at many years behind bars and upon release could face reprisals by the terrorists who might suspect that you tipped us off. Is that how you see it, Monsieur Duris?"

"Sure, that's how I see it. At the time I did what I felt I had to do ... didn't see it any other way. But now ... I guess ... I hoped ... you might be grateful. If your team hadn't saved the hostages you, the Ambassador, Paris, even the country, would have a public relations nightmare on your hands ... a big black mark. Is that how you see it, Inspector?" Eric asked the question in a soft voice. He was not surly. He made his statement, his defense.

Boileau looked from one of his officers to the other and back to Duris. He made his decision—implanting a GPS microchip in the redhead's arm if he accepted the conditions. "Have you heard of letting someone serve their prison time on the outside if they wear an ankle bracelet?"

Eric nodded, yes.

"Instead of wearing an ankle bracelet with a chip to monitor your whereabouts, have you heard of an implanted chip, sometimes called a veriChip, that is inserted under the skin?"

"Like a way to find a lost dog?" Eric asked.

"Yes, only much more sophisticated. An ankle bracelet is easily removed whereas an implant would necessitate cutting in to one's skin. They can also be planted deeper in the body to the point where voluntary removal could be dangerous, even life-threatening, eliminating the chance one might take to remove it with a pocketknife. Implants are much smaller and less obtrusive than the bulky ankle bracelets. Once inserted, the device will be tracked by satellite, and your location, movements, and vital signs can be stored in a database. The information will be sent from the GPS satellites to the database wirelessly through the internet. On a monitor in their cars, my law enforcement officers would have access to your exact position ... at all times."

"Where do you implant this device?"

"Usually the arm."

"So you track me for eighteen years? Seems like a long time," Eric said rubbing his neck.

"Well, you would be *free* to go about your business, living your life *freely*. Of course in your case, given the severity of your actions, I only offer the implantation of a veriChip in return for information. You see my men were very careful not to let on that you tipped us off. As you said when you called, you could help more at the farmhouse than in my office. So I assume your fellow terrorists in this heinous act believe you are our prisoner—rightly so."

"So you want me to snitch on them?"

"You would be an informant. We will take you immediately to a safe house where a doctor will implant the chip. An officer, your contact, will brief you on the chip, how the tracking works, about the information we will be gathering. You will feel nothing. When the doctor says you are completely healed and your contact says you are ready, you will be released. You will go about your life. Let your friends come to you, check you out, so they are comfortable, believe you are with them. What do you say, Monsieur Duris?" Boileau asked. He studied Eric, his body language. He couldn't read his face. Was he going to take the offer?

———

In the afternoon a bulletin was released to the media regarding the successful operation, the hostage rescue. It was explained that five of the terrorists were killed, three captured, and an unknown number fled vanishing into the hayfields.

The bulletin concluded by saying that an extensive investigation had started to identify the group. Questions remained. Were they part of a larger known terrorist organization, or were they a rogue outfit? Answers to these questions would be given to the press as warranted.

Two months later another bulletin was issued about those members of the group who had been captured during the rescue operation conducted by Inspector Andrew Boileau's elite SWAT team. Two were being held for further interrogation and one was released as having been an unwitting accomplice.

That night under a moonless sky, a man with red hair and one hand stepped out of a small house in a rundown Paris neighborhood. Head bent down against a squally spring rain, he walked briskly down the quiet street disappearing in the darkness.

Epilogue

———

To: Eric@ReddPepper.com
Date: April 1, 2013
Time: 11:30 p.m.
From: LeighDobrev@gmail.com
Subject: Belated Happy New Year

Dear Eric (other's may know you as Redd but you will always be Eric to me.).

Sorry it's taken me so long to answer your last email but my life has been in a whirl since moving to the States, Newburyport to be specific.

Did I tell you that Marie came with me? She's on a one-year exchange with the high school here teaching French, of course. We are staying with Kathy Scott for now. In fact I'm sitting with the computer on my lap, on my bed, third floor of her townhouse built in 1850. Sooo absolutely charming. Marie is asleep in the other third-floor bedroom.

Don't tell anyone, but she's dating, well, two dates, with a professor at Harvard. I haven't seen her the last two weekends, but then I'm with Rawly, or he's with me, helping with my business.

That's right, I said my business. The Beckers, owners of a chocolate shop, Newburyport (NBPT from here on) want to retire. Well, oh my, so much to say ... you see, there's a wonderful bakery, Greta's Great Grains, here in NBPT, and low and behold a shop next door turned up vacant.

I made a deal with the Beckers—Rawly and Tyler helped me. Anyway, the Beckers moved their shop into the vacant one BECAUSE there wasn't enough space to accommodate a factory in back at their original location. Their candy-making operation was a couple of blocks away. Very inconvenient if *my hands are in chocolate checking the temperature and I'm called to the front of the store to help a customer.*

So, the Beckers and I are running the shop together for one year, and then they're moving to Florida. Port Orange, I believe. They'll retire with a percent of the business until I buy them out. The plan, and I think we can do it, is that we will be up and running by May, June at the latest. Rawleigh Dobrev Chocolates. How do you like that?

Tyler, you met him, and Sandy (his fiancée) —I love her like a sister—anyway, they are getting married this coming December, Christmas week. Well, I've been here at Christmas time. Beautiful—Christmas in New England, snowflakes … yum.

I was thrilled with your email—playing at a bar in Giverny in the evenings and a tour guide at the Monet Estate in the afternoon. But the most amazing piece of news in your email was your plan to buy the bar. Oh, Eric, I hope it works out. Just think … you and I owning our own businesses on either side of the big pond. HaHa. That's what Kathy AND Marie call the Atlantic Ocean.

How about you and Giselle? She's so pretty—warm, kind, friendly. I could go on and on about how much I like her even if it was only a picture. I could see you and she was a hot item, the way you two looked at each other in the photo.

Ah, the Claude Monet website is incredible, but creepy feelings remain from the farmhouse memories … enough of that. I still have nightmares but living with Kathy and Marie—my two angel mothers, with their love and understanding—I'm beginning to push past those hours. Eric, I know, I know, you don't want me to say it, but I'll never be able to thank you enough. YOU SAVED MY LIFE!

By the way, Madame Betsy Marceau finally convinced the police that she was not in cahoots with the terrorists. She had to hire a lawyer, but together they proved that she had no idea she was passing floor plans for the American Embassy and the Ambassador's residence from the Ambassador's butler to the leader of the terrorists, Aalim something. She thought they were playing some kind of game with the code words: that's a beautiful red rose in the yellow hat. She laughs (now, not then) wondering what would have happened if she had changed the hat to green, or what if she had removed it from the window. Anyway, she's planning to visit NBPT the week before the Beckers and I open ... help with the chocolate factory.

Rawly will receive his Master's Degree in June. He hopes he can serve his assignment at Hanscom Air Force Base about thirty minutes North West of Boston. After that ... well ... I don't know. Stay tuned.

So, dear friend, who would have thought that when a nine-year-old-boy by the name of Rawleigh threw a bottle with a message into the water on one side of the pond would have been found over a year later on the beach by a ten-year-old girl by the name of Rawleigh on the other side of the same pond—so many lives changed, so many friends made.

Love from your forever friend,
Leigh

The End

REVIEW REQUEST

IN THE WORDS OF THE AUTHOR

My family lived the event that triggered this story: a bottle with a message thrown into the Atlantic Ocean and found a year later on the shores of France.

For over twelve years the circumstances surrounding the bottle's journey remained in my file drawer. I knew there was a story waiting to be written, but it wasn't until my grandsons grew to young men that the muse released my creative juices.

ACKNOWLEDGEMENTS

This story was triggered by an event that happened to me and my family beginning on the morning of December 29, 1999. My nine-year-old grandson, Matthew, threw a wine bottle with a message into the Atlantic Ocean off the beach of Newburyport, Massachusetts. A year and four months later, his bottle was found by a young boy by the name of Matthieu who was with his grandmother on the beach Saint Jean de Monts, France. Matthieu's English teacher, Marie, placed the call, the telephone number written on the message in the bottle, from the Headmaster's office, Pornic, France, to Matthew's home in Nashua, New Hampshire, USA. The connection, shore to shore, was made.

Following are a few people who were particularly helpful in the development of this novel: **The Message ...** *call me!* I thank you all.

Pornic, France

First, I thank my new friends in Pornic, for without the bottle being found on a beach nearby we never would have met. Matthieu Charpentier, his mother Regine, grandparents Claude and Narcisse welcomed us with kind, warm hospitality, and a most incredible six-course dinner (wines included).

Marie Picard, a wonderful new friend in Pornic, who thankfully facilitated the words, *"... call me!"* The warm character in the story is patterned after this delightful, pretty, English teacher.

And then there is dear Frédéric, owner and bartender extraordinaire of the Le Varech bar in the vintage area of Pornic near the harbor. Thank you for hosting our little group in need of a rest and a little libation.

Newburyport, Massachusetts, USA

Thanks to the Keeney clan: Matthew, RJ, Peg, and Rob. They all lived the main event.

Anne Fraser Boileau developed a stake in Rawly and Leigh's relationship with her research in Newburyport for the cozy, romantic restaurant I had frequented. If not for Anne, none of this would have happened. You see I moved to Newburyport because of the 1850 townhouse (depicted in the story) that Anne showed and then sold to me.

Daytona Beach, Florida, USA

Thanks to Chuck Smith, Angell & Phelps Candy and Gift Shop, Daytona Beach, Florida, for his time enlightening me on the vagaries of working with chocolate in his chocolate factory. Angell & Phelps has been making fine gourmet chocolates since 1925! Chuck specializes in making chocolates the old fashion way, by hand. His boxed chocolates are made using only the freshest ingredients available.

Randy Pepper, Guitar Attic. Thank you, Randy, for your help and insight into playing a guitar with one hand. The YouTube videos and your experience of attending a performance by a such an artist in Key West was very helpful in formulating my character, Redd Pepper. Your shop is a guitar lover's dream, a treat for the eyes: guitars—new, vintage, used—lining the walls floor to ceiling, all polished to a high shine.

————

Thanks as always to the following reviewers who continue to guide me: Roger and Pat Grady, Lorna Prusak, Molly Tredwell, Tasha Hériché, Vera Kuzmyak. To Peggy Keeney a special thanks for her help in keeping the facts straight.

Through my online research I found the following chocolatier training school: Ecole Chocolat, Professional School of Chocolate Arts. The online training represented in this book is a fictional representation of a portion of the training offered by this premier school, with offices in San Francisco, California, and Vancouver, BC Canada.

Books by Mary Jane Forbes

Bradley Farm Series
Bradley Farm, Sadie, Finn
Jeli, Marshall, Georgie

The Baker Girl
One Summer, Promises

Twists of Fate Series
The Fisherman, a love story
The Witness, living a lie
Twists of Fate, daring to dream

Murder by Design, Series:
Murder by Design
Labeled in Seattle
Choices, And the Courage to Risk

Elizabeth Stitchway, PI, Series
The Mailbox, Black Magic,
The Painter, Twister

House of Beads Mystery Series
Murder in the House of Beads
Intercept, Checkmate
Identity Theft

Novels - standalone
The Baby Quilt … a mystery!
The Message…Call Me!

Short Stories
Once Upon a Christmas Eve, a Romantic Fairy Tale
The Christmas Angel and the Magic Holiday Tree

Visit: www.MaryJaneForbes.com

www.ingramcontent.com/pod-product-compliance
Lightning Source LLC
Chambersburg PA
CBHW070620130626
46556CB00001B/418